Reality isn't ι

—Jonathan Lyons

Machina

Jonathan Lyons

the-foundry.net

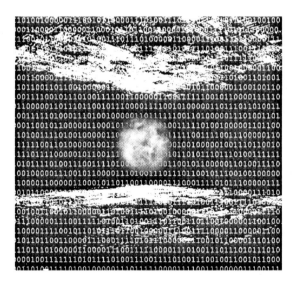

A Double Dragon Press Book

Published by
Double Dragon Publishing, Inc.
PO Box 54016
1-5762 Highway 7 East
Markham, Ontario L3P 7Y4 Canada
http://www.double-dragon-ebooks.com

ISBN: 1-55404-179-1

A DDP First Edition October 28th, 2004

Book Layout and
Cover Art by Deron Douglas

To Karline

From the Author

As someone deeply interested in the exploration of music and its many modes, I offer the following suggestions as a sort of soundtrack to the novel *Machina*. Some of the following songs are mentioned in *Machina*; others simply seem to complement the moods of certain passages in the book. No relationship with the artists listed below is implied here, other than that this music seems appropriate listening alongside the novel.

Here is the soundtrack, if you will, to Machina:

1. Single Gun Theory | "the point beyond which something will happen"

2. Lycia | "Distant Eastern Glare"

3. Skinny Puppy | "Smothered Hope"

4. William S. Burroughs & the Disposable Heroes of HipHoprisy | "A One God Universe"

5. Controlled Bleeding | "Tides of Heaven"

6. Shriekback | "Gunning for the Buddha"

7. Joined at the Head | "In Penetration"

8. ST37 | "Concrete Island"

9. Head Candy | "Mona Lisa Overdrive"

Acknowledgments

Many of the metaphysical and philosophical questions raised in this novel were inspired variously by the following works: *The Dancing Wu Li Masters*, by Gary Zukov; *The Tao of Physics*, by Fritjof Capra; *The Meditations*, by René Descartes; *The Nature of Reality*, by Richard Morris; and, solely because this was the edition my mother bought for me many years ago, *The New American Standard Bible*.

Additionally, long, late-night conversations with many friends over the years have gestated into a sort of extended personal inquiry about the nature of the reality in which we live. The references to Borges are thanks to Juvenal Acosta, who introduced me to the writer's work.

Prologue

How many times has your airplane been destroyed? asked the Elder. *I can no longer tell.*

Sinclair, itchy sweat prickling at his pores, clenched his eyelids tightly closed, fistlike, trying to muster his concentration.

"Seven," he said finally, quietly, his voice awash on the whooshing sea of airplane noise. "None … now."

There was a long, uncomfortable pause.

I can no longer tell when things have changed. You have fended it off every time, said the Elder. *You are learning.*

Sinclair swallowed against a sandpapery catch in his throat, fighting the fear and fatigue. "So far, yeah. It goes 'kaboom,' then I concentrate, seize everything I can in my mind, and we rewind to just before the explosion. Then we move forward again. The next time through, I don't let the plane explode."

Silence, save for the blare of background noise.

And … the Elder began, pausing distantly. *Your friend Thaddeus is part of it now.*

"Friend," thought Sinclair bitterly.

"Part of Machina," said Sinclair, his voice a dry, papery, autumn leaves sound. "Yes."

Silence again, as the Voice faded into the white noise of the airplane.

"Elder?"

I am here, Sinclair. As I told you I would be.

That's reassuring, Sinclair thought. The voice in my head is there for me.

He was having difficulty keeping his sense of reality together — after all, everything he'd ever thought about good, solid reality had been thrown on its ear. Terra Firma was a concept he'd lost long ago.

"I don't know how to stop it, Elder. I can barely keep it from blowing us all out of the air," Sinclair said wearily. "I mean, what kind of god would do that to everyone on a 737?"

After another long, expansive silence, Elder's voice quietly replied:

The kind that hears your footsteps, Sinclair. The kind that knows you're coming for it. And is worried.

November 1990
Chapter One

The Project

A nervous, edgy feeling took up residence in Major Delphina Hutchings' stomach. She shifted uncomfortably in her seat, her supervisor's arrival in the teleconference node imminent. She was still feeling that odd collision of weariness and exhilaration a hard, well-fought morning Muay Thai workout brought.

Slices of light from the cold East-Coast morning streamed through the blinds, thick, wet snow building on the windowsill, caking on tree branches. The quiet hum of a static generator — a countermeasure to laser eavesdropping devices — played its shifting stream of white noise across the glass.

She saw some new such countermeasure with each visit to Defense Intelligence Operations.

Why did they recall me? she wondered. She missed Jordan already.

She was working to tease out at least some benefit from the bitter vending-machine coffee she'd bought, trying with quick, airy sips to drink it without actually tasting it in the hope that it might sharpen her wits a bit. She felt jet-lagged, and really wasn't a morning person to begin with.

Sitting before an array of cameras didn't make her any more comfortable. Five small screens sat on the desk, a tiny camera mounted atop each one, all pointed toward her. The little red lights indicating the cameras' activation weren't lit, but in the intelligence business, she didn't doubt that she was being watched anyway.

After a quarter of an hour's wait, the middle of the five monitors flickered to life, a momentary flare of white noise matching the snow on the screen.

A little too tightly trained on his face, intentionally dark and unfocused, the screen left Hutchings with the sense of speaking to a disembodied head in a cube.

It was Sapphire. She knew his disguised voice and face, knew that he was a black male and that he was her supervisor, but had little other information about the man. She knew from close listening that the effects array disguising his voice employed:

a pitch bender; some sort of overdrive/distortion effect; and flanging, among other tricks usually reserved for guitars owned by bad-home-perm rock-n-roll wannabes.

All of which left him with an alien voice with preposterously deepened bass.

Vader! she always secretly thought, careful not to let a smile cross her face. She had risen quickly in the ranks of the intelligence community and didn't want to take any chances that a superior officer might find her lacking in maturity.

"Good morning, Agent Dalia," came the calm, soothing, bass-boosted male voice via the monitor's speakers. He was sticking to formalities, addressing her by operative name; he wasn't the only person listening. "I trust your travels brought you no undo difficulties."

"With all due respect, sir, I'd like to know why I was removed from field operations."

"Major, your services as a sender are no longer required on-site."

No longer required? she thought. Were they abandoning surveillance?

She had been stationed at the Soviet – make that former Soviet, now Russian — embassy, channeling out everything she observed.

"Sir," she protested, "it takes months to get an RV sender-receiver pair ready for the field!"

"Major, this is not to say that we don't need a sender on-site — we'll arrange for a replacement. And we know of your work and your reputation: You're a skilled, accomplished officer and agent. But we have another, more pressing assignment for you."

Never any answers with these people, she thought. Never any concern for the feelings and situations and relationships an operative may have. It's always a linguistic dance around the facts. Always some kind of circumlocution. Always the bare minimum of information needed to address the task at hand.

She was deeply afraid that they would move her out of contact with Jordan, her receiver partner. She was the sender, and had established a very intimate relationship with her receiver, an operative who used the codename Kodiak.

She fought down her anxiety; she was an officer and an operative first.

She nodded brusquely and waited for him to fill in whichever blanks he chose.

"The nature of Project Long View has changed while you were in the field, Major. While you were away, Project Long View was re-branded Project Oversight. In its place, a new Project Long View will take up residence to keep the current project's cover. Long View will continue to pursue small-scale goals and intelligence gathering, but will never progress beyond those operations.

"Dalia, you have been reassigned to Oversight. You'll remain with D.I.Ops, but in a much larger, much more important project: Remote Viewing on a vast, sweeping scale. This is a matter of the utmost importance."

"How sweeping?" she asked. "What scale are we discussing here — whole government institutes? Whole complexes?"

"Think bigger. Larger scale," said Sapphire. "We're aiming a bit higher, Major. This project is designed to begin with global observation and expand."

For a moment her military training, her years of discipline, fell by the wayside and her mouth simply fell open in disbelief.

"Begin" with global observation?! she thought.

What kind of program would Project Oversight be? Some sort of Big Brother initiative to keep an eye on everyone, everywhere?

"Pardon me, sir?!" she demanded. "Global observation?"

"I know you heard me correctly Major," he said, his tone stern, but still annoyingly smooth. "We simply haven't got time for indecision here. Something very, very big has happened, and we're reassigning you to help with gathering and training our new group of RVs. Now."

She calmed herself, fixing her best disciplinarian's pokerface, as she had so many times before.

What were they up to? Why begin an operation of such massive scope and ambition so quickly? Whose notice were they trying to avoid?

Or whose government's notice?

Their own?

"I doubt that it can be done, sir," she said evenly. "To the best of my knowledge, we've deployed sender-receiver pairs successfully in the field, but not always with the hoped-for results. The program has never employed more than a dozen full-time RVs at any one time."

"And Long View will continue to operate in exactly that fashion. But Oversight's direction is to differ radically. Our goal in Oversight is not to simply select a target to view for a few moments, but to use our RVs, some old and many new operatives, to view everything."

She did not believe that it either could or should be done.

"Sir, why monitor everyone? If word of the project were ever to get out, the Constitutional arguments alone could put the intelligence community under enough scrutiny to paralyze our efforts. It would certainly bring unwanted attention to us."

"*Not everyone*, Major; I said '*everything*.' This is no longer merely an American matter. From this point on, our conversation is no longer Level Four," he said, citing her security clearance; someone else would be joining the conference. "Observe International Security Protocols and keep specifics of sensitive U.S. materials off the table. Understood?"

She nodded. "Yes sir," she said. Again, she thought painfully of Jordan.

The looming face turned, her supervisor's voice muffled behind the coarse, dry ruffling of a hand closing over the microphone on his end.

A moment later, as he turned to face his camera again, the other monitors flickered to life, each with a shadowed, blurred, too-tightly-zoomed face.

"Gentlemen, I'll need you to give a high overview of the project to Agent Dalia."

"How high of an overview?" asked a male voice, a thick German accent her only clue as to who was addressing her.

"Give her a summary. We can brief her as she settles in," replied Sapphire.

"I see," said the German-sounding man, his voice betraying discomfort. "Well. A high-level summary might go something like this, Agent Dalia: We believe that God may be dead."

"Pardon me, sir?!" she said, the second time she'd taken an under-disciplined tone of demand and disbelief today. But she was angered by her separation from her receiver partner and lover. "'God may be dead'?" Was the German paraphrasing Nietzsche?

"We have suspected as much for quite some time, Agent Dalia," said the German-sounding man. Other disconnected heads in the surrounding monitors nodded with solemn silence. "We have observed phenomena that we can only explain with this theory of God's death."

"Whose 'god,' sir? Allah? Christian Old Testament? Christian New Testament? YHWH?" she asked, incredulous. "How about Brahma? Or are we talking more of a dead-David-Koresh-as-Christ? What the hell are you talking about here?"

"Dalia," said her supervisor, annoyingly cool-voiced, "we aren't claiming to be able to address that question. We have observed certain phenomena and we have speculated upon what they mean."

"'Certain phenomena'?"

"Agent, this is Wachhund," said the German. "Project Oversight was begun in April, not long after the U.S. space agency, NASA, launched Hubble, the first deep-space telescope. The telescope's earliest tests involved peering out toward the stars, looking for a star that had long since been identified from the ground. One designated Andromeda RA 2h12m OS D47°10'.

"Imagine the surprise of NASA ground observers when they were greeted not with brilliant images of Andromeda RA 2h12m OS D47°10', but with only the black emptiness of space. Re-targeting Hubble showed NASA scientists that other stars, other heavenly bodies they wished to view were where they should be, but not the one they sought. When they checked their initial settings again, their target star — and, presumably, any associated planets — were still nowhere to be found."

A look of doubt crossed Agent Dalia's face.

"Hubble was unable to focus properly," she said. "Its mirrors wouldn't allow it to focus on its targets. Everyone knows that — it was a huge international embarrassment for NASA."

"No, Agent," said Sapphire. "Hubble functioned perfectly. It was the universe that wasn't behaving properly."

"And the warped mirrors I've been reading about?"

"A cover story, Agent Dalia," said Wachhund. "You did not truly believe that a credible scientific agency would produce a telescope hobbled by an inability to focus, and then launch it into space anyway, did you? Let alone one with … " he paused, flipping a sheet of paper, "multiple gyroscope failures, power-supply problems, a crumpled solar panel, etc., etc.?" He allowed himself a quick, dismissive laugh.

"But why?" she asked.

"Because the truth was much, much more frightening," said the German, Wachhund. "An entire star system simply winking out of existence? Simply ceasing to be? What consequences could this have for us, for our little planet? Or for our star? Our sun?"

She considered this for a moment. They had thought this important enough to concoct an internationally embarrassing space agency fumble? Surely this could all be explained away scientifically. Perhaps something had simply interfered with the light from the target galaxy, prevented it from reaching Hubble's lenses.

"But why is the telescope in operation today, if there's such a problem?" she asked.

"You must understand, Dalia, scientists who wish to have access to Hubble must first have their projects approved by NASA. And in national security concerns, D.I.Ops outranks NASA. Any astronomy project that has a chance of looking toward the Andromeda galaxy above a certain degree of magnification will disappear into a whirlwind of red tape," said Sapphire.

"What about other ways of spotting Andromeda RA 2 … uh … the star in question?" she asked.

"All of them have been circumvented, save our own," replied Sapphire's disembodied voice.

"This leads you to believe that 'God' is dead? Doesn't that seem like a bit of a leap?" She asked.

"I'm afraid not," said Wachhund. "We began fielding reports from all over the globe from those in the quantum physics community."

"I'm afraid you're likely to lose me here," confessed Dalia. "My physics training was a bit sketchy."

"No matter," said Wachhund dismissively. "There are methods of verifying certain properties by observation. In attempting to verify a well-known paradox light — that it exists as both a wave and as a particle — a few experiments have begun proving unable to find both qualities. So in what was a routine sort of quantum physics experiment, the routine is no longer being encountered; something has changed, or is in the process of changing.

"It is a serious problem, you see? If light and matter begin to misbehave, if stars and their planets are disappearing, the universe may be fading out, may be dying — its rules, the rules that hold it together, may be coming undone. Something about the universe has fundamentally changed."

"Or is in the process of changing fundamentally," Sapphire interjected.

"Correct," said Wachhund. "Of course."

"What does this have to do with a global-surveillance operation? How does a change in the nature of the universe call for Big Brother measures?" she asked.

Sapphire chuckled mildly. "Always with a literary reference, Agent Dalia," came the irritating dismissal.

Wachhund spoke again: "It would take much explaining, Agent Dalia, but let me put it to you this way: We believe that without a God to observe our little planet and every single thing on it, our world may cease to exist, as did our missing star in the Andromeda galaxy when no one was looking. We must construct a massive surveillance mission to observe it all, every gnat, every mountain, every home and its contents, every single thing on the planet. It may be our only chance at surviving the death of a deity.

"We have a list of candidates for your new Remote Viewing team. I am afraid it is quite extensive; you will need many, many sharp, gifted minds at your disposal for Project Oversight to succeed," said Wachhund. "I shall meet with you personally to discuss the details."

Personally? she thought. They're serious enough to breach protocol?

"Under whose auspices is this project being conducted?"

"The project has the cooperation of the world's leading economic powers, albeit on a clandestine level. Your involvement, of course, is sponsored by Defense Intelligence Operations. The other cooperating countries are similarly represented by off-the-books intelligence divisions.

"And Agent Dalia? Under no circumstances is the true motivation for this project to be spoken of — not to our RV candidates, not to those we may have intimate relationships with, not to anyone. Understood?"

"Yes, sir," she replied. Her heart sank.

She understood, all right: She was being ordered not to send — not to even make mental contact — with Jordan.

A strobe of incandescent overhead lights reflected in the lenses of her spectacles as Major Delphina Hutchings' driver piloted a go-cart-like transport along the cool, dusty cement tunnelway far beneath Washington D.C. A breeze rushed past, full of the stale scents of earth and of recycled air.

"Paranormal abilities have been employed by various governments and government agencies since at least 1961, with the formation of Project ULTRA — a series of CIA mind and behavior control experiments also referred to as MKULTRA," droned the monotonous narrator from Dalia's BopBoxä audio player.

"Here, then, is a brief timeline of the U.S. intelligence community's forays into so-called psychic spying: Psychic spying by the U.S. began as a collaboration between the American Society for the Psychical and SRI International's Radio Physics Laboratory in Menlo Park, California. It was here that the term 'Remote Viewing' was first coined. When a simple set of Remote Viewing experiments evolved into successful and more complicated experiments, this collaboration caught the attention of the CIA. The CIA was at the time heavily invested in the Cold War, and had gained information suggesting that the Soviets were investing heavily in psychic spying. If this were the case, the CIA recognized the possibility of a significant threat to the U.S. in terms of intelligence gathering and national security.

"Anxious to avoid being caught off guard, the CIA began looking for ways to check on the success and usefulness of such pursuits. To that end, when word of the Menlo Park experiments made its way to the CIA, the agency decided to investigate, testing the Remote Viewing team at Menlo Park with intelligence-gathering missions involving a number of pre-selected targets. The small team achieved spectacular results, and this in turn led to further investigation into psychic spying, as well as the formation of MKULTRA.

"The political climate of the time convinced the CIA to halt pursuits of any projects that might be deemed controversial, or a waste of taxpayer monies. At this point, the Defense Intelligence Agency took over the Remote Viewing program, giving it the code name 'Grill Flame.' Grill Flame became the division under which the Menlo Park effort was organized, as were a handful of smaller psychic spying projects. By 1978, Grill Flame included psychic spying efforts from various military programs, as well.

"After successful Remote Viewing missions meant to asses U.S. vulnerability to psychic spying, the Dept. of Defense moved from U.S. vulnerability assessment to using RV to gather intelligence on Cold War opponents. But the political climate imperiled controversial military and intelligence spending; reports of $6,000 toilets and $450 wrenches in military budget listings sparked budget outrage among voters and politicians. By 1980, most military psychic spy programs had been shut down or scaled back to the point of rendering them useless.

"In 1983, rancorous debates over the funding of U.S. Government-funded forays into psychic ability drove the remaining Grill Flame paranormal research and reconnaissance projects into secrecy, and oversight of the project was again transferred in an effort to remove mention of Grill Flame from the DIA's budget. At this point, seeing the potential value of Remote Viewing, the Army's Intelligence and Security Command, or INSCOM, gained direct control over the effort, re-branding it the 'INSCOM Center Lane Program.' In military terms, this removal from budgetary entries took the Center Lane Program 'out-of-hide,' or away from direct mention in the budget.

"Under INSCOM, the Center Lane Project evolved a new technique for Remote Viewing: Coordinate Remote Viewing. Coordinate Remote Viewing entailed giving a Remote Viewing operative a set of latitude and longitude coordinates of the target as the main information the operative would get about his or her target. Remarkably, given only map coordinates, RV operative still achieved remarkable levels of detail in their surveillance efforts.

"But the endeavor was not to stop there; in 1986, INSCOM returned control of Center Lane to the DIA. During its brief tenure at the DIA, Center Lane was re-branded 'Sun Streak,' before being transferred yet again, amid fears that Sun Streak would surface during an impending budget audit.

"This time, the project was moved to Defense Intelligence Operations, an agency whose below-radar, 'out-of-hide' existence removed them safely from the scrutiny of elected officials, who were then left to simply approve budget entries for entire departments, rather than for specific projects. As anyone with clearance to hear this recording is aware, the autonomous agency Defense Intelligence Operations was created and funded during the 1970s under the auspices of funding for the CIA departmental budget entry 'misc. covert operations.'"

Great, she thought. Ancient history on RV. I thought I was being briefed. She thumbed the fast-forward icon.

The narrator picked up again: "In an effort to head off any further legislative pursuit of intelligence community projects working on the potential of paranormal spying techniques, a disinformation dossier and false history were provided to D.I.Ops Remote Viewing Project Director McMillan Trull, who was from that point forward purported to be head of a fictitious CIA foray into Remote Viewing. In the dossier, Trull outlined his frustration with supposed ongoing troubles getting his superiors to take the project seriously and to keep it funded. The fictitious Trull dossier closes with complaints that the Remote Viewing effort could never succeed in circumstances in which it operated: ULTRA, he said, had compiled tantalizing, but incomplete and inconclusive data. This led, he felt, to no definitive determination as to whether RV actually worked because of what he called 'derisive attitudes, fear of scorn, and the budget environment of the day' at the CIA. Hence, the dossier stated, ULTRA was shut down and the U.S. intelligence community's exploration of so-called psychic spying came to an end.

"What he did not include in the dossier, as it was intended for public and journalistic consumption, were the numerous successes, particularly in the Cold War era remote examination of Soviet URDFs, or Unidentified Research and Development Facilities; the locations of Soviet submarines under the world's oceans; the location of several clandestine training compounds for guerrilla fighters in the Libyan desert; and the Carter administration's successful use of the unit in locating a downed U.S. spy plane behind the Iron Curtain.

"D.I.Ops directors did not allow Trull to make a public appearance on release of the report, as by this time, Professor Trull, apart from becoming the foremost authority on RV and so-called psychic spying, had also become quite eccentric. It would not do, they reasoned, to add fuel to speculation of any ongoing RV or paranormal spying efforts within the U.S. Government by having an unusual public statement by an intelligence community specialist not merely known as eccentric, but whose exploits were also followed avidly by the listeners of late night conspiracy theorist and coast-to-coast radio talk-show host Art Bell.

"The dossier was instead quietly published in the journal *Studies in Intelligence*, the CIA's journal on the spy trade. Ostensibly an internal periodical, *Studies in Intelligence* is nonetheless included in the National Archives in University Park, Maryland. There, the dossier was eventually uncovered by journalists, as planned. End section one. Commentary by Professor Trull follows."

Hutchings' briefing was mandatory. She sipped from her now-cold, still-bitter vending-machine coffee.

"The nature of the phenomena I am about to discuss with you is, o' course, classified. Since you already work here, you already know what that means," said the voice, presumably, of Professor Trull.

He cleared his throat.

"Now we got that outta the way, I'm afraid I haveta ask ya for a little suspension of yer disbelief, here. Whoever you are, this briefing is supposed to be multi-purpose for D.I.Ops types, and God only knows what you have and haven't been told inside this place and out. So hang on. For summa ya, this is gonna seem a little theoretical. Little pedantic, maybe. Some others might just think the old doctor's a little touched in the head."

January 2023
Chapter Two

Endless Nights

Sleepwalking. In the emotionless, ethereal gray of the night.

It always felt like sleepwalking to Sinclair: The autopilot mode he fell into when he was at work; the spaced-out, undirected feel his emotionless, gray nights had about them.

He turned, surprised, at the end of a row of toilets he didn't recall cleaning, but which he must have cleaned, because they were finished now, and he was at the end of the row, holding his toilet brush.

Sleepwalking.

His only direct contact with people, most times, came around a quarter to 11 or so at night, and again around 7 a.m. or so — the start and stop of his work day — at the middle of three university buildings. The company wasn't stimulating.

Elias Ernst, the crew's lead man, drove in from his aging home on his run-down farm each night and took up a nightly watch like clockwork, parked on his unmotivated ass in an office in the building he cleaned, on the lookout for approaching supervisors' university vehicles. Elias had been a custodian with the campus Physical Plant for 48 years, and was due to retire in June, less than a year away now. These days, he rarely did more than empty the trash cans in the rooms and offices of his building, taking up his watch afterward to avoid being caught doing nothing.

A bitter, dull-witted, self-important old curmudgeon, Elias' contribution to their sign-in and sign-out conversations could be counted on to include some attempt at proving his claim that he hadn't needed a day more of schooling than he'd amassed by the time he'd dropped out of sixth grade.

Sinclair hated the stupid, lazy, old bastard.

Raymond Doyle cleaned building No. 3. He kept a long string of his oily, Brill-Creamed hair spackled moistly over an advancing bald spot, confident in the subtlety of his camouflage. He wafted a cloud of odor wherever he went, a cologne of pungent b.o., the stench of old Marlboro Reds, and Brüt after shave.

Raymond Doyle, as far as Sinclair could tell, also sleepwalked. The point was a given with Elias.

Sinclair had decided to give Raymond a wide berth, once the first heavy snow of Sinclair's first year on the job struck, and Raymond grew himself half a beard.

The lower half.

Raymond shaved his face, but let his hair grow unchecked from a border beginning more or less under his chin and continuing unevenly along his jawline. Cleanshaven above, bramblish growth under his chin and across his neck.

It was to stave off the cold, he told Sinclair.

Sort of a natural-growth scarf.

Raymond didn't get out much.

On autopilot, Sinclair patrolled for refuse in the structure that his Physical Plant supervisors had designated building No. 2: Garraint Walther Hall, an aging, poorly insulated set of less-than-prime offices named for an alumnus who had once donated a generous sum to the university, but who no one really remembered anymore. Its marble stairs bore smooth concavities, worn into them from decades of students' and teaching assistants' foot traffic.

Sleepwalking, he scrubbed the toilets in the second-floor women's room. Sleepwalking, sometimes, he heard things that he later determined couldn't have been there. Sometimes a scream in the distance. Sometimes a word, or the sound of a door closing just down the hall on a night when he knew he was alone in building No. 2.

Tonight, too near his left ear, as he refilled the toilet-paper dispensers, he heard:

I am fading.

He started, whirling about — the voice had been very close.

No – he could see that no one was there with him.

But the second-floor women's room suddenly seemed to have filled with an ancient, invisible all-permeating presence.

Fighting the urge to flee, he made a quick check of the area, and after a few moments had passed, he started trying to remember what movie he had heard that voice in. Where he might have picked up the line for a late-night overactive imagination playback. It had to have come from a movie — right?

He shrugged.

He was feeling pretty spaced out.

Alone in No. 2, save for the occasional late-night encounter with a tenant trying to cram or finish a project that was going down to the wire, Sinclair tried to stretch two hours' work into an eight-hour shift.

The old office spaces in No. 2 tended to fall to teaching assistants, visiting lecturers, those with no clout or seniority in the school. The building didn't stay cool during the summer months, and remained frigid from autumn to spring.

Sinclair didn't really notice.

Around 6:30 a.m., he began putting away his cleaning supplies and gear, watching the clock.

Around 6:45 a.m., still watching the clock, he walked to the center building to meet up with Elias and Raymond.

And sit.

And wait.

When Elias said that his watch said it was 7 a.m., they all left work.

It was all the same. Paint by numbers. Every single night, his nights blurring one into the next. He didn't need to think to do his job; he just did it, his emotionless, gray night blurring into the next gray day.

But tonight (what day was it again?), another night in a long, long string of identical shifts, his trash-dumping Zen was interrupted. He had to pause for a moment and shake his head a bit to clear his thoughts.

Something was different: A light was on in one of the offices. He hadn't even noticed until he was in the cramped, cluttered, third-floor room, realizing that he'd interrupted its sole nocturnal dweller.

"Oh. Uh," Sinclair said, his voice raspy, almost rusty from disuse. "Sorry. Didn't seeya."

"That's all right," said the bespectacled occupant, a youngish thirtysomething, Asian-looking man, his messy black hair sticking up all over, as though he'd been ruffling his hands through it the way someone who's taken too much NoDoze does. He had a slim build and wore the natty, second-hand suit coat and fading brown corduroys Sinclair tended to see worn around campus by youngish academics. On his desk rested a copy of the morning's campus paper, half a dozen entries in the "For Rent" section of the want ads circled in red, all of them struck though.

"I needed a break anyway," he said, smiling at the janitor.

Sinclair glanced at the series of graphs and figures scrawled on a dry-marker board behind the office's tenant. They seemed as though they should be familiar, but no bells were ringing for him.

He pulled the used waste liners, dropping them into his larger trashcan, and replaced them without making eye contact with the office-dweller again. Relief washed over him as he retreated from the office and its late-night, out-of-place occupant. Relief that he could get back to sleepwalking. He wasn't used to running into people at work.

After that, the night was routine. Uneventful. Mostly predictable.

As he sat with Elias and Doyle, the two of them resting on folding chairs kept in the older man's janitor closet, the two talked about last night's game. Sinclair sat on the floor, staring, unfocused, at a spot on the wall directly before him.

When Elias decided that his watch said it was 7:00 a.m., they shuffled wearily out to the parking lot, the pale winter sun to the east barely potent enough to render the skies a cold, emotionless monochrome.

On Sinclair's car radio, a cold, bleak, removed piece, Lycia's "Distant Eastern Glare," drifted appropriately from KRUI, the university's alternative-music station.

The scenery on the route home seemed like an endless, smudgy wall of old-building brick. It always seemed strange: In the morning's rush-hour traffic, he could be less than six feet from other people, at times, but have no contact whatsoever with them; most of his direct contact with people he wasn't rooming with was with other janitors, and then, only with the two he worked closest to. And he saw them only twice a night; they rarely ventured over between II p.m. and 7 a.m.

Through his windshield he could see them by the thousands: others staring off into the dirty morning air, stopped dead in gridlocked traffic. Lots of people sleep-walked like he did, he noticed.

Sinclair pulled into the Zip-In Mart on his drive homeward, pumping a few bucks in gas into the tank and liberating a cheap 40-ouncer from the cooler. The clerk handed him the beer in a made-to-fit plain brown bag, and Sinclair pushed his way back into traffic and toward the aging house where he rented a room.

As he made his way up the creaking stairs, searching his pockets for his keys, he noticed that Room #4 was available for rent again. Someone must have bailed out.

In the morning, Sinclair liked to have a beer or two after work, and he liked to drink them on the front steps of the smog-stained building where he rented a room. When he was bored, he'd pick off bits of flaking gray paint from the entryway door as he watched the daytimers going by, crisp and clean. Hair perfect. People perfumed. Puffiness around their eyes betraying interrupted sleep. He felt completely out of sync with them — the regular people working regular jobs and regular hours.

Every once in a while, a daytimer would scowl at Sinclair for drinking his big, cheap beer from a plain-brown bag so early in the day, out where everyone could see him. He had obviously either been out all night drinking or was drinking first thing in the morning. When the occasional daytimer disapproved of this, he'd smile broadly and tip the 40-ouncer toward them in a good-morning salute.

This morning, as he headed in for bed, he heard voices and music from the renters' communal living room. Peering around the corner, he caught sight of Rhys, Beckett, Liam, and Jonas, all of them tenants as well as friends, and Burt with a cute brunette girl Sinclair didn't recognize. Her tassled, brown-leather coat and bell-bottom jeans struck Sinclair as hippie-like.

The six of them were grouped around the television that some previous tenant had abandoned, a big black spot obscuring a palm-sized region of the screen's upper-right corner. They were chuckling, trying to keep their laughter in check as someone's rented "Naked Lunch" DVD played. They'd been at it for a while, he guessed.

"And what are you naughty boys and girls up to?" he asked the high-strung group, their pupils dilated wide, like little black discs.

"Exceeding the recommended dosage, clearly," said a grinning Burt, his Scottish accent beginning to show signs of tempering from exposure to his Midwesterner friends.

"Hey, Sync?" Beckett called out, his voice tattered at the edges with barely restrained, acid-driven panic over the movie. "Want a dose? Yo."

This "Yo" business was all affectation on Beckett's part; everyone in his department's Literature and Culture of Late 20th Century America focus sounded just like him, slipping outmoded slang into their everyday talk. Lots of "Yo"'s and referring to people as "G," that sort of thing.

Sinclair pondered his options: It was still early, and he knew he could sweep floors and clean toilets with a hangover if need be.

With a shrug, he decided he could afford to join them, their faces etched in acid-driven near-panic as a typewriter-cum-intelligent-insect spoke to William S. Burroughs' surrogate in the movie, issuing a new set of spy-mission directives via an orifice under its shelled wings — an orifice that rather revoltingly resembled an anus.

"'Naked Lunch,'" said Sinclair appreciatively. "A classic."

Not a surprising choice for Beckett, given that the movie had been released in the early 1990s.

A nervous, high-strung, acid-tightened titter shivered through the group.

Sinclair accepted the little blue paper square from Beckett, placing it on his tongue and letting its payload slowly diffuse into his system.

"Number four's open again, dig? Know anyone who's looking?"

"Not really, Beckett," said Sinclair. "I'll ask around."

"Right. Yo, best to have a friend move in, right?"

"Right."

Sinclair's beer had relaxed him a bit, and he'd felt like sleeping only a few minutes before. Now, as the acid dissolved and made its way into his system, he began to perk up, the edges of his reality already teeming with subtle vibrations and imagined new life appearing in the shadows.

Dozens of candles melted themselves down under the appetites of their tiny flames, a lavalike flow freezing in a column from the little beer-can-cluttered coffee table to the worn wooden floor below.

On the flawed TV screen, a slice of unreality unfolded: " ... and be sure and make it *rrreal* tasty!" said the typewriter bug's anus-mouth, instructing the Burroughs-surrogate to commit murder.

Suddenly, the typewriter-insect seemed horrific to Sinclair.

He relaxed, let the acid wash over him for the next few hours, tittered nervously at the disturbing visions wrought by the video. As the acid settled into his system, he watched as a pile of brown corduroy throw pillows that had been piled in the corner to clear seating for everyone became animate, an arm tugging upward out of the pile. The pile of pillows had, Sinclair lysergically deduced, merged to form a new entity.

A mouth formed near the front of the pile and tried to open, tried to speak, but (horribly, it seemed to Sinclair) was unable to open sufficiently due to the restraining cords of the brown corduroy laced vertically across its new orifice.

Sinclair smiled a maniacal grin borne of acid-speed and terror and spectacular curiosity. He wondered whether he should get a steak knife and help it open its mouth. His eyes were peeled wide enough, his pupils large enough, now, to attract attention anywhere on earth, save this one, safe room.

Sinclair could no longer be bothered with the movie; the freakshow right there in the room with him was much, much more interesting.

Life from nothing, he thought. Whoa.

He'd had absolutely no inkling Beckett's acid would be this potent. But it was all OK, man, as long as he could keep the reality separate from the illusion – as long as he could tell them apart.

When he awoke that afternoon, his head felt thick, as though a newly cauterized layer of brain tissue was slowing the speed of signals getting into and out of his brain. He did not, for example, recall having made his way to his room. Or getting mostly undressed; he wore no pants, only his work shirt and socks.

As he tried to clear the post-LSD haze from his head, he realized that he knew where he'd seen one of the figures on the dry-marker board of the late-night tenant's office the night before: On a diagram explaining something about electrons. At least that's what he thought it said.

He knew he'd seen it before; why couldn't he get his head to clear and recall the diagram, and where he'd seen it and what it meant?

Slowly, thickly, he dragged the memory to the surface.

He'd seen the diagram in a book on quantum physics — the oddball field of physics the mere mention of which made the physics grad students he'd met turn nervous and defensive. It tended to deal with areas of physics where the hard, certain Newtonian rules governing reality didn't apply.

He also realized that he had begun to run out of money. Again. As always. He couldn't even make it from paycheck to paycheck anymore. And he hadn't even bought the acid!

When he arrived at building No. 1 for work, he fished a discarded campus newspaper from the trash and began looking through the classifieds, hoping to find some sort of short-term work to help him get by.

There were plenty of ads for McJobs like his — low-wage, low-dignity, no-benefits jobs, as he saw them — but most required face time with anxious, irritable customers. That was an irritant he didn't need to add to the equation.

He'd already pushed any dreams of finishing his own degree work back into the deepest recesses of his brain, and on a daily basis dealt with a sense of guilt over his failure to afford school.

The added aggravation wouldn't help.

He worked through the Help Wanted section, and moved to the Miscellaneous heading, mostly to pass the last few minutes before his shift began.

There wasn't much available, but a small, simple ad near the bottom of the page caught his eye:

"Male Volunteers Needed, Ages 22-40, nonsmokers, for test of new antihistamine. Compensation."

He folded the paper and tucked it into his coat pocket.

Maybe he could earn a little cash as a guinea pig.

Chapter Three

From the Desk of Dr. E. Mannheim, Director

Dr. Errol Mannheim, Ph.D. in parapsychology, assistant director of the Geller Metaphysics Institute, rubbed his weary eyes with his left hand, his right balancing his pop-bottle-bottomed spectacles as it rested on a stack of folders. The folders were expandable, the sort that have accordian-like folds along the bottom and both sides, allowing them to hold quite a number of printouts. Each folder was marked with a case number.

Glancing up, Mannheim noted the hour – an alarming 2:45 a.m.

Where were all of these reports coming from, all of the sudden? Why were there suddenly so many supposed hauntings? Why the sudden spike in sightings of so-called Men In Black? And reports of reincarnation were suddenly spiking, as well.

The institute typically received a few thousand contacts regarding paranormal phenomena in any given year. Of these, the number that would distill down from initial report to pursuable case would reliably be reduced by an order of magnitude.

At least, that was what had generally occurred.

Now, though, he had sheafs of data, lists of interviews to conduct with supposed eyewitnesses, even people claiming to have captured spectral visitors on videotape.

What was going on? What had changed? Was there just some new paranormal fad happening?

He recalled the spate of Bigfoot sightings in Minnesota and Northern Iowa that had caused a rash of reports to the institute's Xenobiology Department back in 1999 and 2000. It was the stuff of legend in his field: In the space of a few weeks, the idea of a previously undiscovered hominid roaming North America had gone from fringe belief embraced only by a small crop of oddball enthusiasts to credible topic fit for coverage on the evening news. People were even claiming to have seen a bigfoot in the heart of the Minne-apple's downtown.

Newspapers in Minneapolis began to run reports of police (or some related agency) having captured a "Bigfoot-like creature," though they could not confirm such reports.

The Institute's Xenobiology Department had been flooded with sightings of eight-foot-tall humanoid creatures roaming all over the state.

Then, as quickly as it came, the craze left, and the people in the Xenobiology

Dept. were able to return to 40-hour-a-week schedules.

But this flood – the one Mannheim was dealing with now – was different.

The reports had begun coming in slowly. Ghostly figures appearing in the hallways of families' locked homes, appearing in a recurring way, and always mysteriously impossible to trace when the haunted family attempted to investigate. Men in Black seen striding out from solid walls. So-called Smart Guy Abductions were up.

The title text topping one of the field reports caught his eye: "Remarkable past-life memories in Maharashtra state, India."

OK, he thought. *Let's have a look.* He opened the report:

"Remarkable past-life memories in Maharashtra state, India.

"Synopsis compiled from reports by GMI Field Investigators Mario Pastore and Nancy Hyde Krueger.

"On April 20, 2017, a 10-year-old boy named Pradeep died of small pox at his family's home in Niphad, in the District of Ahmadnagar, in India. Pradeep's father, Sri Digambar Mishra, related the story to Mario Pastore, an investigator from the Geller Metaphysics Institute, but found dealing with Nancy Hyde Krueger difficult, due to markedly different standards of gender relations in India.

"On April 21, 2017, Sri Krishnachand Nagar and his wife, Saraswati, residents of Chandvad, gave birth to a son, who they named Ravindra. Ravindra's behavior was perfectly normal, according to his father, until October of 2021, at the age of four and one-half, during an episode of illness. One night, according to his mother's statement, he did not recognize his mother, and claimed that he was from Niphad, and had never heard of Chandvad.

"A few days later, after recovering from the illness, he began what was to be an oft-repeated and unexplained behavior: He would suddenly stop whatever he was doing, whether playing with his toys, or eating, or whatever pursuit he might be engaged in, and would run from the family's house. He would then tell alarmed family members who ran after him to check on the disturbance that he belonged in Niphad. He also insisted that his father's name was Digambar, rather than Krishnachand.

"Ravindra begged to be taken to Niphad with such insistence during these episodes, that an older cousin named Prajit decided to pretend to go along with his wishes. To test the boy's knowledge of Niphad, he took the young Ravindra on a bus headed the wrong direction, away from Niphad. Remarkably, the boy — only four and a half years old, remember — noticed that they were heading in the wrong direction, and again pleaded to be taken to Niphad. Impressed by this, Prajit gave in and took the boy to the correct bus.

"When they arrived in Niphad, the boy claimed to recognize Sri Digambar Mishra's chai shop as his father's establishment; interested in seeing how much young Ravi knew and how much he was inventing, Prajit took the child inside to meet the family.

"Ravindra somehow recalled the names of Pradeep's close relatives and friends, whom he had never met, and ran at one point to Pradeep's toy box, pulling out what the Mishra family said had been Pradeep's favorite toys. Upon returning home to Chandvad, Prajit reported himself deeply impressed with the boy's knowledge of people he could not possibly have met.

"Whether out of superstition or out of fear of losing their son to the Mishras (Nagar family accounts vary on this), the Nagars attempted several folk practices to 'cure' Ravindra of his memories of being another child. These included turning him counter-clockwise on a potter's wheel, which supposedly impairs memory.

"In October of 2022 Sri Digambar Mishra was in Chandvad on business, and ran across Ravindra by chance. Ravi recognized Digambar, and insisted that he — Digambar — was Ravindra's father. He begged Digambar to take him 'home' to Niphad. Digambar did not do so, leaving Ravindra, of course, with the Nagar family.

"A few days later, Pradeep's mother and older sister and brother visited Chandvad to meet Ravi. Ravindra reportedly wept with joy upon seeing Pradeep's mother and siblings, and the visiting Mishras convinced Ravindra's family to allow the boy to visit them in Niphad. During this visit, the young Ravi again recognized and named relatives he had not seen or been introduced to previously.

"The Mishra family became convinced that Ravindra was Pradeep reborn, and this generated a great deal of distrust between the two families. The visit rekindled Ravindra's desire to 'return' to the Mishra family home in Niphad. In an effort to deter the boy from acting on these supposed memories, Krishnachand began punishing the boy.

"Tensions between the Nagar and Mishra families has led the Nagar family to become uncooperative with GMI investigators."

Mannheim was intrigued. If all of what was imparted in the field report were true, how could the boy, Ravindra, have retained memories that seemingly belonged to a deceased child named Pradeep? How could he know Pradeep's favorite toys and their locations, let alone be able to call Pradeep's family members by name? Unless, of course, Ravindra had somehow received at least some of the information Pradeep had learned during his brief life.

He leafed forward through the paperwork, pulling out another file — a report summary detailing a purported case from Brazil:

"Dona Henrique, who went by the nickname Catarina, was born in 1997, was reportedly happy with the solitary life of a young woman growing up on a farm in the state of Paraná. But such a life can be very lonely, as one might imagine. Catarina kept busy with chores around the farm as she was able, tending to the sheep with her father and fetching water from the family's well as it was needed in the house.

"To give his daughter a chance to meet other children and make friends, Bira Henrique periodically took the young Catarina to the nearest town, a village called Adapa.

"In Adapa, at the age of 17, Catarina met and became friends with Ida Dos Santos, the wife of an Adapa shop owner. Ida was about six months older than Catarina.

"Catarina became romantically involved with a young man from Adapa named Tapecar Cantou. But Bira Henrique did not approve of Cantou, and demanded that she end the relationship. And so, with reluctance, Catarina broke off her blossoming relationship with Cantou. When she struck up a friendship with another young man from Adapa, this time a schoolteacher named Manoel Marinho, her father again disapproved.

"According to statements Bira Henrique and Ida Dos Santos made to GMI investigators, the rejection sent Catarina into a deep depression. Catarina began living more dangerously, taking chances with her safety that she would not have taken previously. She would cross the roads near their home without looking up to check for traffic, for example, and was otherwise deeply depressed and unmotivated.

"Eventually, when none of her more dangerous behavior proved fatal, she simply laid down on the road after nightfall and waited for a car or truck to run her over. Her father did not actually realize she had gone away from the house until later; the driver of the vehicle that killed Catarina drove off without attempting to render assistance.

"About eight and one-half months later, Ida Dos Santos gave birth to a daughter, who she named Helena. At about three years of age, Helena began to recall and relate details about the life of Catarina. The first such occurrence was between Helena and her older sister, Idalina, as they walked back from playing in a field used by local children as a park. According to a statement by Idalina, Helena asked that Idalina carry her back to the house. When Idalina refused, Helena reportedly said: 'When you were little and I was big, I used to carry you around, Idalina!'

"Idalina replied, 'Oh you did now, did you? When have you been bigger than me?'

"'When I tended the sheep at the farm with my father,' Helena replied.

"At the time, Idalina Dos Santos dismissed the story as a product of a little girl's active imagination. When Idalina reported the story to her mother, Ida sought out Helena and told her that she, Ida, had never lived on a farm with the children.

"'No, you didn't live there,' replied Helena.

"'And did my little Helena have any brothers or sisters?' asked Ida.

"'No,' said Helena sadly. 'And I was called Catarina.'"

"Over time, Helena went on to make hundreds of accurate statements on matters and details about the life of Catarina (detailed in the full report, enclosed) that she could not possibly have learned about independently, including the names of the two men she had fallen in love with, and information Catarina had learned during conversations she had when she visited Ida."

Mannheim stroked his goatee thoughtfully, considering the report summary.

There were more – dozens more – in the reincarnation stack.

His eyes passed in a dazed sort of way over the stack before him. Shortly, he knew, he would need to request funding for a research assistant, extended hours on the clock, and extra resources to tackle this unexplained swell in cases.

Chapter Four

Nocturnes and Sanity

Sinclair rolled the top of the paper bag down around the neck of his 40, donning a big, clumsy set of grandpa-ish shades, the kind meant to fit over your regular glasses, except that he didn't wear regular glasses. To him, the wide, wrap-around style referenced one of the four replacement supermen who turned up when DC Comics, in a marketing ploy, had killed off Superman for a few issues.

But Sinclair's friends and neighbors had a different perception of things: To his friends and neighbors, these were Sinclair's grandpa shades.

No one else was up in the house where he rented his closetlike room, a claustrophobic 10 by 12 feet, bathroom and kitchen facilities shared between himself and the other denizens of the ancient, dilapidated rental on South Dodge.

Sinclair actually needed the shades to fend off the glare of sunrise from his East-facing steps, his eyes made sensitive to the daylight by his overnight schedule.

A big beer, in all its trashy, 40-ounce glory, was one of the little fixtures he counted on. One of the steps he took to stay sane.

He was a little surprised when he realized the beer was over, so to speak, and he'd only gotten to watch half a dozen people shuffle past, ready to start the day, trying nervously not to eye him as they passed.

You must help me, he heard with a start, from close, far too close on his left. He looked quickly around, but could see no one. The voice had been male, he'd thought, and old and tired. It had had the wasted-away, papery quality of dry leaves being crushed underfoot. And again, he could feel the sudden, ancient presence. It felt like he was surrounded by ... something. He didn't know what to call it.

After giving his nerves a moment to settle, Sinclair decided to call it a day, and headed into the shadows of the old wreck of a building, seeking shelter from the sun, worn floorboards creaking in protest as he walked, shuffling past a pair of tenants, Rhys and Beckett, as they crunched their cereal in the ratty communal kitchen.

He wearily climbed the stairs to his floor and made his way to the room at the end of the hall to try to sleep.

Sinclair was riding in the family's fire-engine-red minivan. His father — his father before he'd squandered what little money the family had on a synthetic meth-amphetamine habit — drove. His mother — a young, healthy woman with the aversion to alcohol she'd had when he was growing up, not the miserable, abandoned woman who picked up the bottle and eventually, in despairing loneliness, had taken her own life — sat up front on the passenger side.

This was how they were, before his family had caved in; how they would be today had things not gone so completely bad, his parents not divorced, then gone on to suicide or synth, rather than their own lives.

He awoke with a start, sheets sticking to him with a cold, uncomfortable sweat. He never dreamt pleasant dreams, as he thought most people must; his were only nightmares — sometimes nightmares of how things were supposed to be.

He reached out, tugging back the shade covering the window next to his bed to spy the backlit ashy gray of the early-evening sun. He'd set his alarm for 5 p.m. (hadn't he? It was set for 5 now); it read 4:51 as he looked it over, so he flicked its dial to the "off" position and popped in an aging cassette copy of Controlled Bleeding's "Songs from the Ashes," a bleak, post-industrial requiem to start the day. He'd been in a hurry when he made the cassette copy, and had forgotten to write down the song titles, so now he knew which songs he liked most on the album, but had no idea what their titles might be.

Outside, a chilling, steady drizzle and overcast skies made his late-afternoon morning cold and dark.

He caught a campus bus to the medical campus building cited in the "Male Volunteers Needed" ad, and was offered $400 in exchange for taking part in a clinical study of a new antihistamine.

Needing the money to avoid another eviction and emergency late-night relocation, Sinclair signed on the dotted line and took his first dose.

The hours before work were so repetitive, so much a paint-by-numbers game, that he could coax little joy from them. But he had the added color, this evening, of trying to figure out which of his boxes of books contained which of his old philosophy and related texts, and which of those contained the diagram he'd seen in the tenant's office. Didn't the diagram mean something disturbing about reality?

The memory was dim.

(When he had had to give up on trying to afford school, Sinclair had boxed up most of his books for easy and frequent moves to cheap places around town. He hadn't been proud of it, but had needed to move without paying back rent three times so far to avoid becoming homeless, and never completely unpacked anymore.)

It had been so long since he'd taken an interest that he'd forgotten which book the diagram was in. Been so long, he realized, that he felt vaguely as though he was beginning to awaken from some long, difficult to explain, mind-numbing sleep.

The same sort everyone seemed to be sleeping. He thought he'd noticed more people being spaced out more often since he'd taken the night janitor job with the university Physical Plant, but he wasn't sure whether the observation were true, or whether he was noticing more inattentiveness simply because he worked with such mentally absent people.

Which was the reality, really?

Not that it mattered much, either way; he still had to get back to his pre-work routine, so that he could prepare for his work routine. He had to get ready for more sleep-janitoring.

At No. 2, the mystery tenant's lights were out; Sinclair let himself into the office with his building's master key and examined the contents of the dry-marker board. He borrowed a pad and pen, and scribbled down what he found: A graph with the label "space" at its horizontal axis, "time" at its vertical. A four-dimensional event, then.

He spotted several "e-" labels. That meant "electron," right? Some sort of particle-collision sketch?

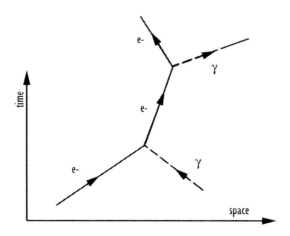

Sinclair was trying to recall how, exactly, to read the diagram; he had a hazy recollection of its having something to do with a strange, but somehow audacious idea about subatomic reality. Or had he dreamt that part? Sometimes his dreams were alarmingly realistic.

He couldn't remember. Maybe this wasn't even the same thing he thought he remembered. He shook his clouded head, his vision trembling and distorting, as he tried to clear years of accumulated cobwebs from his skull.

He folded up the sketch and pushed it down into the pocket of his work shirt, behind an embroidery that said "Physical Plant," unable to decipher the sketch, but hoping to compare it, later, to the diagram in one of the two books he'd dug out.

The rain outside had stopped, he noticed.

The passing rain had taken its cold front with it. The night was warmer — even pleasant. For a change of pace, something to keep him from going insane with the sameness of his routine, he decided to take his coffee break on the roof of No. 2, alone. Through the thick cover of cobwebbing overlaying his brain, he daydreamed as he stared out over the city in the night.

And then it happened.

He thought.

Hadn't it?

Out of the corner of his eye, he saw a woman wandering home on the walk below, not paying attention. He wasn't really paying attention to her. She seemed to be sleepwalking, as he always did. Then he saw her — or thought he saw her — not notice; saw her neglect to avoid a lamppost. Thought he saw her not collide with it. Thought he saw her pass through it!

He was startled, uncertain — he turned his attention toward her, and the world seemed solid enough under his discerning gaze — but he was certain that she had walked in a straight line, through the lamppost in front of No. 2.

What happened?, he wondered, watching as the woman's shoulder collided roughly with a stop sign on the corner. Hadn't he flushed all of Beckett's acid out of his system? He should have by now!

But if she passed through the lamppost like some ghost, why didn't she pass through the street sign?, he wondered. He began trying to convince himself that it was all some sort of optical illusion. He hadn't been paying much attention, he realized. He worked to assure himself that maybe it hadn't happened that way at all.

It couldn't have actually happened.

Right?

A thought from the other night, tripping among his friends, drifted into his mind: It was all OK, man, as long as he could keep the reality separate from the illusion – as long as he could tell them apart.

Soon, said the voice, at his side again, suddenly, as though hovering at his left ear. Sinclair jumped, gagging on an inadvertently inhaled mouthful of coffee at the sudden reappearance of the voice. Why was he imagining it so frequently? Was it schizophrenics who heard voices? Was that his problem – some sort of mental illness just beginning to show itself?

A nervous laugh raced through him as he recalled an old drug-war-era claim that a person could be considered legally insane after his fourth dose of LSD.

He'd certainly long passed that mile-marker.

An acidic, uncomfortable spot formed in his stomach. He was honestly, deeply afraid that he might not be able to trust what his senses told him.

Or worse: That his mind, his ability to interpret what his senses told him, was untrustworthy.

Chapter Five

Observations

On Delphina Hutchings' briefing, Professor MacMillan Trull drawled on: "Rene Descartes," he informed her, "in his *Meditations*, postulated that the essence of reality consists in it – reality, that is – being observed. That is, he argued that in order for all things to exist, some omniscient consciousness must be perceiving those things at all times. That consciousness, he argued, was God." You could almost hear Trull's shrug of indifference: "Fair enough, I 'spose. Keep it in mind when I describe the need for observing things."

A piece of the justification Sapphire and Wachhund had made to her suddenly clicked into place: If pieces of the universe are disappearing, maybe it's because there's no omniscient consciousness – no God - there to observe them anymore.

Now she understood that part, anyway.

Her little transport buzzed down the labyrinthine tunnelways under Defense Intelligence Operations headquarters, zipping past a blur of (she assumed) D.I.Ops people, some, like herself, in military dress, others in the depressingly plain, black formalwear that seemed to be the de facto dress code of the intelligence community.

The tunnelways were separated into four lanes: one each direction for the little transport carts, one each way for foot traffic between the D.I.Ops buildings and other facilities, a lifeless, pallid overhead lighting system stretching along for miles.

"Now then," Trull continued, "Remote Viewing. That's the title o' this next part. 'Cause that's what we do — least, that's what I do, and I'm doing the briefing. And since you're hearin' this, these facts make me think that's probably what you do, too. In Controlled Remote Viewing, which we usually shorten to 'Remote Viewing,' or 'RV,' a specially trained agent of our government attempts to gain information about remote places, objects such as documents, or people. Or all of the above — sometimes you don't know what to expect. Ennahway, here are a few things to remember: It works. We know it works, and we know damn well, 'cause we do it. All the time. Get loads of great intelligence gathering out of it. If you've got a problem with just accepting that, you should probably take off your headphones and request reassignment, 'cause that's just chicken scratchins. Small puhtatahs."

Hutchings gave a single, perturbed huff of a laugh at Trull's abrasiveness, careful not to draw the attention of her driver. *Like I have any choice,* she thought.

Trull paused meaningfully in her headphones, providing the skeptical with time to hit the "stop" button.

"'K, now they're gone," he said, clearing his throat.

"Deal is, as you probably know by now, your government's pretty good at rewriting public perceptions of things. By now, some of you know about Hubble, our first deep-space telescope: Big damned fiasco, public money spent on a contraption doesn't work worth a damn. Unless your clearance is high enough, 'n which case you know Hubble saw things just fine, and that the problem lies with people with enough authority not liking what Hubble was telling them. A few other good ones:

The 'single bullet theory'

The War on Drugs

The supposedly natural evolution of HIV

The first lunar landing

"With enough clearance to hear this, you know that:

"One: A single bullet does not make many holes in many people from many different angles. And it certainly doesn't pause politely in mid-air for several seconds while considering its next move;

"Two: With all due respect to former commanders-in-chief, what better way to deflect attention from your role as a drug trafficker than to begin a high-profile campaign against drugs and drug use? The government trafficked in drugs to fund the president's pet projects during the so-called 'drug war' during the '80s. It's not nice, but it's true; it has been, and will continue to be, funded enough to keep it in the headlines, but not enough to ever have any chance of success. Mark my words;

"Three: Can't talk too much about this one, but if you're hearin' this, again, your clearance is high enough to keep me outta the dog house. Just think about the 1932 United States Public Health Service (PHASE) and Tuskegee Institute study in Macon County, Alabama, to determine the effects of untreated syphilis; 399 black males, all deliberately infected and allowed to die of a perfectly treatable disease."

His tone changed, becoming mocking.

"In the interest of science, y'all understand, of course."

"And Four — this one's my favorite: The whole thing was staged on a set out in the dunes near Roswell, New Mexico.

"See, we didn't really have the science in place to make a lunar landing happen. We do now, but then? No way. Send a guy inta orbit, sure, but to the moon, to land on the moon, to launch again, then come back? Nope.

"Y'all who think this is a joke can watch the landing and liftoff of the lunar module on file tape. There's no blast crater from either. And there should be. There definitely should be.

"But the best part's this: Due to hysteria in the military and the media following the 1947 crash of a weather balloon, folks already thought there were crashed UFOs and aliens in frozen storage or somethin' at Area 51 — we got nothin' like that, but have I got a hell of a nice lunar landscape to show you!

"Not like they'd ever really let me show you. Again, though, mark my words.

"Hell, we make sure — damned sure — that we make a public effort to discredit the folks think we got a crashed UFO. Looks like we're hidin' somethin'. And we are; just ain't what they think it is!"

Trull broke into a gusty, gravelly laugh as Hutchings' jaw swung open in amazement.

"'K, that's enough 'bout big — ah — re-envisionings on your employer's part to make mah point, I think.

"Now then. Remote Viewing. This idea — or analogs thereof — can be found in the pre-modern cultures of Egypt, parts of Africa, Babylon, America — among Native Americans — Australia, Greece, Scandinavia, Siberia, Persia, many Polynesian Islander cultures, and in ancient Indian Yoga teachings.

"One researcher of record, a Mr. Theodore Angelis, reviewed anthropological data from research done on a sample of 60 separate cultures; he found that 54 of them made at least some mention of a state similar enough to RV to be useful for our purposes. Keep in mind that despite the expected wide range of differences in cultures and traditions, and despite a wide variety in terminology used to describe the phenomenon we call RV, what he found was a shared belief in this ability across cultural lines.

"While varyin' somewhat," he paused to cough, "I've encountered ideas in each o' the aforementioned cultures that are more or less similar to what we think of when we say 'Remote Viewing,' and which likewise correspond to Angelis' research."

The little transport jumped suddenly, bouncing over a seam in the concrete floor of the tunnelway. Hutchings righted herself, shooting a look of reprimand toward her driver, but he acted as though he hadn't noticed a thing.

"In a somewhat more modern vein, the term 'Out of Body Experience,' or OBE, or even OOBE, may be thought of as relatin' to RV. It's also relevant to us as a way o' broadening what we're talking about in a historical context. Our term is the new kid onna block here. Take the Theosophists: Theosophist thought envisions a human being as comprising a series of 'bodies,' each more subtle than its — ah — predecessor. They teach of seven separate 'planes' of existence, and a corresponding body of sorts for each. The astral plane and its correspondin' body are what concern us in terms o' their teaching, 'cause it's the astral body these folks, and others like 'em, talk about when they talk about having an OBE. And when they talk about OBE, they're talking about observation of places and people and things that are outside the usual range of the five senses traditionally recognized in the West.

"Get it? In all the ways that matter, we're talking about the same thing.

"The Theosophists teach that anyone can be trained to do this; we believed so, too, and in practice, that's the way it's worked out. So we're talking about an innate human ability. A means of sensory perception beyond the range normally expected for the human senses, but a perfectly natural means of sensory perception, nonetheless.

"Now, while there is significant historical background for this sorta viewing at a distance, mention of the phenomenon has been slowly canonized outta modern scientific and historical texts.

"I don't mind telling you that from what I understand, that took some work.

"While this information survived in oral traditions in most cases, ancient Yogic texts contained written references to a kind of super power they refer to as a 'siddhi.' Siddhi is a Sanskrit term, and that's a problem, 'cause English ain't quite so flexible and elegant, and so what I'm saying when I talk about a siddhi is gonna be simplified a bit, outta necessity and the limits of the language. Now, I'm dumbin' the Sanskrit term down a lot to say a siddhi is a super power, but for now, that'll have to do. You wanna go study up on Sanskrit, that's fine by me. Broaden your horizons."

Trull paused to laugh at his own joke.

"Anyway, there are lots of siddhis. Between seven and 20, dependin' on your source and translation. And they branch out into more 'n a hundred. Think of 'em as sort of highly evolved senses no one knows they have. So we can loosely call a siddhi a super power of the mind and body that extends beyond the local limits we usually conceive of for our senses. That's close 'nuff for our purposes.

"Of all of 'em, the one we're concerned with is a siddhi for distance seeing. It's mentioned around 200 BC, so we know the concept and practice have been around for a while.

"Now then, as to the types of RV:

"Coordinate Remote Viewing, or CRV - With or without a partner agent, or "sender" — that's an individual sent to the target site to act as a beacon or a transmitter for the remote viewer — on the site being viewed, this method seeks to gather intelligence about a remote location. Sender-receiver pairs train exhaustively before the sender is sent into the field to the site which will be observed. In surveillance missions utilizing the CRV method with no sender, map coordinates, some details, even surveillance photos might be provided to the RV sensitive.

"Extended Remote Viewing (ERV)- a hybrid relaxation/meditative-based method known to program personnel as "extended remote viewing," or ERV is sometimes employed.

"Written Remote Viewing (WRV) - a hybrid of both channeling and automatic writing. Strangely, WRV was adopted very quickly as an official method for performing intelligence missions.

"Automatic writing was made most famous by renowned supposed psychic Edgar Cayce. You may read up on Mr. Cayce in any public library.

"Both CRV and ERV methods had been heavily evaluated and refined before being put into service on "live" intelligence collection and surveillance missions. WRV was adopted without the careful evaluation that either CRV or ERV had undergone.

"Senders and beacons were used in early RV experiments, and continued to be used for trainees to provide a connection with the site to be viewed that the beginning RVer could easily grasp … "

Her silent chauffeur slowed, taxiing the last few yards to her drop-off point; he deposited her beneath another wing of the D.I.Ops building and, without a word, drove back the way he came. The elevator took her to her new office on floor 14 of the D.I.Ops West wing. (It was actually the thirteenth floor from ground level, but, strangely, D.I.Ops had apparently clung to superstitions marking the number as unlucky, and so her elevator passed floor 12 and stopped at 14, without ever actually passing a floor unlucky enough to be designated 13.)

An Army lieutenant in full uniform stood outside the office Sapphire had dispatched her to. The doorway was opaque – solid metal of some sort, polished until reflective, a massive, imposing thing she could not have moved aside on her own. A standard-issue keycard lock was mounted to the right of the steel monster.

The lieutenant shifted uncomfortably, checking his watch, then straightening, embarrassed, as he noticed her approach.

"Major," he said with a tight salute, snapping to attention. Something in his body language – she couldn't place what, exactly — suggested discomfort. He was young – perhaps 28 – and Caucasian, as far as she could tell, his hair a stubbly military Brillo pad growing from his head.

She returned the salute. "Waiting for me, lieutenant?"

"Yes ma'am," he replied in the pseudo-Southern twang so many in the military affect. "Lieutenant Rifkin reporting, ma'am." He presented an envelope full of paperwork. "I've been assigned to assist you."

"Assist me how, lieutenant?" she asked. "Not just anyone gets a role in a project like this one."

Again, he shifted uncomfortably.

"No, ma'am. I have been authorized to help you get whatever equipment you want, contact whoever you'd like to interview, and generally do whatever is necessary to facilitate Project Oversight."

"At ease, lieutenant. What's bothering you?"

He relaxed a bit, shifting his weight and meeting her gaze.

"Permission to speak freely?" he asked.

She nodded.

"I'm a military man, major. I've been trying to figure out what I might have done to get assigned to something like this."

She arched her eyebrows.

"'Like this,' lieutenant?"

"Yeah. Hocus pocus," he said, then, a little too quickly, "Uh, ma'am."

Great, she thought. An unwilling assistant.

"Well, your clearance must be rock solid to be assigned to this, so I wouldn't view it as punishment, if I were you," she said. But then, she still wondered whether she was being punished by being reassigned.

Don't think about Jordan don't think about Jordan don't think about Jordan, she thought, fighting off a wave of grief.

But how couldn't she think about him?

It still didn't make sense to her, but then, it didn't have to make sense. Not to her, anyway. She was in the intelligence business. She was given orders, and those orders were to be followed, regardless of whether she was given enough information to put any real faith into the task at hand. If she was to head up some expanded Remote Viewing effort, so be it. She had come as close as she would ever come to being allowed to complain outright during her meeting with Sapphire.

She produced a keycard from the new packet Sapphire had provided, swiped it through the lock mechanism. With a faint card-shuffle stutter of clicks, the readout light on the lock flipped from red to green, and the massive door slid aside to reveal a stadium-like open work area. She was taken aback; she had expected to get a simple office with a work area to follow, eventually, when she had begun to form her team.

Inside, Wachhund awaited, a file of dossiers open on the worktable before him, and box after file-folder box of them behind him on a fold-out table. He flapped down the file he had been reviewing, its echo rebounding off the distant, barren walls and ceiling.

The lieutenant whistled, marveling at the size of facility their new Project Oversight had been assigned.

"Ah, major. Good you could get to this wing so quickly," he said, his thick German accent turning all of his th's to d's.

"Time is of the essence. Lieutenant ... ?" he asked.

"Sir!" said the young officer, snapping again to attention.

"This operation, more so than any you have ever been or ever will be a part of, absolutely requires one element: faith on your part in the project. Do you understand me?" he asked. "Understand perfectly?"

"Sir, yes sir!" replied Rifkin. His military conditioning would keep him in line, his sir-yes-sir reply assured them. He knew the drill.

"If you ever have doubt about our – ah – 'hocus pocus' here, you must inform me immediately. A lack of faith here could destroy our project. Do you understand, lieutenant?"

Rifkin's gaze remained fixed forward. "Sir, yes sir!"

"Ah. Good," said Wachhund. "And, ah, you need only say 'Yes sir' to get the point across to me, lieutenant; I am no military man."

"Sir, y – uh – yes sir!" Rifkin stuttered.

"Major, a good deal of equipment is on its way. I think that the lieutenant may oversee receipt and installation of all of that while you and I concentrate on a list of possible recruits."

She was taken aback a bit; she was in charge of this, right?

Still, Wachhund was much more informed on the specifics of the new Project

Oversight, and had been sent to aid her in its formation. And in intelligence community terms, he did outrank her.

"Sounds good, sir. What sort of equipment is on the way?"

"Oh, the usual when setting up a large covert operation: Desks, cabinets, computers, coffee makers ... the nuts and bolts, you might say."

Chapter Six

Friendship

Standing in the big shared bathroom, Sinclair remembered his additional dose — he was to take two of the experimental antihistamine tablets per day; any less would have no effect, and more would have him feeling his hair crawl around on his head on its own.

That weirded him out.

He was already dealing with voices in his head, and had no desire to add to the paranoia he felt when they spoke up suddenly, scaring the hell out of him.

This afternoon, he could smell someone's cooking wafting up from the cramped kitchen they shared.

"Afternoon, Sync," Beckett called to him from the kitchen as Sinclair rounded the landing and stepped into the first floor hallway. The hall was a straight shot beginning at the front door and continuing, unlit, through to the kitchen, at the rear of the house. Partway down, on the left, was the unlit entry to the evidently unoccupied living room.

A faint, pallid light shone into the hall from the waning sun of another frosty, overcast day — the kind of day that made him feel like the gods were cold and distant.

The sickly glow backlit the man's odd, unruly frock of hair in a curly locked halo; Beckett's hair was longer in front than in the back, brown curls spilling down over his eyes.

"Beckett," Sinclair replied, yawning.

"You're up and dressed early, G," said Beckett, scraping with a spatula at something burnt to the bottom of his trusty wrought-iron pan. With little provocation, Beckett could burst into a 15-minute jag about how great, useful, durable, whatever, wrought-iron pans were, and Sinclair had experienced the speech fully six times now. He was affecting the ridiculous hip-hop style that had gotten popular in the late '90s, his elastic-waist jeans pulled down a few inches to reveal designer-label boxers.

"Your ass is hanging out again, Beckett," Sinclair chided, smirking.

Beckett paid no attention. He had his thang on, and no one was going to dis it.

He had a habit of making home DVDs to stock hour after hour of late '80s and '90s music. His DVD reader was swimming its way through a track from Single Gun

Theory; Jacqui Hunt's dreamy, chantlike vocals drifted forth amid the chaos of Beckett's clanging of dishes and pans:

"At the point beyond which something will happen …

"At the point beyond which something will occur …"

Her voice recalled chords struck and held, blasting soothingly from a church organ during Easter Sunday service. Sinclair didn't have much use for church these days. How did they do that?

He found himself wondering idly what the lyrics meant, anyway.

What is "the point beyond which something will happen"? he wondered. He shook himself out of it.

"Yeah," he replied. "Wanted to catch a cuppa joe at the Java House before work."

"Yo, check it out," said Beckett, waving imprecisely toward the table. "Another S.G.A," he said.

On the table Sinclair spotted a copy of *Fringe Inquirer* next to the .22 Beckett kept around to shoot at rats. Every now and then the weird bastard actually hit one. It was cheaper than calling an exterminator, he said, and the building's owners had made it clear that pests were the tenants' problem. It was a small enough caliber weapon that Sinclair was pretty sure the bullets couldn't get through the walls or floors.

Fringe Inquirer was a UFO/alien-abduction/Bigfoot-type supermarket tabloid Beckett counted on for all the stories the governments were keeping out of the mainstream press.

"S.G.A.?" Sinclair asked warily.

"Smart Guy Abduction," came the distracted reply, as Beckett continued to scrape at the burnt whatever on the pan. "They think it's related to appearances of Men In Black. Got some Japanese professor this time."

Sinclair had no idea what the hell Beckett was talking about, and he knew it didn't matter; next month Beckett would be talking about the Louisiana Alligator Man or something.

"Hey, I hate to bring it up, but do you have a rent check ready yet? Old Man Tomlin's coming by tomorrow to pick 'em all up. Likes me to round 'em up," Beckett said distantly, his attention still focused on the pan.

Thank God for drug studies, Sinclair thought.

"I'll have to post-date it a few days, but I can have it ready."

"That's cool, Sync, that's cool. Seen Liam yet?"

"Liam? No. I just got up and going. Why?"

"He pitched himself off his bike."

Alarm hit Sinclair. Liam worked as a bicycle courier. The guy rode his bike like some demonically possessed steroid popper. No one anywhere near him was safe while he was on a delivery mission, ignoring traffic rules, charging in front of trucks, zipping through the too-small openings between moving vehicles, his parcel strapped across his back …

The mental image made Sinclair shudder.

"Is he all right?"

"Yeah," said Beckett indifferently, changing his angle to get better leverage in his struggle against the burnt stuff.

"How'd he do it? I mean, was he hurt?"

Beckett shrugged, grinning. "Go ask him."

Sinclair made his way back up the stairs to the aged, loosely hung door of Liam's rented room and knocked.

"Hey Liam — you in there?"

The door swung open suddenly, the room's occupant standing there in a bath towel, his eyes wide and puffy, as though he'd just awakened from a nightmare.

"Sync. Hey. I, um," he took a deep, mucousy snort and swallowed moistly, smacking his lips distractedly. Sinclair winced. "Yeah. Um. Trashed my bike."

Liam's social skills seemed pretty dull to Sinclair; he wondered how the guy ever managed to get a date. His voice was hoarse and monotonous, his delivery filled with abrupt, inexplicable, mid-sentence halts. And the mucous thing. That was no bonus, either.

"Are you OK?"

"Yeah. Yeah," he snorted deeply again and swallowed, smacking his lips a bit. Then after a moment: "No. Needed 12 sutures in my scalp."

He turned his head and showed Sinclair a small, shaved lump and its stitching in his scalp, on the top of his head.

"What the hell happened?"

"Well. Um." He sorted and swallowed again. "I was taking this corner kind of fast."

"Yeah … ?"

"Yeah. And, um, there was a patch of sand."

"Yes?"

"And — you know where the youth center pool is? That big window that faces the road?"

Sinclair nodded impatiently.

"Well, there were some girls there, in these, like, really great swimsuits."

"'Great' meaning 'skimpy?'"

Liam was moving like lava, not grasping anything with much speed today. "Well, yeah," he said. "Duh."

"Spit it out, Liam," Sinclair said impatiently. Sometimes the painstaking process of dragging a story out of him was more of a struggle than it was worth.

"Well, I noticed my sock was all loose. Fell down around my ankle, so I was pulling it up."

Liam wore tube socks.

"You took a corner at your best speed while you were pulling up your sock with one hand and watching girls in bathing suits?!"

Liam nodded.

"Exactly," he said. "Yeah.

"So I hit all this, like, sand. And just. Like. Flipped over my handlebars and landed on my head."

"I can't believe you aren't dead yet," said an incredulous Sinclair. "You do stuff like this all the time!"

"Yeah. You know it's, like, $350 if an ambulance worker helps you get into the ambulance? So I had to kinda fend this guy off and climb in on my own."

Sinclair's jaw swung open in disbelief.

"Jesus, Liam, try being careful once in a while."

On his way around the landing again, Beckett called out: "Catchya."

"Yeah," said Sinclair, pulling on his long, heavy, Army-surplus trench coat.

The walk to Java House isn't too bad, Sinclair thought, but he wanted to splurge some of his drug-study money on a decent cup of coffee, a rarity with his budget constraints. He usually had to make do with whatever coffee he could clandestinely spoon into a zip-lock bag from the offices he cleaned.

Sinclair thought about the graph again as he made his way downtown: Space on one arm and time on the other meant that the graph was depicting something in 3D that was happening over time — a four-dimensional graph. He thought so, anyway. It had been a long time since he'd read the book's accompanying explanation. He pulled out the sketch of it he'd jotted down.

An electron (labeled e-) was part of it, but there were other symbols, too, whose meanings he didn't recall, whose paths crossed that of the electron. Why hadn't he remembered that before?

He hastily folded up the sketch and pushed it down into his pocket again.

"Americano," he said to the skillfully down-dressed coffeehouse cashier.

"One shot or two?"

"Two. My day's just getting started," replied Sinclair.

He could almost — almost — taste the coffee from its potent aroma alone. God, he missed good coffee.

As the attendant collected his money, she noticed his janitor's workshirt.

"Hey, cool shirt. D'you get it at Secondhand Sally's Alley?"

"Last one," he replied, smiling.

Java House was Sinclair's favorite: Painted in subdued, flat tones and decked out with secondhand furniture, it was a great place to just get lost for an afternoon. Usually.

As he eyed an old, unoccupied lounger near a small table and lamp, he recognized Dannie. Short for Dannielle. His ex. The two had had a tumultuous two-year relationship accented with angry spats that came on when they were drinking together. In his mind's eye, he recalled dulled flashes of the worst moments: the fights over money, the beer and too-frequent acid, violence in what turned out to be their final fight. He'd seen violence between his parents when he was very, very young and promised it would never be a part of his relationships; then, one night, she had slugged his groin as they argued in bed.

Even now, more than a year later, his stomach soured at the thought of speaking with her. The idea brought a dull, distant ache to the testicle she had struck.

"To go," he told the cashier, trying to avoid notice.

It was too early for work, but he was already halfway there. He gathered up his cuppa and headed back out into the night.

Building No. 2 wasn't much, and it wasn't fun being there any longer than he needed to be, but he didn't really have anywhere else to go. To kill time, he started to walk the halls, sipping his cooled coffee. The light was on again in the third-floor office that was home to the late-night guy and his diagram.

Sinclair peered into the office and found the rumpled thirtysomething man in again, sifting through another edition of the classifieds, now marked up and resting on his desk.

The occupant noticed Sinclair, recognizing him after a moment.

"Hi," he said cheerfully. "Another late one. Don't mind me."

"Oh. No problem," replied Sinclair.

"Is it that late, or are you early?"

"I'm a little early. Thought I'd have a look around."

"Ah."

Sinclair stepped into the office, eyeing the board.

"What is that? I think I saw it in a book I read when I was in school."

The tenant looked confused, mesmerized for a moment, then shook his head and pulled himself together.

"Really? That's cool!" he replied. "It's an idea about sub-atomic particles and how we see time. I'd — somehow I'd completely forgotten about putting it up there. Sheesh — I was half asleep!"

"Oh yeah?"

The tenant scratched his scalp.

"Yeah — weird. Well, anyway, the diagram is a way of saying that sometimes, at least, electrons aren't always with whatever they're part of. That they're really just waiting there for us in a specific span of time and space."

Sinclair gazed for a long time at the diagram.

"I see," he said, not seeing.

"Where do you get yours?" the occupant asked, pointing toward Sinclair's paper coffee mug.

"Java House, when I can."

"That's a great little shop. I don't really have time to run all the way down there much, so I brought my espresso maker to campus." With an air of devotion and pride, he slid back a cabinet door to reveal the polished-steel marvel.

"Want one?"

Sinclair smiled, nodding.

"My name's Thaddeus MacKenzie. Call me Deuce. It's easier than 'Thaddeus,' and doesn't sound as lame as being called 'Thad.'"

Sinclair shook MacKenzie's hand.

"Sinclair Stauffer," he replied, as the other man began setting up the machine.

After they'd been talking for a while, Sinclair confessed that he had, in the past, read interesting, challenging material.

"But I don't know what happened. Once it sunk in that school was out for me, y'know, that I couldn't afford to go back and that I was a janitor, I just sort of stopped caring. I don't even know when it happened — I just kind of went on auto-pilot. My life was pretty strange for a couple of years anyway."

"Strange? How's that?"

Sinclair paused, uncertain whether he should really discuss details of his private life with someone he hardly knew.

"Bad relationship," he said. "A long, bad one."

Deuce nodded thoughtfully.

"I've just been trying to dig out from under all that."

"You kept a taste for good coffee."

Sinclair laughed a little. "This is a luxury. I usually can't afford to blow three bucks on a cup of coffee."

Then he realized that time was catching up with him. Sinclair thanked Deuce MacKenzie for the espresso and made his way to the middle building to sign in for work.

Deuce MacKenzie pulled out the cup with the spent coffee grounds and up-ending it, tapping the grounds out over the side of his desk, aiming for a small trash can that was there earlier.

Wasn't it?

Too late, after he'd dumped the grounds, he noticed that he couldn't actually see the trash can.

Peeking over the edge, he found the grounds resting on the floor, no trash can in sight.

Chapter Seven

The Observers

Wachhund, as it turned out, was to be a sort of overseer of Major Hutchings from the inner circle of the international intelligence community whose shadowy countenances and computer-disguised voices she'd met following her transfer. She was certainly in charge from a military standpoint, but his actions, his words, made it clear that he felt himself to be in charge from a political and administrative perspective; she was still to act on his words, whether he phrased them as orders or not.

Fine, she thought, for the time being.

Hutchings had no interest in having another person on her project who might generate confusion by giving project operatives orders that might contradict hers.

She had a team to build from the remnants of the old Project Long View, and sank her energy into that job. She had a small group, some two dozen experienced remote viewers, to begin working with. But from their case reports, despite what amounted to spectacular psychic spying results from the perspective of a military intelligence officer, she no longer had the luxury of evaluating the results on that basis.

No, the task at hand was much, much larger: She needed to parse out an ongoing watch of everything on Earth, break it down into individual areas large enough to be observed by a single RV sensitive. The equivalent of having a night watchman dedicated to monitoring a single security video. And she didn't know where to begin on deciding how much of an area one sensitive could watch over how much time and still achieve the hoped-for results.

That sort of quantification would have to come later, she decided, gauged as the project moved forward. She noted it in the margins of her project schedule. Wachhund was there to help explain the D.I.Ops' theories on the matter, and to help her with gaps in her training in the RV field. She was, after all, a field operative in only one type of RV. Her audio briefing had convinced her that she still had much to learn about the various agencies' scientific, theoretical, and even metaphysical perspectives on the project and the problem it was being created to address.

Her assistant, the lieutenant, turned out to be good for little more than helping to keep her schedule running smoothly as she interviewed Project Long View operatives and began reactivating them for duty on Project Oversight.

As soon as she could get their commissions reactivated, the operatives began RV testing and training to gauge the ability of each to observe targets remotely, and to determine the extent of their range and just how much they could view remotely.

By and large, the operatives could observe a small area — say, an unoccupied parcel of landing spanning several acres, or a single four-bedroom home — with remarkable accuracy. But when larger areas were named as targets, the observations grew hazier — and much too general to prove useful for Oversight's needs.

Hutchings rubbed her temples, trying to massage away a growing frustration headache. The task was just too large. How could they ever get enough of these operatives together — operatives who had to gain sufficient security clearance and be given proper training in an obscure field — to observe what Wachhund blithely referred to with a global sweep of his hand as "all of it"?

And, she idly wondered, if this Trull person is the one doing the briefings, why don't I ever hear his name from Wachhund?

Two months into the project, with the number of operatives on the group approaching 150, she voiced her concerns to Wachhund, who dismissed them with a wave.

"These are our parameters, Major. This is the framework within which we build our project," he said evenly, his eyes firmly locked on her. "This is the framework which we were given."

"We need more, Wachhund," she said. "It can't be done. Not like this. We need to be able to remotely view more — much, much more — than we can with the operatives. And to solve this problem, I need to know more, a great deal more, about the problem and what we know about how it all works together."

"This is my position," he said firmly, crossing his arms. "What can I tell you?"

Wachhund wasn't going to budge. He'd fallen back into territorial pissing mode. He seemed to understand the magnitude of the problem, but was unable to envision a solution outside the guidelines he had been handed.

"Where is Dr. MacMillan Trull?" she asked. "Why don't you ever mention him or his work?"

Wachhund eyed her coolly; they were no longer on the same side.

"Herr Doktor is no longer with the agency," he said carefully.

"Then reactivate him," she said. "We need his expertise if we're to have a chance at this. I just don't have the knowledge he does on this stuff."

"Major," he said, "Herr Doktor was part of the cover story in which Remote Viewing was ended within U.S. intelligence. Reactivating Trull presents us with the larger problem, potentially, of exposing that cover story as a fiction."

"Don't announce his reactivation — "

"It will be noticed by someone ... "

"Then concoct another fiction, Wachhund — reactivate him in an unrelated project. Oversight has no chance of success without his specialized knowledge of the field. None. And you know what's at stake. You know we can't afford not to succeed."

Wacchund relented, pulling back. He would have to establish another line of defense for later confrontations.

Chapter Eight

Dr. MacMillan Trull, fan of LSD, tie-die wearer, and certified supra-genius, CIA (retired), sat on his green vinyl lawnchair in his wide-open back yard, eating a breakfast of granola with banana slices, and wondered what sort of reaction he'd get if he were ever to describe what his job had been like back at the CIA.

"Trull? The nutty professor?" his former undergraduate students would chuckle. He watched, as, after nearly any of his lectures, he could see one or more of his students making a quick motion of the hand over the head to one another, as if to say: That cruised right over my head!

"Give me half a dose of whatever he's on!"

His joint appointments in parapsychology and physics had made him something of an oddball even at John F. Kennedy University, one of the few schools where studies in parapsychology were part of the curriculum at all. Trull was also one of the youngest professors in the faculty's history.

He was full of ideas about how it all worked together, but as far as he was concerned, he was an armchair philosopher at best, only paying attention to those papers, articles, and books dealing with his favorite topic for light reading: the nature of reality.

But to 18-year-olds fresh from the public education system, people struggling with the concept of producing a simple, brief, scholarly paper when so assigned, even broaching the subject of parapsychology — or the study thereof — incited laughter. Get him going during his lecture in "Nature of Consciousness: Western Perspectives," and students could get a real show.

He loved to drag students unawares to the abyss at the end of Newtonian physics, where quantum reality took over, and the observer's decisions could be shown to have a direct impact on an experiment's results. He went into incredible detail, exploring to the point of excruciating minutiae the concepts behind Shroedinger's wave equation and its corresponding victim, the hypothetical Schoedinger's Cat.

He was fascinated with the debate over the collapse of that wave. That and the death of the cat.

"It's named after an Austrian physicist named Erwin Schroedinger. Bright fella. It goes like this: Now the whole idea is that the number of possible effects resulting from a causal event is mapped in what we call the Schroedinger wave — a probability wave — sometimes small, sometimes infinitely vast!" he'd begin, his voice already raised in excitement. "When all of that probability is replaced in the wave by a single point — the actual effect — we call that the collapse of the Schroedinger wave. But the question is, when does the wave collapse?

"We know, for example, that choices made by the experimenter decide ultimately whether his experiment proves that light is a wave or a particle, right? So," he almost howled, "we can also see how the choices other experimenters make might affect the outcomes of their experiments. Take the cat. Schroedinger's theoretical cat. We'll call him 'Spot.'

"Now then, we take Spot here, and stick him in a box. Since it's Schroedinger's cat Spot, it's also Schroedinger's box. 'Cause I said so. Now, this is a helluva box. Nothing — no light, no sound, no smell — nothing, an' sure as hell nothing the size of a cat, escapes the box. The vast array of things that can happen in this experiment can be thought of in terms of Schroedinger's wave.

"You with me? Who said 'No'? Catch up, boy, I'm dumbin' this down as much as I can.

"Now, some day the cat dies inside Schroedinger's box. But when? If we aren't directly observing the cat, we don't know, do we? Say we wait three months, then we open the box. We find poor, dead ol' Spot. But when did he die? I mean, at some point, Mr. Schroedinger's cat Spot died, and his probability wave collapsed to the single point representing the end effect. In this case, that's poor ol' dead Spot.

"But *when* did the Schroedinger wave collapse? When the cat died? We don't know when that was, now, do we? Or did the wave collapse when we observed it — when we opened the box and found poor ol' dead Spot?

"'Cause y'see, kids, in the Schroedinger wave, there's a point beyond which something will happen. A point beyond which something will occur. That point is elusive. The collapse of the Schroedinger wave and the results to which it collapses are directly affected by our choices and our observations."

Students would laugh quietly and nervously at this point. What the hell was the nutty professor even talking about?

"I'll tell ya: I do not know. Nor do a helluva lot o' people leaps and bounds brighter than I am. How and when we open the box affects how and when the wave collapses, and what final effect we find. Get it? Your choices affect the very quantum fabric of the teeny-tiny corner of reality that includes your experiment. And woe be unto Spot if you get your act together a little too late.

"So y'see, students, your homework exercises are not likely so harmless as you imagine."

Seeing a hand timidly raised about halfway back, Trull pointed and yelled, "Yes?!"

"But sir — uh — professor," the student, inevitably one of the kids who thought he was signing up for a blow-off class he could simply breeze through, would stammer. "How does this relate to the nature of consciousness?" he would ask, citing the course title.

"Jumpin' Jesus, boy, "Trull would bellow. "Ain't you payin' any god-damned attention?!"

The Schroedinger summary lecture was usually enough to clear out about a third of the class, so Trull made sure to give it early on. Those who remained aboard the reality-cruising deck of Trull's class, though, received no mercy.

Time-traveling subatomic particles. The multiple realities represented by the many worlds theory, a chaotic means of explaining how the universe dealt with both the Schroedinger wave and its myriad possible collapses.

Those were the days.

Then came the CIA's sudden realization that the world might be more complicated than they thought, and that the Soviets had realized that fact a little sooner than they had, and suddenly there was a pair of G-Men in dull black suits knocking at his office door as he read an issue of *Fortean Times*.

"Professor Trull," said the apparent man in charge, or at least the more outgoing of the two, "Your country needs you to help in the ongoing battle against the evils of Communism."

To which Trull promptly replied, "Fuck off." After which he promptly returned his attention to his reading.

It was the beginning of a beautiful, professional relationship.

In coming months, the CIA recruiters racked their brains trying to find ways to entice the eccentric professor from his post at JFK. But Trull had tenure, liked living in a small university town where he could get psilocybin or high-quality blotter acid when he felt like giving his brains a mini-vacation.

Better salary?

Nope.

New sports car?

No.

A new house?

Nada.

Trull, fan of LSD, tie-die wearer, and certified supra-genius, did not particularly wish to surround himself with dull-witted low-level government spies who would have no idea what he was talking about or what he was up to. He was happy where he was, didn't really want or need more money, or a gas-guzzling sports car, and he liked his modest home in his little university town just fine.

So, in effect, they drafted him.

In retrospective, Trull had always wondered whether during that first encounter with G-men he should have instead informed them that concepts such as public education, a right to health care, and a right not to starve to death — all embraced by socialism and communism — seemed like pretty good ones, and asked whether the G-men in their dull black suits had meant to say "totalitarianism," rather than

"Communism." After all, as he loved to point out to ROTC students in his courses, the world hadn't actually seen a government practicing communism, no matter what some governments said; instead, places like the Soviet Union practiced a probably doomed internal economic system of state-controlled capitalism.

In retrospect, though, he was pretty sure it wouldn't have made a difference, and that he still would have gotten dragged away to serve God and country. The G-men hadn't seemed very interested in banter.

And the "Fuck off" had brought a succinct sort of satisfaction to his protest.

In due time, under the watchful supervision of an operative code-named Wachhund, he was bitterly scribbling away at the conceptual designs for the evolution of the CIA's Remote Viewing program. While grudgingly admitting that what the spooks at the agency had managed to develop was quite a lot more than he had given them credit for (he felt a wave of relief when he learned that much of the program's successes and techniques had actually been developed outside the agency), he nonetheless saw much room for expansion and improvement.

Remote Viewing, in his opinion, should be recast to head in new directions. While the project had achieved impressive results developing what appeared to be a perfectly natural human sense, it seemed a little light on the theoretical side of things. What result did these Remote Viewing missions have on the targets? Were these clandestine observations clouded with details provided by the imaginations of the RV operatives involved? If so, did their imagined details become imprinted upon the reality of the targets being observed – did they alter what they observed, as happened in experiments conducted on the quantum level? If so, could RV be wielded by an RV operative as a sort of Remote Assault? If a tree fell in the forest, but it was being observed by an RVer, did it make any noise?

He drove his CIA handlers nuts with his questions. He did so with a certain relish.

Morons, he thought.

But what could he do? To convince him to stay and work for them, they had confiscated his little psilocybin lab, carefully sealed away his strip of a dozens hits of acid in a protective plastic evidence bag, and threatened him with the era's draconian Zero-Tolerance laws on drug possession. He was stuck.

"Just produce the conceptual designs, professor," Wachhund advised him. "Do us our little favor and you're free to go."

"Fuck off," said Trull, adding, thoughtfully, "Kraut."

He was far from nationalistic, particularly in his present CIA company, but this Wachhund character pissed him off. Particularly because, though he could lash out verbally, he knew he couldn't just quit and walk out of the building. (That and the fact that Wacchund's thick German accent grated on Trull's nerves.)

Trull's options reminded him of those open to people suffering under restrictive totalitarian regimes.

Trull labored on the sorts of questions that needed to be asked, the kinds of riddles that the new, evolved RV project would need to consider as part of its mission.

Six months laboring on the sorts of questions to ask, the sorts of individuals to train, and the sorts of knowledge in which to train them in order to ensure a proper scientific, philosophical, and theoretical grounding in the RVers. Six months of sleeping in an underground apartment 50 yards from his office, only allowed to venture outside to a secure, enclosed CIA courtyard. And, as suddenly as they had first shown up, the two CIA recruiters who'd drafted Trull reappeared in his life, entering his little office.

"Time to pack it up, professor," the more outgoing of the two said. "Center Lane is getting a new home. Box up your possessions and place these labels on each box."

The man in the dull-black suit passed Trull a handful of stickers marked, simply, "Grill Flame."

"Fuck off," said Trull helpfully.

"Right now, professor," said the CIA agent, more authority in his tone this time. "You're going over to the DIA."

"How much do you boys shell-game these hush-hush projects of yours around?" Trull asked disdainfully. Then the agent's words sunk in. "Uh — wait a sec. You've got it wrong; I'm done. I've written the visionary document you spooks wanted from me so bad. Now I'm done. That was the deal."

"I'm afraid the deal's been restructured, professor."

"Like hell it has," replied Trull, red-faced. "You spooks have got your program running, and now you've got a conceptual design outline to guide further research. I'm done. What the hell's the DIA, anyway?"

Setting the Grill Flame labels on Trull's desk, the agent said, impassively: "You'll be working for the Defense Intelligence Agency."

Trull watched sullenly as the agents left his CIA office and wondered how long he'd be stuck in this gig.

As it turned out, he and the RV project wound up being shuffled through many more changes of name and controlling organization. In 1986, as the project was re-branded "Sun Streak," and shuffled again to the DIA, Trull was finally allowed to retire to a quiet, remote home with a view of the Rocky Mountains and a secrecy pledge.

Which was where he sat today, tripping a mild trip in his back yard, on his lawn chair with its green-vinyl slats, as an unmarked sedan with government plates pulled up to his driveway, and another unremarkable agent in a dull black suit stepped from it, and approached.

"Professor Trull?" asked the man, obviously an agent from one of the agencies who'd kept Trull manacled to its RV project.

"Fuck off," said Trull, enjoying the visual trails the man left in the air as he walked from the sedan.

Unmoved, the agent said, "Can't do that, sir. We've got a problem. A serious problem. We need you to help fix it."

"What kind of problem?" Trull asked mildly.

"I'm not privy to that information, sir — they just sent me to collect you," the agent replied.

"Then I refer you," Trull said magnanimously, "to my previous response."

The now 53-year-old MacMillan Trull trudged sullenly back into employment on the intelligence community's RV program, whatever the hell they were calling it these days.

After introductions and a half-hearted "Fuck off" to the man still using the code name Wachhund, Trull learned of the group — now branded Project Oversight — and its current concerns and mission.

Major Hutchings related the difficulties of hurriedly recruiting not merely hundreds, but thousands of recruits for the RV effort. To date, she had managed only to get the number of acceptable RV operatives to just under 600, with an additional 74 listed as possible call-backs. There was simply no mechanism in place for recruiting, evaluating, and training a number of Remote Viewers on this scale. No one had ever attempted to do so before.

Something lit up behind Trull's eyes as Hutchings explained Oversight's efforts, and though he tried to resist it, an eager, almost maniacal grin began to spread, crawling bit by bit across his face.

"So you're screwed," Trull said appraisingly.

Hutchings was struck speechless by this.

"That's not really what I had you reactivated to tell me, professor," she said evenly.

"Nope. Screwed. What you need is a different approach."

"What do you mean, Professor Trull?" asked Wachhund.

"Problem is, you've got lots o' things to observe, and nowhere near enough separate, individual RVers to observe it all. So that solution won't work," he replied, appalled at himself for enjoying this. He had an idea that might be the solution to the riddle they posed, and he loved solving riddles such as this.

"What do you propose, professor?" asked Wachhund. "That we scrap the whole project and just wait for the world to come unravelled at the seams?"

"No, no, no, no, no, no, no," said Trull quickly, flapping both hands dismissively in the air. "Don't be so damned melodramatic! Lots o' little brains working separately observing lots o' little patches of space won't do it, so we gotta think outside that box. Think of the lots o' little brains working together — increasing their performance exponentially by functioning as one big brain! A big brain to observe a lot of things, all of the time!"

Wachhung stared blankly at him. "Herr professor gets like this all the time … " he began dismissively.

"Just a minute, Wachhund," said Hutchings. "Professor, how do you propose going about getting this big brain together?"

"We need to devise a means of getting the minds to synchronize, to get into harmony and begin to function as a single mind. I feel we are going to require a great deal of equipment," said Trull, the toothy grin of a speed freak now plastered across his face.

"What kind of equipment do you mean, Professor Trull?" asked Hutchings.

"Biomechanical. When I left, classified work was being done in the DIA creating computers that function with biological, as well as mechanical components," he replied, leading her toward the back, toward one of many separate rooms and offices lining the main work area. "We need to build a tool using that technology to let our operatives get their minds synchronized, get 'em working as a single unit, rather than separately, as a disorganized mess."

Trull waved a hand distractedly at the cavernous main workspace of Project Oversight. "We gotta get all o' that the hell outta here. Need the space."

Hutchings eyed the professor standing before her, panting and washing his hands feverishly in the air.

An obvious loon.

"We need the space for what, professor?" she asked carefully.

"Jumpin' Jesus! Aren't you paying any god-damned attention, girl?" Trull demanded. "For the machine!"

Chapter Nine

Awakening

Sinclair felt oddly aware of the things he was doing, the tasks he performed as he moved through the paces of his job. No mysterious already-finished toilets in his path tonight. During his 1 a.m. break, he listened to an AM radio all-news channel.

At his 3 a.m. lunch break, he took his lunch up to the roof again, hoping that the brisk, cold night air would revive him.

And as his 5 a.m. coffee break approached, and he began to dustmop the second floor hallway, he started suddenly, letting out a panicked yelp when the voice, too close to his ear, said: Soon, Sinclair.

His hair tingling on his scalp, a ringing echo from his yell still in the air, Sinclair spun around to find no one. Again, the area seemed to fill with a dust-dry, ancient presence. It was all around him.

"Wh—who's there?" he demanded.

Silence.

"I mean it! Who the hell are you?"

"Sinclair?" came Elias' distant voice from the stairwell. "Who're y'all yellin' at?"

Sinclair looked around, caught his breath, and replied: "No one, Ernst. Just thought a noise on my BopBoxä was something in the building."

"Oh," the old man said disinterestedly. "Just came over to tell ya'll Zubroski phoned. He's gonna send a supervisor through in half an hour to see how we're doin' tonight."

"OK," said Sinclair, still looking around.

As he made his way home, big clunky wrap-around shades in place against the colorless brightness of a gray morning sky, Sinclair wondered what the hell was going on with him. Why was he hallucinating? And why had he felt aware, all night, more aware than he had in months?

He had no idea.

Grabbing a 40 from the Zip-In, Sinclair eased into his end-of-the-day routine.

Out there, in the waning night, somewhere, he could feel someone not speaking to him. Could feel a presence lurking just over his shoulder, just out of sight. Waiting.

Although he was a graduate student, within some limitations, Deuce MacKenzie still set his schedule to include as few morning hours as he wanted. He was a fan of late nights and sleeping in. He always seemed to have breakthroughs on problems he was trying to solve late at night.

He just felt more lucid then.

For a while, now, he'd been feeling a bit out of sorts during the day — just not getting up to speed mentally until later in the day. So he'd adjusted his schedule accordingly. A sort of malaise seemed to have settled over the entire department over the past few months. And being filed away in a shared office space with people from different departments and disciplines meant that he and his officemates rarely had the chance to discuss their ideas and studies with one another. His department seemed to be crumbling and he could find no easy avenue for intellectual discussion in his office, where there were so many people from so many different fields, and yet none who really understood what the others did.

Then there was the problem of finding a place to live. He'd been renting a condo for the first few months of the semester, but its owner had given him two weeks' notice that she was going to be needing it herself.

So he'd been trying to find a livable apartment in the university area that wasn't close to either the noisy greek-system houses or underclassmen's dorms.

Thaddeus MacKenzie chose the name Deuce over his mother's favored diminutive: Thad. "Thad" was a word that sounded to Deuce like someone with a lisp making fun of his name. And to his ear, "Tad" sounded vaguely fishy. No, neither of those would do, he'd decided, and took to introducing himself early on as Deuce.

When he arrived in the cramped shared office space, the sun was already beginning to set. This was a good time of day to come in, anyway, as the others who had desks here tended clear out for the day by six or so.

Deuce admired the diagram he'd copied onto his dry-marker board; it depicted one of his favorite mind-benders. It was the sort of simple idea that keeps people up at night because it suggested that the certain, solid world we see around us, the world in which we humans make choices that affect the world around them, might actually be nothing like that at all.

He scrawled the word "SAVE" on the board and circled it.

Now that he remembered what it meant, he was dying to explain its implications to his officemates, but they never brought it up.

Maybe it would make a nice tattoo.

Tucked away in an office with comparative literature teaching assistants and people doing research in religious studies, though, the diagram that raised the Big Question to him as an armchair philosopher drew only an occasional confused look from the others.

And the sketch didn't go over well with his hard-science counterparts, either. Physics was supposed to explain the world, not make it all more confusing.

He always thought that his favored field — quantum physics — kept him more in the company of the religious studies people anyway, but they understood what he did no better than people from his own department.

So it made his pulse race a bit when the night janitor noticed the diagram and remembered seeing it before somewhere. The guy had seemed very, very spaced out when they'd first met, but it didn't seem all that out of place to him: It was the middle of the night, right? This guy, Sinclair, probably just didn't see people much when he worked, and Deuce had never seen any other custodians cleaning Walther.

Besides, the guy was a night owl, as well — probably the only person he'd likely have a coherent conversation with around the office anytime soon, with the hours he kept.

While he chipped away at his thesis, he savored the idea of having someone to talk quantum reality with, and hoped Sinclair would be up to the task.

And suddenly, ideas were clicking. The crumpled notes on fast-food napkins and folded post-it notes seemed to be coming together, jelling into a coherent argument.

When he looked up to check the time, he found he'd been wrapped up enough in his own work that he hadn't lifted his eyes from his work in hours. It was getting late, just before sunrise now. He decided to take a break to collect his thoughts. Hot java outside in the chilly night air sounded like a recipe to keep him sharp.

Out in the courtyard between the three campus halls, he found Sinclair reading a newspaper.

"Sinclair?"

Sinclair jumped, startled. He did his best to cover the fear he felt, worrying at first that he was hearing voices again.

Not voices, he corrected himself. The voice. Singular.

"Deuce! I'm not used to people just showing up when I'm at work," he said, wondering just how paranoid his tone of voice sounded.

"Hey, sorry, Sinclair. Just taking a break."

"Me too. I get a lunch break and a couple of coffee breaks. Don't really like the guys who do the other buildings much, so I usually stay over here. I like the solitude better than their company." He could feel his pulse easing toward calm again.

"It looked like it. You really jumped!"

Sinclair felt foolish. "Yeah." No sense letting the only human contact he had between 11 and seven know that he had voices — correction: a voice — in his head, talking to him.

"Listen," said Deuce, "You were interested in that diagram. Did you study quantum physics in college or something?"

"No. I was a liberal arts student, kind of into philosophy. I read a couple of layman's books on it, though."

"Cool. What were you into in philosophy?"

Sinclair thought about it for a moment.

"Well, I never really staked claim to anything formally. I got interested in the nature of reality."

Deuce became more excited. Maybe he and Sinclair could talk about the weird ideas everyone else around him seemed to steer clear of.

"I don't remember now, what the diagram meant," Sinclair confessed.

"Do you have some time left on break?"

Sinclair held his watch up to read it in the harsh glare of the parking-lot light. "Sure."

The two made their way back indoors and headed up the stairs of Garraint Walther, toward the office of Deuce MacKenzie.

"You can read the diagram like this: An electron moves forward in time until it collides with a photon and absorbs it, changing directions in space; after the collision, the electron continues moving forward in time and eventually emits the photon, changing direction in space again."

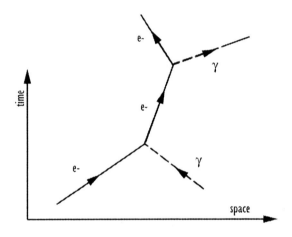

Sinclair waited for a revelation; the diagram still didn't mean anything to him.

Deuce could see that he hadn't made his point yet. He sighed impatiently.

"It's a Feynman diagram of an event called an electron-photon scattering. The dashed lines are the photons. What we need to do is take a few liberties with this; Feynman diagrams can be rotated around any way we like. When we rotate the graph, change our perspective a bit, the electron's adventure changes. See, if you reverse the directions indicated in the diagram and reverse the charge, so we get the electron's anti-particle – a positron – we have the same event occurring, but for a positron. So it looks like this:"

He began drawing on the board again.

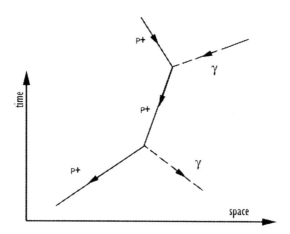

But another way to look at it is like this: The second diagram's event is the same as the first diagram's event moving backwards in time. In one diagram the process moves forward in time; in the other, the same process is viewed, but moving backwards in time. All space-time diagrams can be altered like this, reversing the direction they move in through time and replacing the particle with its antiparticle."

"Antiparticle?" Sinclair asked, trying not to give away how much he'd forgotten. But it was coming back to him now.

"Same as the particle in the first case, but with the opposite charge. An electron has a negative charge, a positron has a positive charge."

"What's the photon's antiparticle?"

"Well, light's kind of strange. In a lot of ways, really. But since a photon has no charge, it acts as its own antiparticle. And you know what happens when a particle collides with its antiparticle?"

Sinclair shook his head.

"They annihilate each other — they disappear and two photons instantly depart from the scene in opposite directions."

"The destruction of the particle and antiparticle creates light?"

"Exactly. Physical matter becomes energy. And it works the other way, too: The collision and annihilation of a pair of photons can also create an electron and a proton."

"Weird."

"Yeah. Look," he said, scribbling a new diagram out in dry-marker. "Here's another one – and it's related. This is the one that excites me. It takes what happened in the first diagrams a bit further."

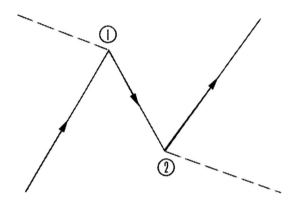

"When we look at a scattering this way, an electron traveling forward in time emits a photon at point number 1 and begins traveling backward in time until this point," he tapped the board next to point number 2 on the diagram, "where it absorbs the photon — the same one — and begins to travel forward in time again."

Deuce grinned excitedly, awaiting Sinclair's reaction.

Sinclair, for his part, shook his head, remembering now the passage where he'd first seen the diagram.

"The electron moves backward in time, along its own timeline, until it emits the photon it absorbed, right?" he asked Deuce.

"Right."

"Then it moves forward in time until it collides with and absorbs that photon."

"So sometimes things travel backward in time?" Sinclair asked. "That's cool."

"But the diagram implies more, Sinclair," Deuce replied excitedly. "If subatomic particles exist like this, in a loop, as the new diagram shows them, then at least sometimes they exist in a finite stretch of space and time."

"So?"

"So, philosophy guy, if electrons aren't actually moving around with the molecules they belong to in, say, a chair, or you, or me, if they're just waiting there, in the future somewhere, for us to catch up with them ... "

Sinclair swallowed, a horrified understanding settling over him.

"Then ... then the fact that we'll eventually be there is predestined," Sinclair said quietly, almost whispering. "Oh shit."

"Yes!" Deuce howled gleefully. "Do you have any idea how much that bugs the rest of my department?"

But Sinclair was busy re-realizing the fear he'd felt when he first encountered this diagram. One of his deepest fears about what the diagram meant. How had he forgotten?

"I had an experience that shook me up a little only a few nights ago, when I took a larger dose of acid than I really meant to. I've never managed to get hold of peyote, but I tried a variety of LSD recipes, and I managed to sample magic mushrooms.

"Anyway, I'd done acid for months, off and on, and had fun, paranoia, saw minor vibrations in my peripheral vision, that kind of effect. But that night … "

"Yes?" MacKenzie interjected, amused.

"Well. A bunch of my friends scored acid for us all, and I interrupted their nighter. When they pulled out the acid for me, it looked different than the hits I'd seen before; the paper hits were larger — I mean a lot larger. About four times the size of the usual tabs we'd seen before. That worried me a little, but they told me it was 'really clean,'" he said, a slight smile forming. "I misinterpreted that as meaning that the tabs were larger because they were a little weak, so I took two of the big blue squares."

"How much had you had at a time in the past?"

"Only one."

"So you had eight times the dose of acid you'd usually had in the past?! I've never even taken the stuff, but that still sounds nuts! Are you nuts?"

"For a little while now, I think," Sinclair smiled meekly. "I was surprised at how hard it hit me. See, the acid was stronger than any of us had had before. While I watched, a pile of pillows in the corner spontaneously animated. An arm tried to pull free of all the stitching. A mouth kept trying to open and tell me something, but the corduroy would only let it open a little. Strings of it ran from the top of its new mouth to the bottom, so it couldn't open its mouth very far. It was amazing, Deuce.

"Another time, when I dosed with a friend, a guy named Jonah Thompson, I got stir crazy about three hours into the trip, and had to go out. Jonah walked with me to keep me company.

"While we were out walking, I felt time dilate; my perspective separated in to three clean, aligned timelines, one about a second ahead of me, then my perspective, and one about a second afterward. I'd hear Thompson say something, then see my self respond, then I'd respond, then I'd see myself respond again. Three separate, sequential, identical timelines. I could see more than the current instant, but I couldn't vary it."

"Look, I hate to bogeyman your observations, but don't you think the whole 'acid opens your mind' thing is a little done?" said Deuce.

"I'm not really claiming that it opened my mind, Deuce — but those experience changed reality, at least as far as my mind was concerned; for just a little while, they changed my perceptions. I think I just mentioned it because of how slippery the nature of reality seems to be, y'know? How many times have we been presented with separate options and had to figure out which was reality and which was some sort of illusion — or delusion — or whatever — drugs or no drugs?"

"They still sound like a tough couple of nights," laughed Deuce.

But Sinclair wasn't laughing. He'd always thought those experiences had just been hallucinations, but now ...

Now it seemed to fit. Predestiny — if his actions were predestined, even only by a few moments, that might mean it was actually possible to experience things before they happened, as he had that night. Was it another piece of their puzzle?

But he didn't like the idea that some god somewhere had predestined that he'd get involved with a completely incompatible woman who would help him waste two years of his life. Or that, a few years before that, he'd become so debilitated by mono, a fairly common disease, that it would cost him his academic ambitions.

These just had to be his own colossal mistakes and problems, bad events he'd lived through and that he could correct by his own efforts; they couldn't be the perverse play of an indifferent god of some sort.

He couldn't stand it. He was close to broke, and hallucinating voices in his head all on his own without having an idea that fundamentally challenged all of his beliefs on how the world fit together thrown into the mix. He'd thought long and hard about this idea on and off a variety of hallucinogens and concluded that it was unacceptable.

"Of course, it's just an idea," said Deuce.

Sinclair gave him an anxious look.

"Right," said Sinclair. "A big scary mother of an idea.

"See, I like a world of free will. Under free will you can change things. I do not like the idea of a world where nothing I do ever really matters; and if it's all predestined, down to the sub-atomic level, what's the point? Why should I even try to accomplish anything if whether I will or not is already a set fact? I mean, look at the philosophy of the existentialists. Jean-Paul Sartre. They feel in no uncertain terms that absolutely everything comes down to personal responsibility, that you always have and make choices that affect where you are and what you're doing in life. They don't even let slaves off; they argue that the slave has the responsibility to pursue his freedom rather than complain about being born into or sold into slavery. The way the existentialists see it, even in hypothetical cases where the slave has no hope of escape, the slave can still commit suicide if he truly wants to remove himself from his situation."

Deuce's jaw went slack. Where was all of this coming from?

"Predestiny is at the opposite end of the scale," Sinclair continued. "It removes free will, and so removes responsibility for one's actions."

Whew, thought Sinclair as it all came flooding out, raging into his memory. *I really have been sleepwalking.*

Deuce looked into Sinclair's eyes, surprised to find his pupils suddenly dilated so wide they looked like big, round black circles on a white ball. There was no other color.

What the hell?! he thought.

"You're a fucking janitor?!" asked Deuce, laughing. After a few seconds of silence had passed between them, he nervously added, still smiling: "You need a drink? You sound like you need a drink. I need a drink. To take the edge off. I'll get us a beer at the Fuel Pump."

Sinclair didn't answer — just stood his ground, breathing heavily now, a glossy sheen of perspiration coating his face, his eyes focused on some point far out in the cosmos.

Arriving ahead of Sinclair, Deuce pulled into the parking lot of the Fuel Pump, a neighborhood dive open early for third-shifters. The Fuel Pump was a gas station at some point in its history, and still retained the same basic architecture, complete with outmoded, shut-down gas pumps on a concrete island out front.

Not wanting to go alone into a tavern he was unfamiliar with, he punched his radio to a news station and tried to coax some heat from his beater: an '83 Cavalier with a faded blue, somewhat rusting shell. The car he'd had since he was 16.

When Sinclair finally pulled in behind him, Deuce climbed out, locking the beater behind him.

"OK," Deuce continued in a quiet corner booth, over a couple of pints of Leinenkugel's. "You've done more study on the philosophical ramifications of all this than I have. I just thought it was kind of cool. You know? That my field might have a few answers for the big questions religion and philosophy raise."

Sinclair watched him, not blinking, drinking deeply from his pint glass.

Deuce waved a hand back and forth before Sinclair's face.

"Uh — hello? Hello, Sinclair? You in there?"

"Yeah," he replied, his voice low and relaxed. "More than I have been in a long time."

Deuce ignored the comment.

"So I thought, when I started extrapolating meaning from this, that it might be really scary for other departments — not just physics. It might settle the free will vs. determinism argument. Or make the free will people's fight a lot tougher, anyway," chuckled Deuce.

"Man. What's happened to me all this time?" asked Sinclair. "I wasn't even sure I remembered that diagram."

"What do you mean?" Deuce prodded. "Or maybe you want to change the subject?"

"I mean, for some reason my brain feels like it's been half asleep for months. I had a self-loathing way of looking at it: I called it 'sleep-janitoring.' Have you noticed anything like that?"

MacKenzie paused to reflect on the question.

"Actually, yeah, now that you mention it. It's been hard for me to work during the day. But at night, my brain doesn't seem as — I don't know — not as punchy."

Sinclair considered this.

"There's another piece of the puzzle that might bother you, Sinclair."

"What's that?"

"Ever heard of chaos theory? Fractals?"

Sinclair considered the question.

"Heard of it, yes, but I don't know much about it. A friend of mine used to like to play a video demonstrating fractal geometric equations being solved, you know, playing out, when we'd dose."

"Ah. In a nutshell, chaos theory deals in fractals. A truly amazing thing happens when absolutely chaotic numbers are generated at random: Order arises from the chaos."

"Excuse me?"

"The numbers, if charted as they occur, as they're generated from the Mandelbrot Set, for example, create these recurring sort of paisley patterns; absolute randomness eventually settles into absolute order. Know what that means?"

"Another bid for predestiny?" Sinclair guessed.

"It suggests that no matter how random things seem to us, they are en route to a predetermined, ordered pattern. So that's sort of a maybe on predestiny, but it does seem to suggest it. To me it does, anyway."

Sinclair just shook his head, trying to soak it all in. What was predestiny, then? Just a matter of perspective? Did chaos only seem chaotic because he couldn't see enough of the picture — couldn't hold enough of the data in his mind?

"Ever read Descartes, Sinclair?

The custodian arched an eyebrow. "Hmmmm … " he said, rifling through his brain for details. "Yes! It's been a long time. He did the first work I ever read that tried to sort out objectively what the universe was and wasn't."

"I love that guy!" said Deuce. "First guy to tackle the question of God with a capital 'G' from a no-religion perspective."

"You really think that?" Sinclair asked.

"Doesn't everyone?"

"No. But he did something amazing when he tried."

"Tried?" Deuce asked, his eyebrows arching in doubt.

"Right."

"Look, janitor-guy, a lot of people think Descartes proved the existence of God with a capital 'G.'"

"They're wrong."

Sinclair's behavior perplexed him. He wouldn't respond to Deuce's prodding at all.

"OK, how are they wrong, oh wise nocturnal keeper of the toilet scrub-brush?"

Sinclair shot him a look of warning.

Sinclair took a deep breath in through his nose, held it for a moment, and released it through his mouth. He'd learned that sort of breathing from a martial arts instructor when he'd been in junior high school; it was the breathing she taught him for meditation, and he thought of it as a tool for helping calm oneself.

"Cogito, ergo Sum," said Sinclair.

"I think, therefore I am," came the translation, courtesy of Deuce MacKenzie. "Descartes coined that for 'The Meditations.'"

"One of the most important first steps in the pursuit of the truth about reality."

"Truth with a capital 'T,' Sinclair?" Deuce goaded him.

"Right," he replied. "Truth with a capital 'T.' But he panicked."

"Panicked?"

"He gave up. He couldn't face the universe without God with a capital 'G.'"

"See, he started by attempting to prove things around him existed, but he decided that it was possible that his senses could be misleading him. So he decided to start with the one fact he was certain of: His own existence. The fact that he thought proved that part."

"Right."

"But he couldn't get any further. He ran into problems starting at such an absolute level. Could some evil force just be torturing him, for example, by making him hallucinate that he had hands?"

"What do you mean?"

"Well, after a lifetime of believing that you and everyone around you had hands — that humankind was probably smarter than the other animals because of our opposable thumbs, for example — and becoming wholly dependent upon them, what if one day the evil force making you hallucinate that you had hands took the hallucination away? From everyone on Earth? Gone is the opposable thumbs-equals-supremacy argument; the other animals' paws are more functional than ours. How do we take notes? Tie shoes? Do any of that?"

"People who lose use of their hands deal with that all the time."

"They do. In time. What if this evil force made everyone hallucinate having hands, then took away that hallucination? How much of society would just crumble in despair?"

"I think I see what you mean ... "

"OK. Descartes took that idea and ran with it: He decided that his senses could not be trusted. But then he had a problem: No matter what he tried, no matter how bold and calculated a beginning he had made, he couldn't prove that anything else existed.

"So he took a shortcut. His clean, logical start had left him feeling cold, afraid, and alone in a Godless universe ..."

"God with a capital 'G'?" asked Deuce.

Sinclair drained his beer.

"God with a capital 'G'," he confirmed. "He decided that it was OK to accept what his senses told him, because what else did he have? He took it a step further, too. Have you ever heard that philosophical cliché about the tree in the forest?"

Deuce nodded. "If a tree falls in the forest, but no one is there to observe it, does it make any noise?"

"That's the one. Descartes decided that it was wrong to assume that things, say, the next room over, continued to exist when no one was observing them, because then no one could prove by observation that these things in the next room still existed."

"So he's already given up once."

"OK," said Deuce, feeling a little out of his depth.

"But then he couldn't take his proof of things any further. It was maddening to him! He absolutely could not prove that things in the next room, or in a forest, didn't just wink out of existence when someone wasn't observing them."

"Or that, if they did exist, they made noise like they normally would if no one was there to observe it."

"Right. So after failing his own standards for proof and taking a philosophical shortcut to get around it, he'd hit another dead end. He hadn't proven that the universe would wink out when he or someone else wasn't looking, but he hadn't proven that it wouldn't, either. So, rather than decide that it's silly to think that things in the next room disappear when you aren't watching them, he invented another shortcut. He decided that an omniscient Someone — capital 'S' — must be perceiving everything. That Someone must be God. Capital 'G.'"

Deuce was speechless. He'd never heard anyone ruthlessly and casually deconstruct and then utterly dismiss Descartes like this. (Admittedly, he was in the wrong department, but he knew the philosophy majors he'd talked to didn't act this way about René Descartes.)

"Bear with me, Deuce," said Sinclair. "Descartes eventually decided that the universe and everyone and everything in it were essentially automata — just peices of the bigger picture. Or, in his view, cogs in the machinery of the universe. He called it 'The Great Machine.'"

"Which kind of fits with your predestiny idea," said Deuce.

What time is it? thought Deuce.

He'd been listening, stunned, for hours to this man — this night janitor with a diamondlike focus in his eyes, who had only days ago appeared zombielike in the hallways of Garraint Walther. His respect and — something else … camaraderie? — for Sinclair grew.

The Fuel Pump, though, was beginning to get crowded, a mix of retired men having a beer with the morning paper and third-shift workers washing down the end of the day filling the place. The crowd made Thaddeus MacKenzie feel self-conscious.

"Listen," he said, "I'm a grad student and you're a night janitor, so I doubt either of us has any cash to spare. I'm running out of money. I'd suggest my place, but the owner's moving back in soon. I'm kind of supposed to be cleaning it up for her right now."

"I have beer at home. Want to pick up where we left off there?"

Sinclair glanced at his watch, then realized that he just didn't care if he had to call in sick tonight. He was having too much fun, his mind awake for the first time in years. He pulled his morning drug-trial antihistamine from his pocket and washed it back with the last of his beer.

He couldn't recall, off-hand, whether he was supposed to avoid mixing the drug with alcohol.

Oh well.

"Sounds good, Deuce."

In his car, he kept an eye on his rearview mirror as Deuce MacKenzie followed him back to his apartment.

Sinclair felt a chill that pricked up the hairs on the back of his neck. He felt like he was being watched.

"Nice little place," said Deuce as they made their way into the dilapidated house where Sinclair rented out a room. As Sinclair began to lead them up the stairs, he could hear muffled laughter from some of the tenants in the living room.

"It's a little dismal, but it's OK. Besides," Sinclair chuckled, "We try to make sure we know and like someone before we let them move in."

He pulled a pair of bottles from the mini-fridge in his room, pulled a magnet-backed bottle opener from the fridge door, and pried off the caps.

"Thanks," said Deuce, accepting one.

Sinclair led Deuce down the hallway to room four. The door opened to a quiet, dark, mostly empty space, the air within already still and stale from disuse. Sinclair flicked on the overhead bulb.

"This one's open right now," he said.

"Perfect!" exclaimed Deuce. "How much is it?"

"Are you serious?" he asked, surprised.

MacKenzie looked around, taking in the small room.

"Are your roommates OK? Quiet?"

Sinclair laughed. "No, not quiet, but they're good people, and this old building's insulated enough to keep their party noise out of the room."

"When can I meet them?" asked Deuce excitedly.

From downstairs, Sinclair could hear muffled laughter from the living room. Another long movie night.

Do those guys ever really stop tripping? he wondered.

Pushing his hair back from his eyes, Sinclair said, "I think they're available."

In the shared living room, Sinclair and Deuce, new beers in hand, found Rhys, Beckett, and Jonah, along with Burt and the girl Sinclair thought dressed like a hippie.

"'Ey mate," Burt said in his Scottish-Midwestern accent, "you two joining us?"

He offered them a saucer littered with small squares of paper.

On the damaged screen played "Hellraiser." The group was enthralled as the lead cenobite, the demon with row after row of nails embedded in his graph-scarred scalp, rasped: "Ahhh, the suffering! The sweet suffering!"

Sinclair looked to Deuce, then back to Burt.

"Thanks. We're just gonna have a few beers upstairs," Sinclair replied. He led Deuce up the aging stairs to his room.

"I think maybe it's best to meet them for the first time sometime when they aren't slippery with LSD," said Sinclair.

"Um — how about my place?" asked Deuce.

"Yeah," said Sinclair, brightening. "Yeah, that sounds cool."

"So I was thinking on the way here," said Deuce, back at his little efficiency apartment. "I'm almost afraid to bring it up after how that last bit of quantum weirdness stirred you up. But anyway, I was thinking: There's a basic paradox we can't get past in quantum physics. Have you ever read anything about the wave-particle dichotomy?"

Sinclair took a pull from the beer.

"Do you mean that light can be thought of as both waves and particles?"

"That it is both," he said, with emphasis on the 'is.' "The only things we can do to pinpoint it as either affects how it behaves."

"How it behaves?"

"Right. How it's observed affects how it behaves."

"I'm not following you."

"Well, there are ways to look for qualities that would tell us what we're seeing is a particle and qualities that would tell us that it's a wave. With light, sometimes a photon acts like a particle, sometimes it acts like a wave. Individual events are particle-like, while wave behavior is detected as a statistical pattern — a probability wave.

"There's an experiment that's often cited about this: we have a light source which is fired through a single slit and onto a photographic plate. We know the velocity and direction of the light, its origin, direction, and its target, so it stands to reason that we could predict where the photon will land on the photographic plate. Light behaves like a particle.

"But when the same experiment is performed with two slits open to allow light through to the photographic plate, we encounter a problem. We still know the initial conditions of the experiment, and the light is still aimed at a photographic plate. The only difference is that a second slit is also open. Because we have the same figures, conditions, and formulas as in the first experiment, we should be able to conclude that the light will land in exactly the same place. But instead, the light, fired through two slits, does not land in the same place; instead, light from one source traveling through one slit interferes with light from that source traveling through another. Light behaves like a wave.

"And it gets weirder. Part of this is something called Heisenberg's uncertainty principal."

"What's that?"

"Heisenberg discovered that we can never learn both the position and momentum of a particle with absolute precision. We can approximate both, but the more precise we are about one, the less we can know about the other."

"But doesn't that just have to do with limitations in the equipment they use?"

"No. It's actually just impossible to know both accurately. The conclusion that's been reached in quantum physics is that by observing the experiment, we make choices that determine how the light will behave. Get it? By observing, we affect the outcome of these experiments. By observing, we affect how light behaves!"

Sinclair was leaning forward now, listening attentively.

"So Niels Bohr developed an idea called 'complementarity,' part of which states that we actually can't observe without altering what we see. After that, it gets out into weird metaphysical territory. But think about it: Descartes might have been right about not trusting what his senses told him, if by observing things, he was affecting them."

"I read something really weird about subatomic particles communicating over great distance once," said Sinclair. "In this old Orson Scott Card novel, *Ender's Game*, I think, but I think Ursula K. Le Guin coined the term — they had a way of communicating over interstellar distances faster than the speed of light — instantaneously. They called it an 'ansible.'"

Deuce scratched his scalp for a moment, thinking.

"Riiiight," he said. "OK, it's been a long time since I read up on this, but bear with me. I think you're talking about a property of electrons called spin. Here's the deal, and it's related to Bohr's idea of complementarity: Electrons have spin, even though it's not quite spin like you and I think of when, say, someone spins a basketball."

"With you so far."

"OK. The spin can be 'up' or 'down' only. There are ways to associate a couple of electrons with one another so that their total spin, one spinning up and one spinning down, will equal a value of one. It just means that the two are spinning in direct opposition to one another. And once this associating is done, the two become an indivisible whole, no matter the distance. Now, as an experimenter, you measure spin by choosing an axis on which to measure that *spin*."

"OK ... "

"So physicists found out that they could take these two particles with their associated spin and separate them by any distance — even vast distances — and by measuring the first electron's spin, we automatically learn the spin of the second."

"Why's that sound odd to you?"

"Because of how the experimenter measures the spin. It's the experimenter who chooses an axis on which to measure the spin; that affects the value of the spin measurement itself. See, according to quantum theory, the two electrons about any axis will be opposite, but the values of their spins exist only as potentialities until the experimenter actually chooses an axis to measure by and does the actual measurement of the spin of the first electron. Once we know those two qualities of the first electron, the second instantly acquires definite, opposite properties. And this can be accomplished when separating the two electrons by any distance, rendering this — ah — communication of information between the two electrons faster than light-speed.

"Einstein hated the faster-than-light-speed part. But then, this communication isn't done by signals in the sense that we are used to, because the two electrons are locked in an instantaneous, nonlocal connection that goes beyond our current concepts of transfer of information."

"That's what Le Guin and Card were writing about," said Sinclair. "A communications device that depended on that indivisible whole that the two-particle system becomes."

"Interesting application, but we are talking about science fiction there ... "

Deuce suddenly realized that Sinclair was gazing intently at him.

Sinclair had never respected anyone's mind, someone's intelligence, so much — never felt himself so honestly, unabashedly attracted to anyone. Without hesitation, emboldened a bit by the alcohol, he leaned toward Deuce MacKenzie and suddenly they were together, their mouths together, then exploring one another, their clothes frantically tugged aside.

Sinclair didn't even realize until later that he had never found a man attractive before.

Chapter Ten

From the desk of: [name classified]
Operative codename: Sapphire
News Release:

Approved with changes, as noted
Rejected _____
For Immediate Release 08.28.01

For Immediate Release 08.28.01

~~Radical changes appear to be taking place within what have been thought of as immutable constants in the field of physics~~ **Some fundamental laws of physics change slightly with the passage of vast amounts of time**, according to a research project being conducted by an international team of astrophysicists. The project, begun in 1989 at the 30-foot-wide Keck Telescope on Mauna Kea, in Hawaii, the world's largest single telescope, studied the absorption of light from quasars as it passed through interstellar clouds containing hydrogen and helium, as well as heavier elements, such as chromium, silicon, zinc and aluminum atoms ~~over the past 12 years~~ up to 12 billion light years from Earth.

The project found that light behaved in a very unexpected manner as it was absorbed by interstellar gas clouds between earth and the quasars – behaved in ways so unexpected that they could only be explained by changes in the fine structure constant (defined as the charge of the electron squared divided by the product of Planck's constant and the speed of light), which involves the strength of attraction between electrically charged particles, over the past 10 years **in ways that can only be explained by very slight changes in a so-called constant in physics over the course of billions of years**.

If the finding is confirmed, it could mean that other constants regarded as immutable in physics~~, such as the speed of light, or the charge of an electron,~~ may also have changed over the ~~past 12 years~~ **history of the cosmos~~, and may still be shifting. The charge of an electron, for example, appears to be growing. The size of~~**

~~the fine structure constant, denoted in physics by the greek letter alpha, determines how well atoms hold together and what types of light atoms will emit when heated up. If the charge held by electrons is growing, as appears to be the case, the consequences could range from the alarming to the bizarre: The electrons in our bodies and our world could move into tighter and tighter orbits, causing everything to shrink over time; long molecules in our cells could begin to fold up differently and stop working over time.~~

If the speed of light were slowly decreasing, for example, we might never know it, because our measuring apparatus might be shrinking at the same time. The current value of the fine structure constant — roughly 1/137 — could not have been very different in the past, as that would have spelled trouble for our very existence. A variation in the constant by more than a factor of ten would imply that carbon atoms could not be stable, and organic life could not have arisen.

The findings are to be published in the Sept. 1 edition of the prestigious Letters in New Physics journal.

Those involved in the project have urged caution, noting that although they have encountered no errors in the course of their studies, such a sweeping finding must be thoroughly checked and re-checked.

Because the consequences for science would be so far-reaching and because the differences from the expected measurements are so drastic, m Many scientists are expressing skepticism that the discovery will stand the test of time, and say they will await independent verification.

The finding would, however, fit with some theorists' views of the universe, which are expressed in the field of string theory. String theory predicts that the universe may contain as many as 10 dimensions, rather than the four we usually think of. It also predicts that such constants can change. ~~String theory does not predict, however, that such radical changes would occur in those constants as have been found in this project.~~

String theory postulates that space contains tiny, unseen dimensions. Changes in the size of those dimensions — much like the expansion of the universe in the space we are familiar with — could change quantities like the fine structure constant, said Dr. David Brookhaven, a physicist at Philadelphia State University.

Brookhaven said that string theory predicts that those changes will have occurred in the first seconds of the universe's life. They expect that because of this, those changes would be virtually unobservable by astronomers today.

The project, headed by Dr. Darius Engelby of Princeton University, is being conducted by scientists in the United States, Australia and Britain.

"If our results stand up under the scrutiny of our peers, we will have made the discovery of a lifetime, and a most disturbing discovery, at that," said Engelby.

Astrophysicist Dr. Roland Crenson, with the Fermi National Accelerator Laboratory, said the finding could force revisions in cosmology, the science of how the universe began and evolved, and could also add credence to string theory, which thus far remains unproven. Crenson was not involved in the project.

"The implication would just be so enormous that it would upset the apple cart, in terms of the laws of physics as we understand them," said Crenson.

The magnitude of the change reported by the group is ~~surprisingly large~~ **minute**, amounting to about ~~1 part in 100~~ **1 part in 100,000** in a number called the fine structure constant over ~~the past 12 years~~ 12 billion years. The fine structure constant is defined in terms of the speed of light and the strength of electronic attractions within atoms.

The absorption of light by metal atoms present in interstellar clouds creates dark spikes at various wavelengths in the quasar's spectrum, with a pattern so well-defined that it is often likened to a fingerprint. The value of those wavelengths — that fingerprint — is directly related to the value of the fine structure constant.

But the fingerprint seemed to change in time, Engelby said, indicating that the constant grows **very slightly** larger as one goes nearer to the present, and so was not actually constant at all.

But because the project's findings deal with changes to widely accepted constants in the field of physics, many scientists are expressing deep skepticism, and say that they will withhold final judgment on the findings until they have been thoroughly checked by astrophysicists independent of the project. Most predict that the finding will be proven the result of human error.

End release.

From the desk of: [name classified]

Operative codename: Sapphire

News Release:

Approved <u>with changes, as noted</u>

Rejected _____

For Immediate Release 02.16.02

Researchers at the Long Island National Laboratory reported findings today that a subatomic particle deviated ~~more than expected~~ **very slightly** from its expected behavior in experiments. That **tiny** deviation ~~provides support~~ **may provide support** for exotic theories such as supersymmetry, which hypothesizes that every particle has a much heavier, yet-to-be-observed counterpart. ~~It may also be an indication of changes taking place within what have, until now, been thought to be constants in the field of physics.~~

The Standard model, the set of rules upon which much of physics today is based, is a set of equations that describe how all fundamental forces interact with known particles. Scientists looking into supersymmetry have been designing and carrying out experiments to challenge the Standard Model for three decades.

Although ~~p~~ Physicists and researchers involved with the experiment cautioned that the case is not yet proven, the Long Island experiments appear to be the first time physicists have contradicted the Standard Model.

The Long Island experiment looked at the behavior of muons, subatomic particles that are heavier relatives of electrons, suspended in a powerful magnetic field. In a magnetic field, a muon modifies its spin.

Similar experiments conducted earlier had found a spin modification close to that predicted by the Standard Model. But the Long Island experiment was several times more precise than the earlier measurements, and concluded that the actual change in the muons' spin **very slightly** differed from predictions **by just a few parts in a million**.

That **small** discrepancy suggests there is something lacking in the Standard Model~~, or that something about the Standard Model is undergoing change over time~~.

Should the results hold up under further testing, an outcome declared unlikely by physicists univolved with the experiment, ~~tT~~he most likely explanation for the anomalous result is ~~some sort of change in the constants used in the Standard Model~~ supersymmetry, a theory that states that every known particle has a much heavier counterpart paired with it. Unlike the Standard Model, the theory has a place for gravity, and explains why the various particles have the masses they do.

Physicists contacted for comment have reported skepticism, generally saying that they expect that the results will eventually be credited to human error.

End release.

From the desk of: [name classified]

Operative codename: Sapphire

News Release:

Approved <u>with changes, as noted</u>

Rejected _____

For Immediate Release 02.16.02

Physicists conducting research jointly at Harvard and Cambridge universities have managed to ~~bring the speed of light to a dead halt~~ **slow the speed of light somewhat** from its speed in a vacuum of 186,000 miles per second — long thought of as a constant — to ~~a point of stasis at which the light simply hangs in the air~~ **a speed of only 170 meters per second, or about 380 miles per hour**. At that speed, light traveling from the Sun would ~~, of course, never have made~~ **take 30 years to make** the journey to Earth, rather than the 8 and 1/3 minutes that the journey from the Sun to the Earth requires now.

Then again, at 380 miles per hour, light would be moving swiftly enough to violate speed limits on highways everywhere.

When asked about his group's results, project lead physicist Dr. Frederick Kirchofeldt commented, "It's fascinating to see a pulse of light ~~come to a complete standstill~~ **affected in a laboratory setup.**"

Researchers pursued an effect referred to as "electromagnetically induced transparency" in test substances. The process makes opaque vapor transparent by illuminating it with specially tuned laser light. A recently discovered kind of quantum-mechanical interference turns the vapor transparent, allowing the vapor to bend and slow light traveling through it.

Electromagnetically induced transparency increases the vapor's non-linear index of refraction, an index that measures how much a material slows and bends light. This increase ~~, stunningly,~~ is accompanied by a ~~halting of the light being tested~~ **drop in light speed**. Those involved in the project have been working to test similar means of refracting and ~~bringing light to a standstill~~ **slowing light in extremely difficult-to-achieve circumstances unlikely to occur in nature**.

~~The surprise in the researchers' finding was not that light slows;~~ Though Einstein declared the speed of light to be constant, physicists have long been aware that certain substances can slow the speed of light **somewhat**. ~~the surprise came in the ability to halt the progress of light entirely, leaving it suspended in the laser-tuned vapor environment.~~

The experiments were carried out at room temperature, yielding results that surprised the physicists involved, who assumed super-cooling to a temperature at or near absolute zero — approximately -273 degrees Celsius, and about -460 degrees Fahrenheit, 0 degrees Kelvin — would be required to significantly affect the speed of light.

The vapor atoms through which light was passed in the experiment were contained in a Bose-Einstein condensate, a condition created when matter is cooled almost to absolute zero zero — approximately -273 degrees Celsius, and about -460 degrees Fahrenheit, 0 degrees Kelvin — the lowest temperature theoretically possible. So the scientists involved quite literally put light into a deep freeze in their experiments.

But the project's results also raise grave questions for the state of the universe we have all come to regard as being governed by reliable rules and constants: If light can be halted, as it is in the case of an extremely powerful gravitational force, such as a black hole, what becomes of time, which relies upon light as an interacting factor?

In a black hole, gravitational forces so powerful that they even halt light result in a complete cessation of all motion and, as a result, the complete halting of the flow of time within the black hole itself.

Consider: If an atomic weapon were to be detonated in a region of zero light speed, would it simply do nothing? In the famous formula describing the relationship between matter and energy, the energy E released when some mass m is destroyed is given by the formula $E=MC^2$.

But consider the effect of a detonation within a region of light speed c slowed to zero; would such a region provide a defense against such an explosion?

Consider: If an atomic weapon were to be detonated in a region of slowed light speed, would it fizzle, rather than explode? In the famous formula describing the relationship between matter and energy, the energy E released when some mass m is destroyed is given by the formula $E=MC^2$.

But consider the effect of a detonation within a region of light speed c slowed by a factor of 20,000,000 times; would only a little energy be generated? Would that energy move much more slowly, once released in such a region?

These questions are, naturally, moot, since the conditions involved in making this experiment possible cannot be duplicated in the field, away from Kirchofeldt's uniquely specialized laboratory environment.

Chapter Eleven

On the Road

Delphina Hutchings, ex-D.I.Ops agent, ex-director of an ultra-secret government project, looked up from the road for a moment, pushing up a genuinely severe-looking pair of contoured, reflective shades to rub her dry, weary eyes and consider the sanity of what she was doing: She had spent 33 years heading the operation that had been the only fighting chance her world had left if there were no God left to observe and, thereby, preserve it. And as stars billions of light years away quietly ceased to exist, she had to admit that, speaking in the strictest of terms, Project Oversight had been a success. At least so far.

But at what price?

Now, in 2023, she looked out into the flat expanse of blandly green, almost featureless Iowa farmland, row after row, acre after acre, mile after mile of mind-numblingly similar cornfields fanning out on either side of the highway as if toward some bizarre, nonexistent pastoral-Americana infinity. She fought to ignore the forceful aroma of animal shit being spread on the fields, caught up again in a struggle of self-doubt and angst over why she had left the project.

At this point, could she really make a difference? Could anyone?

She emptied one vial of ginseng/gingko concentrate into her cup of gas-station coffee that had cooked down into a vile, thick, burnt substance as it awaited a customer. Discarding the first vial, she opened and emptied another, the monotonous hum of the car's wheels against the pavement, the uneventful landscape, the 26 hours behind the wheel all colluding to drag her into the murky depths of sleep.

She had managed to spend 33 years on Project Oversight, the energy of Awareness and creation sustaining her. Thirty-three years since the machine had devoured every RV operative in a milewide radius. Thirty-three years since the machine had consumed Jordan.

She hadn't aged a day in her years basking in Machina's energies. Lived those years, but not aged during them. Now, having lived 64 years, she knew that the small part of godhood she had spirited away would continue to make her body resistant to aging, at least for the time being.

When she had realized that she could take no more of the shadowy world of unnamed government agencies and international black ops collusion she had been a part of for such a very, very long time, she had managed to get herself away from it all. She had disappeared from the project and from its files, hit the road at a desperate pace, hadn't stopped running and had never looked back.

That was barely more than a day ago now, but they didn't seem to be tracking her.

If they were, how long could I really last? she wondered. Even with her unique camouflaging abilities, she knew the machine could find her sooner or later.

But it was still possible that Machina hadn't yet discovered her ruse.

As her drivetime mix DVD spun to its next track, she couldn't help but laugh; she was in Iowa City to catch up with a young Midwestern college drop-out who was most likely the only hope against Project Oversight. And he probably had no idea.

The track was an old one: "Gunning for the Buddha," by Shriekback.

We're on the road, and we're gunning for the Buddha;

We know his name, and he mustn't get away;

We're on the road, and we're gunning for the Buddha, it would

Take one shot … to blow him away!

Talk about paradoxes. "If you meet the Buddha on the road," the old riddle went, "what do you do?"

The answer, she recalled, was: "Kill him immediately." It had something to do with it being impossible for the Buddha to actually exist, because upon enlightenment, a Buddha escaped the sorrow-bringing confines of the cycle of rebirth. Or something like that. She was fuzzy on the details. A Buddhist would know, she was sure.

But the song resonated for her.

Here she was, on the road.

Here she was, an ex-black-ops director meddling in perhaps the most divine of affairs.

Here she was, gunning for the divine.

If Shriekback only knew, she thought, allowing a tired smile.

She knew about Sinclair Stauffer from the files kept by the FBI and accessible to internal agencies such as D.I.Ops. He was a young man, Caucasian, had a less-than-exemplary record of college performance.

Parents divorced, mother remarried, then another divorce. He'd had serious relationships in his time, but none listed as "current" in his file. Financially not well off, but, hey, he was a college student.

But this file was empty of any information that might suggest what she needed to know – and that meant that neither the FBI nor D.I.Ops knew what she had glimpsed.

Now she was navigating like a spider, her senses attuned to the fabric of reality, waiting for errant vibrations in that fabric as an arachnid awaits the vibrations that inform it of the arrival and snaring of insect prey in its web.

She'd been feeling Machina's manipulations setting off tremblings in the web of the universe's fabric. The machine was up to something. She could tell by the cold, metallic aftertaste Machina's manipulations of the web brought her – a quasi-conscious lack of concern.

A disconnected indifference.

The terrified disbelief of hundreds and hundreds of voices raised in a chaotic psychic chorus.

A cold colder than the deepest, most lifeless regions of the dead galaxies, the ones they had been too slow to save. Too slow to build Machina.

But then she'd felt another tremble, one that left behind an entirely different aftertaste. One with the flavors of naïvete and youth and life; one that hadn't even grasped the raw creational power in its manipulation of the web. A naïvete that suggested that whoever it was did not even realize that they had reshaped creation on some infinitesimal scale.

And, as she recalled, the Bible had implied that on such matters, size and scale meant nothing   a concept that Machina had never grasped.

She remembered the passage, in which disciples failed to cast out a demon:

"Then the disciples came to Jesus privately and said, 'Why could we not cast it out?'

"And He said to them, 'Because of the littleness of your faith; for truly if you have faith as a mustard seed, you shall say to this mountain, "Move from here to there," and it shall move; and nothing shall be impossible to you."

But could someone with no idea what, if anything, had happened, or whether anything had happened at all, possibly have faith in it?

In those tremblings in the fabric of the web, she glimpsed a night janitor, a college dropout, a beaten young man named Sinclair Stauffer. That had gotten her this far.

So she had come to the Midwest, to Iowa City, smallish home of the State University of Iowa campus. She had to find this flunked out janitor before the machine found out about him.

Here, she was listening more closely for vibrations in the web – nearby vibrations – when a coarse, close manipulation set the web trembling, leaving behind a metallic aftertaste.

Damnit!, she thought. The machine had sent out feelers, feelers that had created trembling in the web of reality within a few miles of where she was. She had hoped her attempt to locate Stauffer would take her to him; now, Machina's reality-warping seemed so close, she feared it may have found Stauffer before she could. With so much at stake, she couldn't risk doing anything that would attract the machine's attention. If Machina felt a manipulation of the fabric of reality, it would discover the missing energy she had absconded with, and it would come after her.

And she knew she wasn't up to a confrontation on that scale.

She'd have to try to home in on the epicenter of the vibrations, then make her way there by more conventional means.

She bore down on the car's accelerator.

Chapter Twelve

Early/Late

In the night, the nightmare visions came to Sinclair again: His family, the storybook version of his family, all successful, all happily together at least some of the time. His father driving their big red minivan, mother in the passenger-side seat, Sinclair himself sitting in the rear, all innocent of the trials, failures, and changes that would transmogrify them all. No one dead by their own hand. No one dying the slow death of synthetic methamphetamine addiction.

But real life wasn't like that; his mother had taken her own life, desperately alone and suffering for it, her child having grown old enough to leave the nest, her husband choosing addiction over her; his father was withering away in shame and premature age brought on by devoting all of one's life and resources to the pursuit of synth.

And Sinclair could do nothing to right it. His mother was already dead, and he'd been at an impasse with his father for his entire adult life.

In the darkness of the night, Sinclair screamed out an unintelligible plea for help. Deuce MacKenzie was there to hold and comfort him.

"Shhh, Sinclair," he said, hugging him reassuringly. "It's only a bad dream. Let it pass. Just let it go … "

"But my 'bad' dreams, Deuce," Sinclair said, his voice choked. "My nightmares are dreams of the good things — the way things are supposed to be."

Dreams that remind me how badly we've all failed, he thought.

Sinclair awoke to the smell of coffee — the smell of a sort of coffee he generally couldn't afford — and the clatter of dishes in the little kitchenette of Deuce MacKenzie's efficiency.

Pulling on his shirt and pants from the previous day, Sinclair made his way out from the unfamiliar bedroom to find Deuce.

Bed-head aside, MacKenzie's Amerasian good looks were a sight to Sinclair, who hadn't been with anyone since his rocky relationship with Dannie had finally crashed and burned, leaving his emotional and interpersonal life a smoldering crater. He hadn't even realized it until that moment, but he hadn't been able to trust anyone again until last night.

"Well, Mr. MacKenzie, you certainly taught me something I didn't know about myself," he said with a smile.

"Coffee?" came the reply.

"Sure."

Deuce filled a mug and, smiling, said, "Taught you what?"

"That it was possible for me to find a man attractive."

"Does that bother you?"

Sinclair thought for a moment.

"No. I've had openly gay friends before who seemed to have problems dealing with it, but I never cared whether they liked men or women or both. Why should it matter to me now?"

Deuce smiled and raised his mug, they clinked the two together.

After a long, groggy drink of the coffee, Sinclair looked up again.

"I'm thinking of something a little off-track, Deuce. Have you ever heard of telekinesis? Or psychokinesis?"

MacKenzie pondered the question, swirling his java.

"People bending spoons with brainpower? Uri Geller? That kind of thing?"

"That kind of thing," confirmed Sinclair. "I'm wondering whether something like that, or like what they call psychic photography, all that sort of thing could tie into what we were talking about — into us changing our reality by observation. It reminds me of the hrönir."

"Reminds of the whazzit?"

"Jorges Luis Borges — a literary giant, both in his native Argentinia and world-wide. His work tended toward the metaphysical, the philosophical, and the fantastic. It this short story of his called *Tlön, Uqbar, Orbis Tertius*, people were capable of producing real-world objects — real things — with their minds, either deliberately or by accident. So an archeologist with a potent enough belief in what he was seeking at a dig might accidentally create it with his mind."

"Wouldn't let Descartes hear you saying anything like that! It wouldn't be long before we'd have to endure a Meditation on how God with a capital 'G' doesn't alter things by observing them," chuckled Deuce.

"Think of the implications: If we have but faith the size of a mustard seed ..."

"Sorry?"

"Something attributed to Jesus: '... for truly I say to you, if you have faith as a mustard seed, you shall say to this mountain, "Move from here to there," and it shall move; and nothing will be impossible to you.' It's in the Book of Mark."

"Yeah, but he was talking about faith in Him," said Deuce. "With a capital 'H,'" he added, smirking.

"Maybe. He said it when his disciples couldn't cure a boy of demonic possession by faith alone. Think of the implications! What if by 'faith' the passage referred more to will? Or just a very strong sense of belief? Or some combination of those? What if the passage was trying to tell us that if we had a pittance of will power, we could alter reality? Cast out demons and move mountains?"

"Or bend spoons? Like Uri Geller? Or creates Borges' hrönir? Give me a break!

A lot of people might not take your interpretation very well. Besides, you know Geller was discredited don't you?"

"I know he had his skeptics. But I'm not likely to bring it up to a congregation; I'm just brainstorming with you."

"OK, OK," said Deuce, raising his hands in surrender. "Let's talk about light, again, shall we?"

Sinclair looked at him, confused.

"Light? Why?"

"Well. As I mentioned last night — uh — this morning ... "

"This afternoon. Night-shift reality can get confusing."

"Whatever. Light just gets more metaphysical, the more we know about it."

"How so?"

"Well, Gary Zukav summed it up this way: We ascribe wave-like and particle-like properties to light, but these are properties that belong to our interaction with light — our observation of it — not to light itself."

"So?"

"So by implication, without anyone to interact with it, light might not exist."

"Is this a 'tree in the forest' parallel? You know: If a tree falls in the forest, but there's no one around to see or hear it, does it make any sound?"

"I don't know. Maybe it is. The other end of the implication is a little more frightening: Without light or anything else to interact with, we do not exist."

"Descartes again, then. He had such a tough time proving that anything outside himself existed that he had to build shortcuts into his 'Meditations.' Reason alone couldn't prove it, so he had to trust his senses — had to give up on reason and depend on interactions."

"Interesting connection. What does it mean?"

"I'm not sure, exactly," he said. "Something like: We cannot be separated from our senses. If we are — if, say, a sentient being never receives any sensory input — will it ever actually be a sentient being?"

"This all rings a bell with me about something you said about light earlier."

"What's that?"

"Well, if a particle-antiparticle collision creates light, there's a direct relationship between light and matter. And Bohrs says we actually can't observe anything without altering what we see; and if our observation of light determines how light behaves — whether it acts like a particle or a wave — then that same rule — complementarity — must also apply to matter."

Deuce grinned excitedly. "Then if light, being so metaphysically intertwined with us humans, is so tied to matter, then maybe we can't observe matter without changing it, either."

Sinclair paused for a moment, letting this sink in. "The problem, then, is that our senses can be fooled. We can have hallucinations, or delusions; like in a heavy-duty acid trip, or in some kinds of honest-to-God insanity," he said, a grave tone coming over his voice. "Can we head back to your office for a few minutes? I want to look over the diagram again. I need to work through something, Deuce."

"Sure, Sinclair."

The two of them poured their coffee into travel mugs and snapped down the lids, heading out to Sinclair's car. In the smoggy gray morning, they made their way across campus to Garraint Walther Hall.

"I was up on the roof the other night … " Sinclair started as they entered the office Deuce McKenzie shared.

"Yes … ?"

" … and I saw — I thought I saw — a woman walk through a lamppost. I don't mean she walked close to it, or ran into it. I mean she walked through it like it wasn't even there. I was just spacing off, not paying attention. Not even looking at her directly. When I saw this happen, I paid attention, snapped my eyes toward her to watch … "

"You observed her more closely."

"Right. And she was still walking without paying attention. 'Sleepwalking' is what I called it when I did it at work. She ran into a wall rounding the corner. Once I was paying attention, concentrating on the scene, she couldn't pass through things anymore. She was sleepwalking, like I used to. She had no will power focused on her surroundings — no faith in them. She wasn't even observing them. Not paying attention to them, anyway. But when I focused my attention on it, the matter firmed up and she bumped into it. I changed the properties of the scene by observing it, Deuce. And my assumption of the solidity of the wall — faith in it — made it solid. I'm thinking of Borges again — that same story. In it, there's a doorway that a homeless man visits each day to rest. But when the man dies, and therefore stops coming to the doorway, it ceases to exist."

Deuce ran a hand through his hair, thinking.

"You know," he said, "I had something a little like that happen. Less conspicuously, though. I tried to dump some coffee grounds into a trashcan I thought I'd seen next to my desk. I was sure it was there, just out of sight, so I dumped out the grounds over the edge of my desk. But when I looked, the trashcan was missing — there were just spent coffee grounds on the floor. It was such a small detail, I just wasn't paying attention."

"You weren't paying attention and it — what? — went away? Winked out?"

"I don't know. Maybe."

"What's happening, Deuce?" Sinclair slammed his palm down on the tabletop, worrying about a reality becoming pliable, liquid, when people weren't paying attention, and what that meant for everyone; both men caught themselves glancing quickly down at the desk. Had his palm sent a miniscule ripple across the desktop, like a bug landing on the surface of a calm pond?

"I've been walking around with my brain half-asleep for months," Sinclair said, fear in his voice. "I've seen this sleepwalking in lots of people."

"You know, I just noticed this spring: Partway through the semester I couldn't really concentrate anymore during the day. I thought it was just me, and I haven't talked with anyone else about it — I mean, I'm a Ph.D. student; if I can't concentrate, and word gets around that I'm not up to snuff, intellectually, I won't last long.

"But there's something else. At night, I could concentrate. It was like whatever was clouding my head had less of an effect on me overnight. Like it wasn't working as hard at night. So I started working late hours."

"I wonder why it didn't seem to affect me that way?"

"Maybe because of your situation, Sinclair," Deuce said gently. "You felt you'd fallen a long way when you had to quit school and take a crappy job; maybe you were in a sort of denial. And it isn't as though your job ever really demanded much that might awaken your brain."

After a moment, Sinclair nodded slowly. "Yeah. So what's happening? Is reality softening up on us? Why would people be losing the ability to concentrate?"

Before Deuce could offer his speculations, the office filled with the ancient, permeating presence Sinclair had come to fear.

Sinclair!, said the voice suddenly, a tone of panic behind it. *They are here.*

Sinclair felt fear dig into the walls of his stomach. He looked around wildly, his heart suddenly thumping faster.

"Who's there?!" Sinclair demanded, whirling around. "Who's here?!"

"What's wrong?" asked Deuce, alarmed.

Sinclair felt it first, low in his intestines; then he heard as it built: an unnatural deep bass hum coming from the hallway.

"Who's here?" demanded Sinclair.

Deuce looked at him worriedly, confused.

"What are you talking about, Sinclair?"

The janitor ran to the door of the office, flinging it open, and looked out into the hall. A brick wall in the hallway was pushing outward. Not buckling like brick should, but stretching, like a latex wall with the wall's brick pattern, a skin stretching outside of its usual limits.

Slowly, a point about four feet up pushed outward from the wall. Then, with a little snap, the brick skin gave and peeled back to reveal a finger, then hand, then human-looking arm of someone or something coming through the usually hard, impassible brick. As the stretched fabric of the wall peeled back, he found himself staring, incredulous, at three men whose skin looked an inhuman, poreless porcelain. They were hairless, wearing suits constructed of some shiny black material, and each seemed to have varied mechanical enhancements grafted into his head. The suits themselves looked like a cross between a conservative three-piece, complete with black tie, and some sort of polished-black exoskeleton, heavily reinforced at the joints and neck.

Did the one on the right look Japanese? Hadn't Beckett mentioned a Japanese Smart Guy Abductee?

This confrontation has come too soon! boomed the voice, thundering in Sinclair's ears. He clapped his hands over them, to no avail.

There is no time!

Sinclair felt himself being pushed backward by some unseen force. The room began to lose definition, and the color in his perspective faded to gray, ending in a brief, worldwide Pop!; he tried to yell a warning to Deuce, but MacKenzie didn't seem to hear him. He tried to gesture a warning, but found that he couldn't see his hands.

Deuce MacKenzie looked around, startled at Sinclair's sudden, inexplicable absence.

The three intruders entered the office and seized Deuce MacKenzie; he tried to resist them, but they easily *overpowered* him, hauling him, unconscious, out into the hall.

They didn't seem to notice Sinclair. He walked behind them a few paces and watched in disbelief as the deep bass hum began again. And then, just as they'd arrived, the three hauled Deuce through the brick wall.

With a sudden *Pop!*, his perspective regained color.

He ran down the hall to where they had pushed through brick somehow made pliable; he reached out, running a hand over the surface.

The wall showed no sign that anything had happened.

Then everyone, and everything, slowed to a halt.

Chapter Thirteen

Beginnings | Failings

Before time, because there can be no account of time before there was any way to measure it, there was nothing. For when there is nothing, there are no relative things by which one might measure time. There was no universe, there was no matter. There was no time.

And there was no God.

The words simply seemed to happen in Sinclair's head. It was the voice again, but this time the usually terse hallucination was delivering a monologue.

But where were they? He was surrounded by a glow, a soft, warm, golden glow – and again by that ancient presence – but the details he could make out around him seemed hazy. The ground under his feet felt solid enough.

Outside, he could see Deuce's office frozen in time and space, every single atom motionless.

Can you even have a grasp of nothing, I wonder? The absolute absence of any matter, any darkness, any qualities whatsoever?

It was before even light came into being. Somehow … somehow all that was — which was nothing — became aware that there was nothing: a featureless emptiness lacking warmth or the absence of it, light or the absence of it, anything at all.

The universe was created when the sum of it became aware, and it became two: the universe and the Awareness. There must always be a universe, and with it, there must always be an Awareness. The two are mutually inclusive. They are necessary to one another.

"Who are you? What are you?" *What's happened to Deuce?* He asked silently.

Learn now. I will teach you what I am able, but even now, the memory grows dim and time grows short.

When all that was conceived of nothing, it began the cycle of creation by necessarily creating the opposite of the void: light.

A riot of creation occurred then — an explosion the likes of which has never been seen since. For from the awareness of dark emptiness came creation of light; and from the cold of the emptiness came the necessary opposite: warmth. From immateriality came the material; and so on.

From nothing came chaotic creation, each quality, each characteristic creating, by necessity, its opposite. Creation exploded, and as opposites associated with other new qualities and things, they overlapped; the universe became a realm not merely of black and white, but also of intermediary shades of gray. That second step was like this:

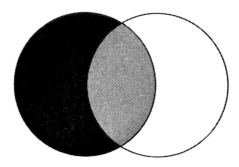

The First Awareness was an Awareness with some sense of self, I think, but not the way you might conceive of self. The First, you see, became caught up, awash in the constantly dividing binary nature of the new universe. Its sense of self became lost in the noise of creation, and its consciousness a diffuse, ambient background presence. Although it took untold millennia, the chaos of this genesis creation eventually became part of the First itself. It lost its sense of self and became, instead, the Great Ocean of Thought.

When the First's own sense of self began dividing as had everything else in this genesis, the universe-Awareness binary system absolutely required that a new Awareness come forth. The creation is automatic; it happens simply as a function of reality.

The Second took on a new function then: It became a shepherd of the Great Ocean of Thought, tending it as it began to infuse life into the organized matter that had been created in the chaotic genesis cycles.

All that is, the Awareness observes, on at least some level; for where the most primitive and meager animal vessels appeared, the Second tied the Great Ocean to them, decanting into them some small measure of the Great Ocean of Thought. The Second made the animals aware, and part of the Awareness of the universe. For while the Second observes everything, the fading away of the individuality of the First became the source of the awareness of all of the creatures that have evolved on Earth.

"Are you telling me that you're God?"

The voice imparted the sense of one made weary by life — an unimaginably long life filled with burdens.

I choose "Awareness"; your people have chosen to call us "God," or "gods," or ascribe us other such titles, and then guessed at what those titles meant.

Sinclair radiated shock. After a moment, he demanded: "If you're God, why didn't you protect Deuce MacKenzie?!"

I cannot. The time is coming for my passing, as the elder Awareness did before me, and the elder who preceded him. It is all part of the cycle.

"Him?"

The Second eventually chose to identify itself as male; I use the term now to simplify communication with you. My binary nature is conjoined with the universe; the Awareness completes the thought-matter binary pair that the universe comprises.

Have you ever wondered why the deity in Judeo-Christian texts exhibits radically differing personae? It is because it is not the same persona from passage to passage at all; I am but one in a long line. The wrathful presence in the Christian Old Testament was another. The one written about in the New Testament another still …

"Which are you?" asked Sinclair doubtfully.

I no longer remember — we share a continuity, we wielders of the Awareness. It becomes muddled.

"I don't understand. The animals are aware, then, the same way we are?"

It is difficult to explain in your terms, Sinclair. The same, but mostly to a lesser degree. Mostly. They receive Awareness, just as your people do, in measures decanted from the Great Ocean of Thought.

"Animals and humans have a piece of God in them?" Sinclair asked, his heart racing.

A portion of the Awareness, yes.

"Is it wrong when we harm them? Or to kill them?"

Is it wrong when one human hurts or kills another? Of course it is. A lesser amount of the Awareness is no justification to cause unnecessary suffering. If it were, humankind would find it acceptable to harm the mentally disabled. Causing unnecessary suffering is evil. It is wrong. And in the end, it is an assault on oneself, and upon the very essence of the Awareness itself, as both assailant and victim will eventually be reunited, their small portions of the Awareness flowing again with the Great Ocean. Do you see? But, Sinclair, you are getting off-track. We have much to discuss. You must prepare.

His mind racing, Sinclair recalled an essay on animal thought. "But – but Noam Chomsky said that nonhuman animals could not think, as such, because they lack language and grammar."

Do you require grammar to avoid a hot fire? What are you thinking when you act very, very quickly? Are you forming words in your mind, carefully forming complete sentences? Or are you acting on what you have learned to protect yourself from injury? Do you require grammar to avoid any other thing that you know from your experience from living and learning would cause you pain or injury? asked the Elder.

No. Neither do they.

"What about instinct?"

Does instinct teach a housecat the name you eventually give it, or does the housecat learn the name?

Sinclair's wits felt sharp — honed to a razor's edge. He was more wide-awake than he could remember ever having been in his life.

"So if you're the current God, we must be standing in Heaven?" Sinclair asked.

There is no such thing, Sinclair. There is only the universe and the Great Ocean of Thought.

"But the Bible …"

Bible, Koran, Torah, the Vedas, Talmud, Tao-te-Ching, Book of Mormon … what does it matter? My hand did not write those tomes; they were penned mostly by well-intentioned people attempting to grasp the nature and will of the divine. In small ways they have, as have some philosophers, glimpsed truths, but humankind's religious texts have ever fallen victim to the political leanings of those overseeing them. Some passages and books are canonized in; others are removed to unofficial apocrypha, depending upon whom is in power in the religions at that moment. New translations yield politically determined reinterpretations. Passages admonishing Christians to put their women to death for wearing the color red, condemnations of entire groups of people … such are the work of those who would use the threat of a vengeful deity to justify their own petty fears, hatreds, and motivations. The Great Ocean flows with none of these.

Ask yourself: Of what interest would it be to the Awareness to mark an entire race of people as descendents of the first murderer?

"So there's no Heaven? No Hell? No Devil?"

No, Sinclair. Those are human constructs. The churches have always argued over who and what the devil was, due to its having so many different names and manifestations in writings that were supposed to be harmonious. The Devil did not even appear in the cloven-hoofed, barb-tailed form with which you are familiar until the early Christian church produced its first official description of him in medieval times. And leaders of various faiths are meeting even now to write out the current fire-and-brimstone description, as it is too outdated to teach believably. And these are articles of faith for millions of your people. When their faiths' leaders conclude, will it mean an instantaneous change in what they believe? Will it mean that they fervently believe in the cloven-hoofed beast until a certain date, and fervently disbelieve in it afterward?

These all arise from humankind's attempts to understand the nature of the universe around him. But they merely guess, grasping at the meager glimpses their perceptions grant them.

Sinclair's head was spinning.

"What about the prophets? Abraham, Mohammad, Jesus — every religion on Earth has prophets. Are you communicating with them?"

Some have glimpsed in some small way information flowing within the Great Ocean of Thought. Others have simply been poor, troubled souls suffering from insanity, their portions of the Awareness imprisoned in flawed organic vessels.

Sinclair struggled to make sense of all this new information, to somehow sort out and analyze all of these new claims. How could humankind have gotten it all so wrong?

All those crosses and stars of David, all the rituals memorized by millions upon millions of people — could it really all just be bad guesswork?

Something about the tale of revolving godhood didn't feel quite right to him. "Why haven't you faded, then, just died out like your predecessors?"

There is interference in the usual cycle of the Awareness.

"Who could possibly interfere with the will of God?"

Humankind is responsible, though once again, I believe its intentions were good.

"What were those things that took Deuce?"

They were human once; now they are the mindless tentacles of that which causes the interference in the cycle of the Awareness. Your neighbor, Jeremy Beckett, identifies them as Men In Black. I am no longer omniscient, but my opponent will never be so.

"I thought you said there was no such thing as the Devil."

I speak not of the devil. I speak of the source of interference in the natural cycle of Awareness.

The source of the interference is biomechanical; those who created it have named the source of the interference Machina. It is not of the Awareness and it is not human, but in order to function, it requires the small amounts of Awareness decanted into individual human beings.

"What do you mean?"

In a manner of speaking, it uses their portion of the Awareness to function. But it does not grasp what the Awareness is, nor even that it is.

"Deuce?"

Yes. Among many, many others.

"But why choose him?"

They did not. They chose you.

Sinclair's mouth hung open in disbelief.

Just before they came after him, you had, with your will, clutched fast to the fabric of reality composing the desktop you hit. When you struck the desktop, you sent a ripple out through all of reality, which Machina interpreted as a potent dose of Awareness — one that it hungered for, and at the same time, one that threatened its function.

I protected you — brought you into a fold in the fabric of reality. Machina does not know that I am still cognizant. I doubt that it knows that I am, at all.

"Why – how could I have caused – what did you call it? A ripple?"

The fabric of the universe is weak now — vulnerable to what you earlier called hrönir. *I have been drawn to you and your ability to influence it. I cannot defeat my opponent, I cannot ascend once more, without your help.*

Sinclair reeled.

"Let me get this straight: God wants me to help him re-ascend to godhood," he said incredulously, more question than a statement.

No. I need you to help me guide the Awareness. Sadly, I am no longer Aware of all that you need to know.

"You said I threatened its function. What function?"

Machina was created to observe all of reality. In the cycle of Awareness, the changeover as one Awareness fades is automatic, a function of the universe-Awareness pair.

Allow me to enlighten you. I no longer have a great deal of influence over reality, but I can still show you images and sounds from the past.

"Wait, voice — oh, what the hell am I supposed to call you, anyway? I don't understand why I need to be here."

I am no longer the Awareness. Now I am merely your Elder. And I am no longer potent enough to confront and subdue Machina; I need you. Your ability to clutch fast to the fabric of reality. I need your assistance.

"Why me?" he asked, fear curdling in his stomach.

I have heard your discussions with Thaddeus MacKenzie. I have seen and felt your ability to grasp and shape reality. But I did not choose you – this is a function of nature, of the universe itself, to maintain the balance. I do not know its reason – perhaps there is none.

The memory is so very dim now, the Elder lamented. *But I need your help to stop the collapse of the universe-Awareness relationship, for without one, the other must surely also disappear.*

"Why can't Machina just take your place?"

Because it is imperfect. Because its creators had only managed to work out part of the nature of reality. Because it does not understand the Great Ocean of Thought. And the Ocean must be tended to — it must have a presiding consciousness.

Sinclair, Machina does not and cannot grasp it all. You and your friend MacKenzie have already found evidence of the weakening of the fabric of reality. Do you recall things becoming less tangible when not directly observed? The woman you fleetingly observed walking through solid objects, half asleep? Did not Descartes predict this? You saw it happen out of the corner of your eye — your level of observation of the obstacle she passed through was not direct enough to maintain the solidity of reality there, and she was mentally asleep, lulled by Machina.

Sinclair had assumed Descartes' argument unlikely to be true; it had seemed too flawed. Besides, Descartes had backed off from that assumption; or rather, he had backed off from it a bit, at least, claiming the need for a god to exist to observe everything so that things would not become insubstantial when not observed by a human.

Machina broadcasts a field that dampens mental energy. It is a defensive function. It is the only way it can use a finite number of human minds to maintain reality; with a planet full of fully conscious people observing their surroundings, daydreaming, making reality shimmer and dance around the edges, it would have too great a battle holding things together.

Sinclair – Machina has forced this confrontation upon us sooner than I had hoped, but it is not yet aware of you, and perhaps not even of me. Shortly, though, when Thaddeus MacKenzie is made a part of Machina, it will learn of you. We cannot risk that.

"What do you mean?" Sinclair asked, a pang of fear in his voice.

Sinclair, we must confront Machina now, before it learns of you and, thus, comes looking for you.

"You can't be serious," shouted a stunned Sinclair. "I'm just a college dropout! I'm a third-shift janitor for God's sake! I'm not even sure I believe that I did anything to attract Machina!"

We have no time, Sinclair, said the Elder resolutely. I am sorry.

Sinclair felt the world shifting around him, the office of Deuce MacKenzie beginning to blur and fade, and another, much, much larger hall, one darkened, save an occasional pale, lifeless overhead and a pulsing, pervasive red glow illuminating a monstrous snarl of mechanical and electronic materials, a low, rumbling thumm emanating from the structure in rhythm with the light. Mechanical, electronic, and, Sinclair now saw, biological materials: Row upon row of dull, metallic-grey figures seemed to be stooped forward, their heads almost completely embedded in the metallic front of the structure. Their bodies knelt, sort of, almost as if in prayer, on black, metal-mesh resting seats, rendering them in a posture suspended partway between standing and kneeling on the floor. A dull, metallic-grey skin covered the figures and the structures evenly.

With the metallic skin, they looked like pieces of a metal sculpture – too unreal, too completely encased in the dull, lifeless metal, too lifeless themselves – to be human.

As the scene solidified before him, he could now make out row upon row of the stooped figures — dozens ... no, hundreds of them! Thousands! — standing there, their heads merged seamlessly into the face of the metallic structure, stacked one atop the other, going up as far as he could see. Farther.

He began to step backward, looking up. Far, far up the wall of embedded figures, their configuration changed: So far up that he could barely make them out, more, many, many more people than he had thought were merged with the machine, their arms and legs spread and outstretched in a sort of X. There were thousands of them! There was no difference in the color of these people or their garments from the surrounding metal; they were included in its dull, grey, seamless skin at this height. Were they the old ones? The first people the Men in Black and the machine had taken? Whatever they had once been, they were now mere cogs and gears and spokes of the thing, forever entombed within it.

Down here, though, on the ground-level row, and for a few rows of the figures up from the ground level, he saw that the figures looked different: Their coloration was not the lifeless grey-metallic sheen. Instead, he could see inhumanly white skin, bodies encased in a shiny, black, mechanized suit. These figures' heads, too, were merged with the face of the structure, but a feeling in the pit of his stomach identified them as, at least until recently, human.

Men in Black.

The ones in rows further up must have been used up, he thought.

Machina, whispered the Elder, as the immense, monstrous girth of the structure gained clarity in Sinclair's gaze.

(No, thought Sinclair, not "the structure." "The machine.")

Sinclair. Conceive of the machine as an inert piece of metal – a solid block. I shall work with you. We must destroy Machina's ability to perceive of itself clearly if we are to defeat it!

"But how?!" yelled Sinclair, fear tainting his voice. "I don't know how!"

You have done this before, boy, more than once! Think of a thing and make it become so! You must wield this ability — you must shape reality with thought!

"Oh, right!" Sinclair bellowed, panic and doubt in his voice. He whipped his head back and forth, wildly around, trying to catch a glimpse of the present-but-invisible Elder. "Just like that, huh?!"

The steady pulsing of the red light, the deafening thrumm of Machina, cycled up in some barely perceptible way, and Sinclair heard a metallic whir, a metallic clank, and saw one of the figures at the far end of the hall disengage and step back from Machina, stand erect, and turn its head toward him.

Sinclair, there is no time for this. Open your mind to me – I must share knowledge with you.

"What do you mean?!" Sinclair yelled, panic in his voice.

Immediately, he was flooded with the conversations he and Deuce had shared, with the content of the books they'd discussed on the subject of reality, and with the Elder's own fleeting memories of godhood.

He had to start small. *With faith the size of a mustard seed, right?* He laughed a paranoid laugh at this.

In his mind's eye, he pictured the figure at the end of the hall as a pillar of the dull-grey metal, as the other, older figures in the rows above were. He concentrated, trying to calm his mind, and suddenly feeling the presence of the Elder's will alongside his, the flickering lights on the figure's suit went out, then back on.

Nothing had happened.

Then the pulsing red glow and deafening thrumm of Machina escalated. The figure's lights flickered again.

Doubt crept into Sinclair's mind. "What am I supposed to do? Is it like praying? I can't do it, Elder! Nothing's happening!"

Machina cannot resist. You and I are more at one with the Awareness than is Machina! came the Elder's reply, beamed into his thoughts with such force that it made him see white for a burning, painful moment.

Sinclair felt a pulsing, throbbing surge of information begin to flow into him. Could he actually do even some small part of what the Elder claimed? A machinegun staccato of emotions clattered through him:

Fear / confidence / panic / brilliance / dullness / power / impotence / Zen calm / unbearable rage / influence / fluidity / shame / libidinousness / profundity / stupidity / strength / crippling weakness / pleasure / pain …

What was happening? If he could just get a grip on this torrent of experience and information, maybe he could …

Suddenly, the universe was reverberating with the deafening thrumm of Machina.

The machine was everywhere, its power smothering the fledgling sliver of potency Sinclair could barely sense he had gained, a torrent of energy asserting itself. From their battleground, perched atop all of reality, it seemed, Sinclair was suddenly awash in a tidal wave of fear and confusion from the Elder. The Elder did not understand why Sinclair was not evolving into the role automatically.

Fear — no, outright panic, he realized — ripped through his body, an icy cut to his core. He began to yell hysterically, submerged suddenly in a sense of inadequacy, a profound feeling that someone like him, someone who hadn't even managed success at school or relationships, could not possibly be the right choice.

The Elder was drowning Sinclair's mind in doubt, and the emotion was becoming Sinclair's own. "But the Elder said that I was the choice the universe itself had made," he thought, battling to hold on.

… insignificance. The flood of emotion and information halted on insignificance.

Sinclair was nothing. He was less than the least undergrad he worked around. Less than his heterosexual friends. Less than people who weren't from broken homes. Less than any single person he could think of.

How could he possibly be the right choice?

Horrified and filled with self-doubt, he realized that he could never restore the cycle of the universe. All of reality was collapsing and Sinclair could do nothing to stop it.

Just as he could do nothing to stop his mother's decision to kill herself.

Or his father's fall into the soul-sucking, money-sucking, life-sucking pit that is synthetic methamphetamine addiction.

He wasn't omnipotent, he was the opposite: The least potent being in the entire god-forsaken universe.

Sinclair was worthless. He was helpless. He might as well die. He felt himself curling into a fetal ball in terror.

Whatever it had once been, the Elder was now lost, as well.

Machina! remembered Sinclair suddenly; he'd gotten so focused on his own sense of worthlessness and self-doubt that he'd almost forgotten about Machina.

Machina struck once, with a concentration that caused all of the embedded Men in Black, row upon ghastly, sickening row, joined to Machina at the head, to shudder, spasming as if electrocution were under way. Blood trickled from the seams around the encased heads.

Its blow shattered the concentration of the two, sending them, simply, away.

From the tidal forces of chaos and dissipation that followed, words appeared in Sinclair's mind:

"For a period immeasurable, all that was was unaware. All that was became aware suddenly with a phrase which might be repeated in another age: 'Cogito Ergo Sum.' There was not form and there was not substance, but the first existence of any sort came of spontaneous consciousness. With thought, all that was created itself. To understand its sum, all that was found that it had created the opposite of sum : nil. 'All that is, I am,' came the realization. Yet this was no longer the case; in existing, all that was had created existence and its counterpart, nil. Comparison had been necessary for that first thought, and so came opposites necessary for comparison. With the inadvertent (but absolutely necessary) creation of opposites, the thought, 'All that is, I am,' spawned something new; in self-contemplation, all that was aware became two from the one which first came to summation. The First's thought mirrored the First, spawning another. There was a sense from the First that the Second was of its like. The First became distinct from this new presence, and fear was created alongside love. There was neither good nor evil just yet, but the First knew that the Second might in some way pose a threat; the Second was its equal.

"The First presence concealed fear and the Second knew love for its predecessor, for surely without that First presence the second could not have come. The First built quickly, the sum of its thoughts creating the sum of existence, conceiving always of new thoughts. A self-serving child, the First began to realize the absoluteness, the totality of creation from will, and conceived of other, lesser presences, like it and the Second, but lacking the gift of creation through thought. This was to be reserved for the First alone, and the Second, quite content with its infant existence, created naught. As that First presence's scope of thought grew, the sum expanded to include lesser presences conceived of by the First, whose sole function was to be to praise the First, and to be grateful for their existence. And the Second discovered something not known before: doubt; doubt in the correctness of the actions of the First. It was then that the possibility of correct or incorrect, of right and of wrong, spawned good and its necessary counterpart: evil.

"As the sum of that First presence's thoughts grew it conceived of a monumental construct: countless lesser bits of awareness would be created, as were the other lesser presences, for what could only be described as the amusement of the First presence. These lesser presences would take innumerable forms; they would clash, competing for supremacy, because the First presence wished it. The creation of this construct would occur solely for the First's pleasure in creation through thought. None would ever be allowed to truly know, to ever truly understand a single thought. Awash and abandoned within the construct they would face endless torture, should they choose not to worship the First presence absolutely. The Second presence became aware of this idea, an absolute enslavement of cognizant beings. The Second, unaware of its equality to every aspect of the First, questioned that First presence. The being that that First presence had become had become acclimated toward whim, toward action without thought, toward action without reason. Having found itself neither questioned nor opposed before, the First reacted with the first reaction of anger ever to occur. The First conceived of a prison, a perpetual torture, and through the sum of its will alone banished the second to the prison. Opposition eliminated, the First embarked upon its construct, part of which was a dark, vaguely formed waste. The First then conceived of light, and the demented play, the enslavement of all cognizant creatures, followed shortly.

"The Deity is a madman."

In overpowering waves of disappointment and frustration and guilt over his own inadequacy — some of the emotions his, some from the Elder — he awoke screaming in his bed, his sheets drenched in sweat.

The Deity is a madman, he thought. What did that mean? Where had the nightmare come from?

He hadn't gotten too worked up about the creation myth in the past. Who was the First? Was it the Elder? Is that the madman the dream seemed to be trying to communicate?

His head ached mightily, and his mouth tasted like a skidmark, like too many beers from the night before.

His heart raced, his pulse thundering painfully in his ears and at his temples. A confrontation between a dying god and an omnipotent machine?

There was no way ... no way that he had actually had that experience.

Was there?

Chapter Fourteen

Faltering

Sinclair jumped at the sudden racket; someone was pounding at his door.

"Yo, Sync! You OK in there?"

It was Beckett.

Sinclair pushed himself up on one elbow.

"Sorry Beckett," he said quickly, hoarsely. "What a nightmare."

"Everything OK, man?" he asked through the door in his distant, wake-and-bake way.

"Yeah. Fine."

After a shower and shave, Sinclair would feel a little better, he told himself.

A little more certain that he had experienced a dream. Everything seemed dull around the edges. Sort of hazy. Like he couldn't think clearly.

On his answering machine were three messages from Jerry Connell, the supervisor he hadn't bothered to call for the day he took off.

Jesus!, he thought, *I haven't gotten far, but I can at least cover my bills now.*

Had he dreamt of sex?

He dragged himself through the mindless ritual of shower and shave, aching from head to toe. He washed down four tablets of painkiller with tapwater stinking so strongly it made him clench his teeth and tighten his throat against the heave of protest from his stomach.

Details of the dream kept leaking into his mind as he washed away the remaining shaving cream and dried his stinging face. His essence crumpled to dry, useless dust in the hands of a failing, imperfect, parasitic machine? A perversion of Descartes' Great Machine idea?

He shivered and forced the memory away.

It took some talking, a manufactured sudden death in the family, and a plea for lenience, but Sinclair managed to keep Jerry and his Physical Plant supervisors from firing him.

At night, as he worked, he badly wanted to forget. He badly wanted to sleep-walk again. So very badly.

In his BopBoxä audio player, the chorus of an old Skinny Puppy song cleaved into him, insinuating itself into the vacant, backgrounded terror he felt, as vocalist Nivek Ogre growled:

"I just don't wanna know … anymore …

"Life shifts up and down, everybody knows it's wrong,

"Life shifts up and down, everybody knows it's wrong,

"Life shifts up and down, everybody knows that it's wrong,

"I just don't wanna know … anymore … "

And in the night, alone, despite his fears poking through from time to time, he was able to space off, to find some relief from the impossible story he'd imagined from the voice.

No, he thought, correcting himself: from the Elder.

Then he was angry at himself, frustrated at his inability to let the nightmare go. He pulled off the BopBoxä, coiling the headphone cord around the audio player, and placed it inside his custodian's cart.

As his 3 a.m. break approached, Sinclair made his way up to the 3rd floor, where the tenant he'd imagined having sex with had his office. Grateful, he found the office light out. As he walked past brick walls just as solid as the area where he'd dreamed of Men In Black pushing their way through a brick wall made somehow pliable, he tried not to think of the nightmare, tried to focus on emptying waste cans.

It was too much, he decided. He hadn't even realized that he'd been trying to figure out why he'd reacted with such fear. It was just that the concept of him, of all the people on the entire planet, facing down some sort of biomechanical demigod, with the fate of all of reality in the balance, was too enormous, the stakes too high. Yes, he decided: It was too much to accept.

And realizing that let him begin to feel better about the decision, whether real or imagined. It was OK, he tried to convince himself, not to accept such a heavy burden.

The easing of his conscience was with him when he opened the door to the office with the diagram (*Don't think about the diagram!* he thought), when he turned on the light and began to empty the trash.

The room began to fill with the ancient, permeating presence Sinclair had come to know, though it seemed weaker than it had when he'd experienced it before.

Sinclair.

"Leave me alone, Elder," he muttered harshly. "I can't afford to see a shrink to buy the pills that'll make you go away!"

I am not alone. Think about Deuce MacKenzie.

"No! Damnit, get out of my head!"

"Sinclair?" asked Deuce, sitting at the desk, his voice having odd acoustics in the office air, like he was far away.

"Deuce? How can you be here?" Sinclair had tears in his eyes now, struggling to understand, struggling to find the sane middle ground where none of it had happened.

"Sinclair, listen. You're awake now, and you know it. We haven't much time. You already resist Machina's dampening field."

"I don't want to … "

"When the Men In Black were strapping me in, integrating me into Machina, I fought. When I understood what Machina was, I grabbed as much of Machina's human-generated Awareness as I could. I know you're awake now, because I reached back through spacetime and started the process to awaken you myself a few weeks back."

Deuce was standing now, an urgent look in his eyes.

"Machina?" asked Sinclair hollowly.

"You know, Sinclair," he said gently. "You know. I can only mask myself from Machina and the Men In Black for a little while. I have possession of a larger measure of God than I once did, but eventually, Machina will figure out that its power has been tapped, and it will find me and overwhelm me and pull me in."

Oh yeah, thought Sinclair: It's all OK, man, as long as you can keep the reality separate from the illusion – as long as you can tell them apart.

So much for that idea.

"What do you want me to do? Come and free you? 'Thaddeus ex Machina'? Deuce out of the machine? Something heroic like that?" Sinclair asked with a short, bitter laugh at his pun.

"No. Forget about me. But don't forget what the Elder told you. Machina must be stopped, or the entire structure that holds together the universe will fail."

"Get someone stronger! I've failed at everything I've ever tried, Deuce," he pleaded.

"You are the only one, Sinclair. There are rules we have to play by."

"How can you be here? You're part of Machina now."

"Machina has no knowledge of the Great Ocean. With no one tending it, some of us are able to hold together our portion of the *Awareness*, rather than reuniting with the Ocean and losing ourselves."

"Jesus, Deuce — are you saying you're a ghost?"

But when he turned toward Deuce for an answer, he found himself alone in the office, holding a trashcan liner.

"Sometimes that happens, my friend," said Deuce's voice, far, far away.

And Sinclair felt pathetic. A maybe-hallucinating loser too frightened to think about things he wasn't even certain had happened.

When he arrived at home, he found Beckett up, despite the early hour, frying something in the kitchen.

"Beckett?" Sinclair asked.

The fuzzy-haired neighbor pulled a tall boy from its plastic six-pack ring and handed it over.

"Want a burger, dude?" he asked.

Sinclair nodded dumbly.

"I know how crazy this'll sound, man, but I really want to talk to you about the Men In Black. Smart Guy Abductions," he said. "Like," with a wave of his beer through the air, "all that."

"It seems really important this morning," Beckett added. "Somehow."

Sinclair reached out a hand and accepted a beer from Beckett, perhaps a shimmer in the air between them, perhaps not. Disoriented, Sinclair shook his head as Beckett scraped the greasy burgers from the black, cast-iron frying pan and plopped them onto burger buns.

In the shared living room of their rental, Beckett began.

"Back in the day, man, Men In Black were a UFO thing. Turned up after flying saucer sightings and badgered witnesses into not talking about what they saw. Supposedly even got the International Flying Saucer Investigation Bureau to shut down back in 1953."

Beckett paused to wash down a bite of the burger with his beer.

"Really?" Sinclair asked.

"Cha, man," Beckett said confidently. Then, "Well, not officially. The head honcho just said he'd solved the UFO mystery, but had been instructed not to talk about it. He'd never say 'Men In Black,' but people knew."

Sinclair took a doubtful pull on the beer.

"'People' knew, huh?" he said. "So what do flying saucers have to do with the Men In Black you read about?"

"Well, no one's sure. The new ones might not be related to the old ones at all. The old description varied a little — sometimes the skin color of the Men In Black was pale, sometimes olive. People say the new ones have a smooth, almost ceramic white skin tone. Kinda inhuman, y'know? Like a porcelain doll.

"And back in the day, the Men In Black favored older black Cadillacs. Like ska dudes, dig?"

"You're kidding," said Sinclair with an incredulous laugh.

"Nope. These days, there aren't many reports of them coming and going, but they get there somehow, and they've been seen kidnapping intelligent people — like, total brainiacs. Big-voltage-brain mothers."

"Smart Guy Abductions," said Sinclair. "What you've been trying to tell me about. Right?"

Beckett nodded.

"So," Sinclair continued, "Does anyone have any idea why Men In Black are abducting bright people instead of threatening people who claim to have seen flying saucers, like in the old days?"

"Like I said, G, these probably are not your father's Men In Black. Unless something big changed in what they're doing — like, in what their mission is."

Sinclair digested this with a swallow of the cold, cheap beer.

"OK, any idea how they're choosing their targets? Are these abductions taking place in a limited area?"

Beckett shook his head. "No, the abductions happen all over. But they like scientists. Or don't like them, depending on your perspective, dig? They choose science guys a lot."

Like Deuce MacKenzie, thought Sinclair.

"Anything else you feel compelled to tell me?"

Beckett scratched his head.

"That's about it, man. Freaky stuff, huh? Yo."

"Freaky stuff," Sinclair agreed.

He hefted the last swallow from his beer and placed the empty can on the wax-dripping-covered table before him. He didn't want to spill the whole story to Beckett – it was crazy enough to have him doubting the sanity of even discussing it.

Carefully, he told Beckett about the voice, and about Deuce's abduction.

"The voice mentioned that its opponent is consuming people," he said cautiously. "Stealing their consciousness, their ability to perceive of the world around them. I think that's why the Men In Black took Deuce. I think they go for smart guys in these Smart Guy Abductions because they're looking for people whose minds can handle a lot of heavy-duty concentration on details."

"Why would this – ah – opponent need to keep gathering smart guys, then?" asked Becket. Then a look of appalled realization crossed his face.

He said: "Is the opponent using them up? Burning them out? Eew! Yo!"

Beckett shook his head back and forth violently to dispel the image.

Sinclair nodded. "I think that's what's happening: I think this opponent is parasitic. The voice said this opponent wasn't even truly 'aware' by itself. It needs organic sources for its awareness."

"Organic sources," said Beckett. "It needs meat? Like, smart guys?"

"Just like smart guys."

Sinclair looked at the hamburger on his plate, and the Elder's words came back to him: Causing unnecessary suffering is evil. It is wrong. And in the end, it is an assault on oneself, and upon the very essence of the Awareness itself, as both offender and victim will eventually be reunited, their small portions of the Awareness flowing again with the Great Ocean. Do you see?

Sinclair put down the hamburger, pushing his plate away.

Beckett said, "Dude, that stuff the voice told you about consciousness all coming from the same source?"

Sinclair looked up. "Yeah?"

"Sounds like some of the stuff in the 'Bhagavad Gita,'" he said proudly.

Sinclair was a bit puzzled.

"When did you read the 'Bhagavad Gita,' Beckett?"

"Second semester Sanskrit, G," he beamed. "There's an idea that sounds like that other one."

"OK ... " said Sinclair, waiting for the explanation.

"OK," said Beckett. "It's kinda like this ... "

"'Kinda'?"

"Hey, it's a tough language!"

"Sorry," said Sinclair.

"So, like, the 'Gita' reveals that Krishna is the cause of all causes — the beginning of everything."

"Krishna?" asked Sinclair. "The kid who's always depicted as greasy-faced from getting in the butter?"

"'Ghee' — clarified butter," said Beckett with confidence. "And yep, that's the one."

"Who chases the peasant women around?"

Beckett tapped his nose in response.

"So he's the source of everything — including the source of the material universes. They call that source the Maha-Visnu. More than any mere incarnation, the 'Gita' says he's the source of all incarnations."

"Is this one of those 'My god is bigger than your god' things? Like when devotees will depict supposedly lesser gods, gods other than their own, with symbols of devotion to their favored deity?"

"Dude, I'm not really very far along," said Beckett glumly. "I don't have any idea."

Lost in thought, Sinclair felt the clouds beginning to clear from his mind once more. Machina had apparently left him to succumb to its thought-dampening transmissions. It must have thought him sufficiently overwhelmed that he could no longer pose a threat. But what about the Elder?

The Deity is a madman.

The thought echoed through his head again, a distant warning from a dream.

Chapter Fifteen

Tremblings

Delphina Hutchings, ex-D.I.Ops agent, ex-director of a super-secret government project, jumped, drew a sharp, shocked breath and looked up from the cup of mediocre coffee she was swilling, her contoured, mirrored shades hopping a bit, then settling on the bridge of her nose.

After sundown, the smoke became so dense in this bar called the Deadwood that she couldn't stand to wait there. Her eyes watered, her nose ran, and her clothes stank without letup the first night she tried. But afternoons such as this, the doors had been open for a few hours, the place had aired out a bit, and the coffee, while nothing to write home about, was a bargain, making the old tavern a cheap place to bide her time, waiting for some action to be played out across the fabric of the Web of reality, waiting for her chance to home in on that activity if it seemed nearby.

Trembling far away, she reasoned, probably wouldn't be caused by the Wünderkind whose trail she was following.

This trembling in the fabric of reality, though, was close enough to make her jump when she sensed it. And it didn't seem to be tainted with the metallic aftertaste she'd come to know from Machina's meddlings.

When she'd sensed the manipulation earlier, it had stunk with Machina's touch. But another scent of sorts – or flavor, or whatever — the naïve one she had sensed earlier, mixed with something older than imagination, had engaged Machina, struggling for control.

Then, abruptly, that had subsided, the new presence had been silenced, and the world again resonated with Machina's dull, grey, metallic aftertaste.

With no idea what had happened, she had decided that she had no choice but to avoid Machina and wait for another instance, another trembling in the reality's fabric.

It had come, and it had the scent of naïvete she had sensed earlier, but mixed with the pain of betrayal and self-doubt this time. Whoever it was, they weren't ready for the task at hand — and she wasn't really even certain what the task at hand was. She had felt tremors in the webwork of reality's fabric, and that had been enough for her to risk it all, to extricate herself from Oversight and from the monstrosity called Machina.

It had started with such good, such truly noble intentions.

But now the thing called Machina was a voracious, parasitic monster failing in its mission and preying upon those it was supposed to protect. For years, Hutchings had seen no choice but to continue with Machina, to try to improve the machine until it could, in fact, observe all things, and to do so before the fabric of reality finished collapsing in what her overseer had called, those long decades ago, the death of God.

Trull had helped her to understand the mission more thoroughly, coaching her on the quantum nature of reality, on quantum field theory and Schroedinger and his wave, and an absolute avalanche of loosely related work and theory, which he fit together like pieces from a hundred jigsaw puzzles.

Wachhund was gone, disappeared into the gaping, murdering maw of Machina's birth. Trull, as well, had been mere fuel to the machine. But Hutchings — it had needed her to keep the project going, to be a liaison with the people who had built it. It preserved her, imbuing her with the energies of creation, an act she later attributed to its self-preservation programming.

There wasn't that much of Iowa City to search, really. But she absolutely had to be cautious. If she managed to attract Machina's attention, it was all over.

But now, hiding out, biding her time, she pursued a hope that the source of the new tremors in the fabric of reality were a sign for hope: Perhaps there was someone or something that could rival Machina, someone or something that could stop the implosion of the universe as she knew it.

But now, sitting here, she felt another tremor with another flavor; she felt the presence of another's meddlings with the fabric, but it was hiding itself. And it did not leave Machina's metallic aftertaste.

Distractedly, she dropped a couple of dollars onto the tabletop of the booth where she'd been sitting and stood, looking from one side to the other. Which way had the tremor come from? In her mind, she reached out, gently caressing the web, trying to sense the source of the tremors while still touching the web gently enough to avoid attracting the attention of the machine.

She walked out into the street, turned slowly, all the way around, working to locate the source of the tremor; pedestrians stared, but simply stepped around her as she turned once, then again, then stopped, looking toward the west. The manipulation had taken place nearby, to the west.

She began walking, concentrating on sensing the web, looking to passersby, she guessed, like a stoned grad student.

West. She pulled out a map of the campus and examined it hazily. To the West lay the Iowa River, then a dozen campus buildings and dormitories.

Determined not to lose the scent, she concentrated on the tremor. She would not allow herself to lose its trail, even if the one who had caused it was hiding.

As night fell, three hours later, she found herself standing before a campus building whose sign proclaimed it Garraint Walther Hall. Whatever the event was that she had sensed, whoever had caused it, it had taken place somewhere inside.

She let herself through the unlocked front entrance and followed the cold, indistinct trail as well as she could. On the third floor, she found herself standing before a section of brick wall alongside a small room — an office for low-ranking academics. What had happened to the wall to leave such a strong aftertaste from Machina?

She stopped. The trail was strongest here. She shoved the locked door; with little protest, it swung open. The building was old and in need of basic maintenance.

She doubted the schools' sports program facilities would be in such shoddy condition.

The echoes of a presence — an individual presence no longer part of humanity, but neither was it a part of Machina — had made its presence known here, then vanished.

But this new presence was not at all the one she had been tracking. What was going on? Was the machine's thought-dampening field beginning to fail? Was someone other than the naïve one she sought able to manipulate the fabric of reality now?

She groaned, slipped off her shades and massaged her temples. How much more trouble would it mean for a collapsing reality if people all over were suddenly able to alter reality?

But there was something else: She tasted the young naïve presence, as well. She concentrated on that for a moment.

Though long gone, she could feel echoes of that one's presence throughout these halls, taste his casual influence on the building. Perhaps he was even unaware that he had influenced the fabric?

She started; how did she now know with certainty that this was a "he" at all? She was getting information about him — details riding the aftertaste of his own minor effect on the local reality.

This was her quarry. This was Sinclair Stauffer. She knew it now.

It was getting dark outside; from the echoes of his presence, she knew that the young, naïve sculptor of reality was here, in this building, frequently.

But there was a third scent on the fabric of reality here, one she did not recognize. It had an ancient, weathered, tired flavor to it.

She pulled out the chair before the desk of someone named Thaddeus MacKenzie and sat down to wait. He — the young sculptor of reality she sought — would turn up eventually.

Chapter Sixteen

The Kid

Sinclair's head was swimming with new information; he fought down his own doubts and self-doubt, walking toward Garraint Walther Hall, and work. He found himself looking nervously over his shoulder, back the way he came.

He couldn't seem to help himself.

What could he possibly do if Machina — or the Elder — decided to stop him?

He tried to put the fear out of his mind, but it would not go.

He rounded the little concrete circle around which the buildings he and the other night janitors cleaned were arrayed, jogging up to the main custodians' closet in the center building. Elias Ernst was there, predictably, ahead of schedule.

His job was his life.

A lifelong janitor, Ernst had held the occupation since his decision to quit school those long decades back, in the late spring of sixth-grade. Later this year, the bitter old bastard would retire.

"Can't believe they let you keep yer job, boy," Ernst bitched, shaking his head. "I'd-a up an' fired ya. Can't get to the job on time, shouldn't have the damn job."

Sinclair punched down his reaction, doing his best to let the old man coast into retirement without the chance to complain to their supervisor.

"On time? It's still early," he said.

The old man sputtered a wordless exhale of affront.

Sinclair punched in and walked off toward Garraint Walther Hall before Ernst could think up a response.

He had a great deal on his mind, but no idea what to do with the information. He simply had to keep his mind on things, watch for any sign of either the Elder or Machina.

He didn't have to wait long: On his first pass of the night, when he made his way from office to office emptying trash cans, he found the shared office of Deuce MacKenzie open. Under other circumstances, this would not have bothered him; young, overworked, undercompensated scholars sharing an office seemed likely enough to simply forget to lock an office when they were finished there.

But he'd seen a lot lately. The Elder had never — as far as he knew, anyway — made changes in Sinclair's world to get his attention. And the machine? It seemed to be ignoring him.

He cautiously let himself in, gazing around the room in the dark, the faint light from a weak, distant streetlamp the only illumination.

Someone was sitting at MacKenzie's desk?! Had Deuce somehow manifested again to talk with him? He swallowed back his fear and felt along the wall for the light switch.

A voice made him jump.

"A little young to be giving my machine so much trouble, aren't you?" asked a woman's voice from Deuce's desk.

He flipped the switch, the hideous, über-white of the overhead tube lighting buzzing irritatingly to life.

At Deuce's desk sat a very fit, somehow menacing woman in dark glasses. She had dark, shoulder-length hair and one of the light, synthetic-material, military-style jackets that had gotten so popular among area post-punks.

A little young? he thought, bewildered; she looked at most three or four years his senior. But there was something about her that made her age difficult to pinpoint.

"Uh — you're not really supposed to be in here after the building's locked up at night," he said. He was no security officer; he'd never really even been in a fistfight. And he was unaccustomed to having to sound either menacing or authoritative.

The woman just smiled coolly at him.

Then something she said sunk in: "What do you mean, 'Giving your machine so much trouble'?"

The smile broadened a bit.

"Sinclair Stauffer: Caucasian male; a less-than-exemplary record of college performance; two younger siblings; parents divorced; mother remarried, then another divorce; had serious relationships in your time, but nothing permanent. Financially not well off," she said, gesturing blandly toward the janitor's cart. "As we see."

Sinclair's reaction was the equivalent of having a giant "?!?" appear over his head in a cartoon. He had no idea how to respond to this.

"Pretty mediocre performance, Mr. Stauffer. So: How is it that you can give the machine a run for its money?" she asked.

He was exasperated. This was too much; who was this woman? And how did she know so much about his background?

"What machine?" he finally blurted; was she with the Men In Black? An ally of theirs he hadn't learned of yet?

The smile began to dissipate. The woman began to look worried.

"You don't know what I'm talking about?" she asked.

He shook his head slowly.

"Ever notice any weird things that only seem to happen to you, Stauffer?" she asked.

"Uh — such as … ?" he responded guardedly.

"I don't know, really — ever seen anyone walk through something solid? Like they were sleepwalking and didn't notice, only it didn't matter? Ever change the shape of something, but completely by accident?"

"Do you mean, like, breaking something?"

"No — more like inadvertently warping it. You know, you touched something and left a handprint when that didn't seem possible."

Sinclair remembered the waves he thought he saw ripple across the tabletop just before Deuce was taken. And the woman who'd walked through a lamppost without seeming to notice it.

"Who are you?" he asked again, this time less guardedly; he wanted to know what her part in all this was, and whether he should be worried, or trying to defend himself somehow. Or running like hell.

"I don't believe it," she said, lifting the shades away from her face to massage her eyes. "You don't even know, do you? I smell your fingerprint all over whatever's been going on around here, and you don't even know."

Maybe this kid was one of the aberrations she had feared when Machina first started to transmit its thought-dampening signal: Someone who was so disproportionately aware of his surroundings that his daydreams would alter reality around him. A sort of demigod/idiot savant.

"Wait," said Sinclair. "I didn't think anyone else knew anything about all this. Has the Elder been talking to you?"

She gave him a look that was even parts ire and confusion.

"What are you talking about, kid?" she demanded.

"Uh," said Sinclair, knowing that to anyone else what he was about to say would merely sound delusional. "You know. Like, a voice. A sort of tired old man's voice."

"You're hearing voices?" she asked. Was the machine behind this?

"Uh — well," he said, "a voice was speaking to me, into my mind, late at night. And it told me to think of it as my Elder."

When she gave no new sign of recognizing any of what he was taking about, he forged ahead: "It saved me when the Men In Black came after my friend. The Elder did."

Suddenly attentive, the woman said, "Men In Black?"

He nodded.

"Describe them."

Sinclair thought back, trying to visualize them; he'd tried to absorb a lot in the past few days.

"They were white — I mean, their skin was really, really white. And hairless," he said. "They were wearing these black, shiny suits made out of plastic or metal or something. Something black and shiny. And they had cables and mech sticking out of them all over."

"Mech?" she asked.

"You know, mechanical-looking stuff. Wires and cables and stuff. Stuck into their heads and over and in their eyes and stuff, too," he said. "It was weird — like somewhere between a black Secret Service suit and an exoskeleton."

Machina's servos, she thought.

After a moment of introspection, she stood.

"Stauffer," she said, "I think you're the one I've been tracking. I've been sensing these weird vibrations — pardon my metaphor, here; it helps me make sense of it all. I've been picking up these tremblings in the fabric of the web of reality. Vibrations that mean someone or something is changing that fabric. I don't know how else to really explain it. But when Machina disturbs reality, it leaves an aftertaste that's cold and metallic. Distant. But you — your changes to reality left a trail that had a different aftertaste; yours was inexperienced. Naïve. Young."

"I don't really know what Machina is," he said. "I've seen it, but I don't understand it."

He looked her over again. She could feel it when someone manipulated reality?

"Where can we go to talk?" she asked. "I have information to share with you. I can tell you all I know about machina. And I need to know about your information, too — about your 'Elder.'"

"You called Machina your machine," he said cautiously. "Are you another piece of it, like the Men In Black?"

She let loose a massive, guffawing, entirely un-ladylike laugh, surprising Sinclair.

"That's great!" she said, slapping the desktop. "I needed that — I really did. No, I'm not one of those poor bastards."

"Are you working for it?" he asked, confused.

"Not anymore," she said. "Not since I learned about your existence."

"Learned of my … ?" he asked. "How?"

"Where can we talk?" she asked again.

"I can't leave. I'll lose my job."

"I'm sure it's a great career, Stauffer," she nodded with a dismissive smirk, "but this is a little bigger than keeping a shitty-paying night janitor job."

Chapter Seventeen

Gods and Monsters

Hutchings pulled up outside Sinclair's rental, parking at the curb out in front. Sinclair led her up the stairs, through the entryway, and up to his room.

The house was empty — everyone must still be out at Joe's Sports Bar or something. (Every tavern in the city seemed to claim it was a sports bar.)

"Want a beer or something?" he asked.

In a way that made the response a terse, all-inclusive order, she replied: "No."

Somewhat surprised, he said, "OK. Tell me about Machina."

"I'm going to skip a lot of history about the project … "

"Project?"

"Yes. It's enough for you to know that before the project's current incarnation, it was all about Remote Viewing. Ever heard of Remote Viewing?"

He paused, thinking back. "Psychic spying, right?"

"Close enough. It's under that umbrella. Anyway, the project's current incarnation started out as a purely well-intentioned endeavor. The people who assigned me to run the effort dubbed it Project Oversight.

"When Project Oversight was begun, its stated mission, simply, was to somehow create a team that could remotely view the contents of the entire world — the scale of that mission grew very quickly to encompass the entire universe — or, should that be impossible, to remotely view enough of it to keep human civilization from perishing.

"You see," she continued, "they had found evidence that God, whoever and whatever 'God' is, had died. Things were disappearing — immense things — from parts of the universe that weren't being observed on a regular basis by humans."

Simple and incredible, all at once. Sinclair's mind boggled as he tried to keep up, tried not to declare the entire idea absurd.

Her life over the past few decades amazed her, she told him.

She had been there when the project was organized, been there when her group of 200 gifted remote viewers failed miserably at their given task. A visionary man, a Professor MacMillan Trull, was recruited onto Project Oversight.

Trull had come up with a new route for the project to take, a new solution to the problem: The project decided that what the project needed to succeed would be many, many more remote viewers. Exponentially more. They needed brilliant people, men and women whose minds burned with a hard, gemlike fire, to grasp so much information, even for a moment.

"Consciousness," Trull had declared to both her and Wachhund. Professor MacMillan Trull, his kaleidoscopic sweater and pants badly mismatched, his shoes (were his shoes from separate pairs?) flapping as he stomped, icebreaker-like, toward them, cleaving the air in his path. "That's what we're missing."

Trull's wild, gray mane made Albert Einstein's hairdresser seem saintly with devotion to order; uneven waves of gray-to-white hair seemed to have exploded outward from his scalp, and not always straight out — some swooped forward with startling, inappropriate suddenness, while other patches went straight up, or outward from the side with mad certainty. "We have yet to achieve that feat. And it is fast becoming a matter of critical import."

And she was there when Wachhund made the critical recommendation that brought both doom and success to the project: Wachund had authorized the forced conscription of however many such brilliant minds they needed. This was more than an issue of national security; it was a matter of the survival of everyone and everything. Period.

Certain liberties must be suspended in these circumstances, he had argued.

Certain sacrifices must be made.

The *Smart Guy Abductions!*, thought Sinclair, astounded.

"A friend of mine — one of my housemates, a guy named Beckett – was telling me about these disappearances. He's a big fan of things like crop circles, sasquatch, the paranormal. Stuff like that," said Sinclair. "Anyway, there's this branch of supposed abductions that he really follows. Not like most UFO abductions, or whatever; the evidence left behind is different, and the abductees never come back. In the tabloids and paranormal 'zines, they're called Smart Guy Abductions, because in these cases, really brilliant people seem to be targeted."

"Yes," said Hutchings gloomily. "Machina's servos."

"Its 'servos'? What do you mean?"

"The brainpower that drives Machina isn't mechanical – it's the combined brainpower of hundreds upon hundreds of the best minds the world has to offer."

Sinclair paused, soaking this in. "Its servos. You're talking about the Men In Black."

Her eyes cast down shamefully, she nodded.

"But if it's running on their brainpower, how can it continue to function when they're separated from it? I've seen them plugged in. Does it get weaker when they separate?"

"No," she said. "It doesn't work like that. Once they're plugged in, their consciousness is transferred into Machina somehow; what's left behind is no longer an independent organism at all. Machina controls them like toys — like remote-control toy cars or airplanes."

Deuce, Sinclair thought painfully; his eyes were welling with tears. "Are they dead?" he asked.

Major Delphina Hutchings had watched, filled with hope for the success of their mission as Wacchund double-checked the specially designed interface helmets, making certain each had the superconductive gel applied at the points where the helmets' dozens of tiny nodes made contact with the scalp. They were kidnappers-to-be, she knew, and exactly the sort of untouchable black op she had always feared the most.

She watched, praying as Wachhund gave a final nod and then, standing near the first row of her carefully chosen, carefully tested Remote Viewers — each of them decked out in the uniform black business suits issued by those running the intelligence community to those working in the intelligence community — signaled for the switch to be thrown to bring the machine online.

Hutchings watched, aghast and powerless, as the room erupted in a deep bass thrumm! and blinding, somehow translucent light, tentacles of the most material beams of light she had ever seen lashed out from the massive construct, seizing the Remote Viewers by their helmets.

A moment later, more of the beams lashed out, whiplike, grappling Remote Viewers throughout the project facility and towing them, helpless, to its side. They did not seem to be able to struggle. The whips of light lashed onto the man she knew only as Wachhund, dragging him in, as well. Then one reached out, stabbing into her own brain.

But it had processed Wacchund, ripping his mind, his consciousness, from him, first; by the time Machina lashed outward for her, it knew on some level that it needed her, that she was the project's leader. The bodies of Wacchund and the hundreds of Remote Viewers arrayed throughout the huge room had sagged momentarily, no mental presence remaining behind in their bodies. Then, erratically, the bodies began to spasm, their feet gradually, mechanically finding the ground beneath them. The ones Machina had held suspended in the air were lowered to the floor, the light-whips now leading to spheres of light which completely enveloped their heads.

My God! Hutchings thought. My God, what have we created?!

But there was no answer from any god of any sort. There was only the all-consuming *thrumm!* of the machine. She could not get a phrase out of her head: "Deus ex Machina," a Latin quote from Menander meaning "god from a machine." It was a way of describing a universe into which a god is introduced to solve a problem. As we have done, she thought: Knowing nothing of the god they presumed dead, they had unwittingly spawned a monstrous, parasitic machine to replace it.

The significance was not lost on her: She decided to code-name the monstrous device "Machina" (which, since her Latin was rusty, she pronounced as though tacking an "uh" to the end of the word "machine.")

On the front and side of the machine, a facelift was taking place: a reconstruction of the machine, by the machine. Ports of some sort were forming, and row after row of Spartan, efficient catwalks, each with row upon row of the ports, all at the same level. And a sloping, angled construction was appearing directly before the ports.

Machina was moving the bodies of the Remote Viewers about the room, some of them picking up tools, others walking stiffly to the machine's side, or up ladders to other levels, toward the ports. When the first of the biomechanically pithed bodies halted before a newly formed port, turned toward it, and kneeled, she realized with revulsion what was about to happen; when the body plunged its head into the port and went motionless, she screamed.

She still shuddered at the memory.

"Effectively, yes, Stauffer," she replied sadly. "Their bodies remain alive, fueled by Machina as it sees fit; their consciousness — all their mental capacity — Machina collects that into a sort of pool of mental energy. It is slowly eroded away to nothing. The individual donors erode away with them."

"So Machina uses them up?" he said sadly. "I'd hoped that wasn't the way it worked. Deuce told me, but … "

"Yes," she said, trying to keep her voice even. "That's not what we intended."

"You tried to build a god and created a monster instead?!" he said. "You created a parasitic monster that feeds on the people you were supposed to save?"

"Not intentionally, Stauffer," she said defensively. "And for whatever reason, Machina has performed its function — as far as it understands that function, anyway: That was in 1991. The Earth is still here; the Solar System, as far as I can tell, is too; but we lost a piece of the Andromeda galaxy early on. And who knows how much else? Without Machina, it would all have collapsed by now."

Sinclair paused for a stunned moment. So that's what happened — that's why the cycle of the Awareness couldn't continue naturally, he thought.

"No," he said with a quiet resolve. "No, it would not have."

"What?!" she demanded. "Did it occur to you that I might know what I'm talking about here, kid? This has been my life's sole mission for the past 33 years, Stauffer. Monstrous as the means may be, the universe has been holding together as a direct result of Project Oversight."

He shook his head slowly, firmly.

"No," he said. "You interfered. You interrupted the natural order of things, disrupted the natural rhythm and flow of the universe. You halted a delicate cycle that has kept all of it in existence for uncounted millennia."

Her face flushed an angry red now.

"What the hell do you think you're talking about? Huh? What's a college dropout night janitor know about 'the natural rhythm and flow of the universe'?" she demanded.

The words stung Sinclair. He knew he was a failure. He didn't need anyone to remind him.

"I know," he said with resolve, biting down his indignance, "about the Elder. And I think that's the missing piece of your Project Oversight. You've made a terrible, terrible mistake."

Chapter Eighteen

Binary

Delphina Hutchings did not, for the life of her, know what the hell Sinclair Stauffer was talking about.

"What do you mean, 'I know about the Elder'?" she demanded. "What's that even supposed to mean?"

"An oversight," Sinclair said, smiling without mirth, "on the part of your project. Your goals were the right ones, as far as your information could inform you. You know? You set out to do the right thing, but you didn't know enough to do it right. Neither did I, for that matter — I had no idea that simply observing as much of the universe as possible could fend off at least part of the collapse that would happen without an Awareness."

"'Awareness'?!"

"Yes. You were right about observation being tied into existence. I can see that now. Your project's partial success shows that much. But that's only a piece of the puzzle — only part of the solution."

"Stauffer ... " she started testily; she did not appreciate being talked down to by this kid, this janitor and dropout. Opting to hear him out, she waved her hand furiously for him to get on with it.

"Information. Knowledge. Those are pieces missing from your solution. I feel dumb as a post right now compared to when the Elder thrust me before Machina and started pouring information into me. When it was happening, each new realization, every revelation about the nature of the universe filled me with more energy, more influence over the fabric of reality."

"Dumb as a post — that might be Machina's thought-dampening transmissions," she offered.

"No, it isn't the same thing," he said. "It's about something the Elder said when he was trying to explain the nature things to me: He told me he had a hard time recalling what it had been like to be one with the Awareness. I never even got close to touching that level of understanding, but I know what he meant now: When someone begins to change, begins to evolve into the Awareness itself, they begin to become capable of knowing everything."

"Omniscience?" she asked.

"Omniscience," he replied. "But I think that the one who becomes the Awareness is the only consciousness in the universe that can truly grasp all of the information and knowledge that that word implies; I started toward the goal and began to be able to hold and grasp the nature of the universe. But when I failed, when Machina beat me back, I lost that understanding. I can't remember it clearly at all. Neither can the Elder."

"Slow down, Stauffer," she demanded, her authoritarian military training snapping to attention. "I didn't understand half of what you just said. Tell me about the Elder. Who or what are you talking about when you say 'the Elder'?"

Sinclair looked down, reaching a hand up to try to massage the tension from the back of his neck.

"OK. The Elder is the consciousness that used to be in control of the Awareness — he literally was the Awareness," Sinclair said. He explained his understanding of the true nature of the universe, as the Elder had explained it to him.

"The Awareness exists somehow in a binary relationship with the stuff of the universe, as I understand it. Somehow, the Awareness is the ephemeral, consciousness-based side of the universe," he said uncertainly. "It's all pretty new to me."

"So the Elder used to be the Awareness?" she asked.

"Yeah," he said. "Kind of. He uses the term interchangeably for the Awareness itself and the consciousness that guides the Awareness."

"Who's the Awareness right now?"

"That's the problem, Hutchings. There's no one in the driver's seat right now," he said. "Machina's sudden appearance on the scene wrested part of the role of being Aware of the universe itself, and everything in it, from the Awareness. I think that that interrupted the cycle of death of one consciousness stewarding the Awareness and the evolution and ascension of the next. From what the Elder told me, these things happen in a sort of cycle. The consciousness that becomes the Awareness itself cycles out and the universe itself cycles a new consciousness into the role."

"The universe just creates one?" she asked skeptically.

"Not exactly," he said. "It's all part of an endless cycle. The universe chooses a successor."

"How?"

"No idea," he shrugged. "But with Machina's interference, the cycle's been interrupted, and it was interrupted before a successor to the Elder could assume the role. I think the function of the Great Ocean of Thought is breaking down."

Hutchings groaned in disbelief.

"'Great Ocean of Thought,' huh?" she chided.

"Yes. That's what the Elder told me."

"The Elder? The voice you've been hearing in your head? Got any more New Age wisdom for me, kid?" she sneered.

"Look, I didn't ask to be involved," he snapped. "The Elder came to me because he was convinced I was awake enough to influence the fabric of reality — a reality that's pretty pliable right now, by the way, thanks to you."

"Stauffer, the only reason you and I are standing here at all, even standing on anything at all, is because of Machina!"

"I don't believe that," he said dismissively.

"No? Tell it to anything that used to be alive on planets orbiting Andromeda RA 2h12m OS D47°10'," she said. "We acted because the star — a whole damned star — just disappeared, Stauffer. And from what we can tell, Project Oversight has managed to keep nearly all of the universe that we're aware of intact."

"No," he said. "The Elder told me. Machina interfered with the natural cycle. If it hadn't, the cycle would have continued, and the Elder's successor would have ascended, and any weaknesses in the fabric of reality would have been restored."

That gave her pause.

Hutchings worked to digest the janitor's words; she had gone AWOL from Project Oversight on a wing and prayer that there might be some other way, any other way to defend reality against collapse — any alternative to the despotic, parasitic rule of Machina, a grotesque shadow of the beautiful, balanced nature Stauffer had described to her. Machina was a self-serving demigod, she knew: It sent out its mindless, modified victims to kidnap an endless stream of brilliant minds to feed its insatiable appetite.

She had left, she knew, for a reason: She had left, she knew, to seek an alternative. And now that alternative — or a chance at realizing that alternative, at least — stood before her.

"We'll need to share our knowledge to make this work," she said, the military edge gone from her voice. "I know I have part of the solution. But you — even if you don't believe you can sculpt the fabric of reality, it's exactly the fact that you've done that that brought me to you. And brought Machina's servos to you, as well."

"The Men In Black?" Sinclair asked.

"The Men In Black," she affirmed. "I think we both have pieces of the puzzle — pieces of the solution. I've been part of Machina, but in a different way than the Men In Black; I've been allowed to bask in the energy of its pool of consciousness …"

Something clicked for Sinclair.

"A pool of consciousness — that's how Machina can do it! It's hoarding consciousness that's supposed to cycle back to the Great Ocean of Thought eventually, not just wind up in a separate reservoir, away from the rest of the Awareness!"

She continued: "Allowing me to soak in its energy was meant mainly to sustain me – to keep me from the damage most people have to face with disease and advancing age — and to allow me to do my job."

"Why didn't it consume you?" Sinclair asked.

"It got Wacchund first, and he very firmly believed in the project's mission. Nothing in the world was more important to him. And he also firmly believed in my position at the head of the project. I think when Machina pulled him in, when it stole his consciousness to add to its pool of mental energy, it inadvertently absorbed those two strongly held ideas."

"This reminds me of a passage I read once in Revelations — something about a 'river of life' flowing from the Lamb's throne, clear as crystal."

"The metaphor sounds similar — did it ever refer to that river of life as an ocean? In earlier translations, or the original, maybe?"

"I have no idea," he said. "I just remembered the similarity to the idea of the Great Ocean. Does Machina only use up the energy of the consciousness from its victims? I'm not sure I'm asking this very clearly — does it keep those consciousnesses intact?" he asked, hopefully. *Could Deuce be freed, somehow?*

She shook her head sadly.

"It doesn't work like that," she said. "Machina retaining anything at all from Wacchund was a fluke; it was young, and hadn't absorbed very many people yet. Relatively speaking."

Sinclair found himself gazing at her, thinking about the rest of her statement.

"Hutchings," he asked the attractive, fit young woman before him; in his grief over the kidnapped Deuce, he hadn't actually noticed her beauty before. *What perfect breasts!*

" ... how old are you, really?"

She smiled. "Nearly old enough to retire," she said.

His mouth fell open.

"When did you say Project Oversight got started?"

"1990. I was 31."

He reeled; he'd just oggled the firm breasts of a 64-year-old.

He shook his head, trying to refocus his attention.

"So," he said peevishly, hoping she hadn't noticed his glance at her chest. "So, uh, where do we start? I think that between my talks with Deuce and with the Elder, I've gotten a lot of it worked out. I remember understanding a lot more, but not what that 'more' consisted of. And you've clearly picked up some insight over the years with Machina. We should find a place where we can sit undisturbed and talk about all of this, try to puzzle out what we can."

She shook her head.

"Let's find the quiet place," she said. "But I've learned a few tricks in four decades in the psychic spying business."

"Oh?" he asked.

She nodded.

"I think I can build a psionic rapport between us," she said.

"What does that mean?"

Her tone was uncomfortable.

"It's sort of like always-on file sharing between two computers, over a network. A piece of my consciousness goes with you, a piece of yours goes to me," she said.

He eyed her suspiciously.

"At what cost?" he asked.

She sighed solemnly, steeling herself.

"We'll never have a private moment. Never keep any secrets. But it's the only way I know of for us to share all of what we know, and perhaps both benefit from our actual experience and training," she said gently. "Think of the consequences if we don't."

He looked away.

"Stauffer?" she said, but he would not look at her.

"Sinclair," she said again, gently. "It's the only way. If we're not strong enough to face extraordinary measures, to take extraordinary steps, we'll never wrest control from Machina. This natural cycle, this nature of the universe you mentioned — it will never return. The universe will never return to its natural balance again."

He still looked down, thinking of the consequences for himself; he didn't know a thing about this woman. But he knew the situation might be worse than she was aware; if Machina kept chipping away at the Awareness, if the Great Ocean of Thought didn't gain a successor to the Elder, the Great Ocean itself would eventually falter and fail. When that happened, there would be no more universe — not even the fading, flawed version they now occupied — left.

The Deity is a madman, he remembered again. Was the Elder a madman? Was that what his dream had tried to warn him of? Or was it the Elder's predecessor?

"I know, Hutchings," he said. "I know we have to."

Sinclair's mind was filled with conflict and doubt; this was a high price to pay, his loss of his privacy, of some portion, even, of himself across a mental gateway of some sort did not sit well. But without it, the price — he could not bear to even think about the price.

The two of them moved uneasily, seating themselves across from one another. Sinclair couldn't help but notice a troubled, distant look in Hutchings' eyes.

"What's the matter?" he asked her gently.

The rapport she had set up with the help of her RV partner, Jordan — the sender in her sender-receiver pair — had long since fallen silent. She hadn't heard a peep across their psionic rapport since a few weeks into her assignment on Project Oversight. What had become of him?

His queries for her across their mental channel had turned to pleas, then to panic, then silence. Had he simply stopped trying to reach across? Was he even alive anymore? It had been decades!

"Nothing," she said, the troubled look remaining.

"Nothing?" he asked doubtfully.

Her eyes snapped up to meet his.

"You'll know soon enough," she said, her tone icy.

"Now relax," she ordered. "Look into my eyes. We need to be gazing into one another's eyes and concentrating very, very lucidly on the same things to accomplish this. It has to do with a sort of synchronization of thoughts that in turn lets us split off and swap a piece of our consciousness. That synchronized bit will never, ever leave us. It will always be a gateway through which we may contact one another and share information much more quickly and efficiently than by any conventional means. It involves a bit of hypnosis to help get us both into the proper frame of mind, let our defenses down enough to make this possible. Are you with me so far?"

Sinclair nodded, trying to steel his courage and beat back his doubts and discomforts.

"OK," she said, her voice taking on a smooth, soothing tone. "Listen to the sound of my voice. Take a very deep breath and quiet your mind. Breathe in through you nose and out through your mouth."

Like meditation, he thought.

She paused for a moment as they both became accustomed to breathing this way, letting it slowly register as the natural thing for them to do.

"Now," she said, her voice soothing, but firm, "I want you to imagine sitting on the white, pure sands of a beach on a peaceful, beautiful tropical island. Visualize the scenes I am describing to the best of your ability, painting in every detail of these pictures in your mind's eye. Make them real, and they will be real to you; perceive the sounds and smells and sensations that accompany your impressions."

She placed her little BopBoxä audio player between them and keyed in a combination. The rising and falling white-noise sounds of waves crashing onto the shore, of gulls and sea breezes, filled the air between them.

"Sense the feeling that this peaceful place creates within you," she said. Firm. Soothing.

Sinclair had never been able to afford a vacation on any of the coasts, but he believed that it would be a relaxing experience. In his beach vision, the sands were white, like on post cards he'd seen from vacation spots in the Caribbean.

"Now," she continued, "it's almost sunrise. It is still dark out, but nearly dawn, now. The sky is just dark enough for you to see the last few stars. The palm trees that line our tropical beach are silhouetted against the sky and the stars. Smell the fresh, salt-tinged sea air, feel it coolly caressing your skin. We are at peace here. Completely at peace. All of our mental and physical needs and desires are sated. We experience immersion in this environment in total peace. We relax, and watch the stars beginning to fade."

In his mind's eye, Sinclair could envision the scene, and the two of them sitting, faced toward one another, their knees touching, on the white-sand beach he envisioned.

"Watch the palm trees. Totally experience this peaceful place and the peaceful sensations it brings us. And as you do, feel your physical body relaxing, your muscles beginning to lose their unnecessary tension. Beginning with both feet at the same time, we feel our feet relaxing. And a wave of relaxation moves slowly now up into our ankles and lower legs, relaxing every muscle, every tendon, as it goes." She paused again, to allow a moment for this to sink in, and for the relaxation to take place.

"And now the wave of relaxation moves slowly up through your knees, permeating every cell and every atom; now into your upper legs, permeating every cell and every atom."

The waves from Hutchings' BopBoxä seemed to have synchronized into a slow, steady, relaxed rhythm, the gulls far off in the distance.

"Our breath will synchronize more now, as we relax. As we relax we become more and more in tune with one another — more and more synchronized. And now the sky is becoming lighter and lighter. All is silent but the gulls in the distance and the lapping of the waves and the wind and our synchronized breathing.

"And as we experience this beautiful, peaceful environment, we feel the relaxing power begin in our fingers. Now the wave of relaxation moves up through our hands. We feel our hands relaxing as we feel the wave of relaxation move up through our wrists, slowly up into our forearms. The wave of relaxing power continues to climb now, relaxing us up through our elbows and our upper arms, and now into our shoulders. Completely relaxing our fingers and hands, our wrists, our forearms, elbows, upper arms, and now the shoulders. And we now become more aware of the gulls announcing the new day, as the sky becomes brighter — bluer."

She was speaking in a low sort of chant now, in rhythm to the sound of the waves crashing on the beach. On cue, the sounds of the gulls rose a bit.

"And the horizon now begins to glow a dull red," she said, then paused for a moment, their universe filled with the sensations of the beach and the sounds of their breathing.

"Now the sun grows redder … now becoming brighter, more orange … its glow now growing to a beautiful, vibrant yellow-gold, as the first rays of the sun touch the top leaves of the palm trees. And now, as the sun rises, we watch its light and warmth and energy slowly move down through the massive leaves of the palm trees, now slowly down the massive trunks of the trees. And within us, we feel relaxation within and along our spines, as we feel the wave of relaxation flow into our spines simultaneously, relaxing our back muscles."

Sinclair, still looking into Hutchings' eyes, now saw the two of them together on the white-sandy beach, and felt the relaxation moving through him, felt their deep breathing and rhythms in perfect synchronization.

"The relaxing power now moves up into your neck and shoulder muscles, which now become loose, limp, completely relaxed. Loose and limp; loose and limp; loose and limp. Completely relaxed. Completely relaxed. Completely relaxed. And now the sun falls across our bodies, suffusing us with golden light and energy. We shiver in response … "

Simultaneously, goosebumps arose on their skins.

" … as we absorb the essence and energy of the sun. Feel the sun on our skins, and perceive it filling our bodies and souls to overflowing with energy, sating our needs and rejuvenating our spirits. The wave of relaxation now moves up into our heads and scalps, relaxing our heads and scalps. And it flows down into our faces, relaxing our facial muscles, our jaws, our throats. Both of our entire bodies are now completely relaxed. We notice the sun reflecting on the surface of the ocean, shimmering with brilliant yellow-gold reflections of the sun's energy and warmth as it rises into a brightening sky. We are absolutely at peace. We enjoy our environment," she said, breathing deeply as she spoke; she breathed in "breathing slowly," exhale, "deeply," inhale, "evenly," exhale.

"And now a new sound enters our environment and begins to relax us even more … even more … even more … "

From the BopBoxä, a steady, faint, low-pitched rhythm began droning in from the distance. It built and built, the two of them experiencing its arrival in their mentally-painted environment over the course of — how long? Five minutes? Ten? Half an hour?

"Our hearts," she said distantly. "Our circulatory systems, our thoughts, move as one now, at precisely the same rhythm."

Then the droning sound faded, and faint, warm, ethereal music arose between them, the sounds of the beach and the far-off gulls still with them.

He could see them in the distance in his mind's eye, shimmering, radiant as the sun, as though they were composed of its energy. Had she slipped that detail in? He could not remember.

"And we are now," she whispered, "relaxed and at ease, our bodies and minds completely synchronized."

She had been speaking, he realized, during the approach of the peaceful droning sound, but he could not recall what she had said. In his mind's eye he saw himself sitting on the beach, gazing into her eyes, down a long, dark tunnel. He realized that he was looking out at her from within a brilliantly luminous place; that the tunnelway ran from his luminous mental space, out through his eyes, and into hers. He gasped when he saw the light at her end of the tunnel open suddenly, the tunnelway suddenly a brilliant arc of shifting light, a sculpture in the air between them.

Suddenly the sounds of the gulls grew closer. He felt momentarily disoriented as the great, glowing flock of luminous creatures suddenly alit through their newly formed tunnelway from both his and her ends, pouring through in both directions.

He marveled at their fantastic, angelic beauty.

Their light was intermingling; the light of her being was traveling across the tunnelway to him, and his across to her.

Sinclair sat, truly happy and at peace for the first time in many, many months, as the angelic flock became a crescendo of light and energy and warmth in the aural sculpture of their mental bridge.

Days later, it seemed, her voice came across between them from the little BopBoxä.

"Wide awake now," it said. "Wide awake now."

Sinclair blinked, suddenly aware that he was in the room, rather than on an idyllic beach of his own creation. But where had the beach gone?

It's the place we'll be able to go to share our thoughts, said Hutchings' voice in his head.

He gasped deeply, startled by the clarity of her thoughts, trickling across like a small, babbling brook.

Suddenly, the tunnelway was like a torrent; like a massive break in a water main was sending a sudden flood of information under unimaginable pressure across their tunnelway. Sinclair reeled, an overpowering sense of vertigo filling him. Suddenly, both were filled with a primitive understanding: Neither had had any form of sexual contact in a while — days, for Sinclair, but years and years for Hutchings.

The least inklings of sexual desire became a raging torrent across their psionic link, a massive eddy of primal urgence threatening to pull them in.

They stared with raw sexual hunger at one another; Sinclair no longer restrained himself from thoroughly oggling her breasts. She, in turn, felt an evaluating once over of Sinclair quickly swell into a thorough, exhaustive, purely physical inquiry.

Sinclair felt himself stiffen so suddenly that it hurt; he pulled at the fabric of his pants, trying to free up room for the sudden erection.

He paused, looking confusedly at the offending organ; under his breath, he bitterly barked, "Oh, for god's sake, make up your mind — is it guys or girls?"

Hutchings sprang on him immediately, forcing him to the ground. Across their psionic link, the already irresistible desire grew exponentially.

Jesus, aural angel-bird-things turned him on!

In a savage, almost panicked blur, they tore the clothes from one another's bodies, and from their own, kissing, biting, clutching, touching, and, with single-minded certainty, fucking each other. He nibbled hungrily at an exposed nipple, at her neck, at anything he could reach. She tore his cock free of its clothing and forcefully mounted him, sending a shiver through both of them, a shiver that crashed across their psionic bridge like a primal, sensual, sexual tidal wave. He rolled to the top for a precarious moment, but she was not to be denied; savagely, she bit into his shoulder, hurling him onto his back and reasserting her dominance.

They were experiencing their instinctive drive and their frighteningly ferocious sex from both perspectives — from Sinclair's and from Hutchings' separate points of view, feeling each sensation from both bodies and minds as one, feeling each thrust as both him pushing in from outside and her drawing him into her body.

Biology, instincts neglected by circumstances and sense of duty in both cases, were no longer the least bit resistible.

When she awoke, so did Sinclair, the sudden brightness and warmth of her consciousness awakening shining like a beacon across their mental bridge. Suddenly, both began to feel wave after wave of self-revulsion, guilt, anger over their lack of self-control. They didn't even like each other that much!

The realizations — the thoughts — were happening simultaneously for both of them. The experience was wrenching for Sinclair, who suddenly felt another wave of vertigo and a sickened pitch to his stomach.

Hutchings, who had not seemed sick to her stomach at all, leaned forward, propping herself up on her arms — her exposed breasts just large and rounded enough to seem somehow deliciously pendulous to him   - and slapped him suddenly, and hard.

"You OK, kid?" she asked him.

He gave no response, merely rubbing his eyes.

"Hey, kid!" she yelled. Then, across their link, she shouted, *Get ahold of yourself! I should have guessed something like that might happen. We couldn't stop it, but we can now. It's all about will power. We're adults, here. We can resist our instincts enough to stop ourselves from masturbating in public, we can sure as hell keep off each other.*

Suddenly, the light spilling in from her side of their link didn't seem quite so warm and inviting.

Damn it, he thought, angry with himself. He felt like a kid in toilet training.

He concentrated, fighting to calm his stomach.

That's better, she said soothingly across their link. It's OK, kid. I couldn't resist it either. The urge was so strong — so primitive!

She smiled. She almost seemed amused. "Are you OK?"

A sheepish grin crossed his face.

"My fucking shoulder hurts," he said.

He picked through their torn and shredded clothing, saw no hope in the remnants, and turned to his closet, pulling out a flannel and military-surplus pants for her, jeans and a pull-over for himself.

It's not much, he said, smiling, but it'll keep you from getting arrested in public.

A sense of balance and truce filled the room, and relief spilled across their psionic bridge in both directions.

Bathroom's across the hall, he said with a chuckle.

Then, sound came thundering across their mental bridge.

Sinclair, said a voice in his head, a voice that was distinctly not Hutchings'. It had the wasted-away, papery quality of dry leaves being crushed underfoot. She turned, alarm spreading across her face as the realization dawned on them both: The Elder had returned.

Chapter Nineteen

Trinary?

Hutchings spun to face Sinclair, hoping to gage his mental state. She wondered: Was Sinclair ready to confront this being again?

She honestly didn't know; but thanks to their rapport, she would know soon enough.

The room was suddenly filled to the brimming point with an ancient, invisible presence, permeating everything.

"What the hell happened to you?!" Sinclair demanded, his fury pouring across the psionic rapport to Hutchings. "Trying to convince me you're a dying god, that you need help, and drag me into a fight with something I didn't even comprehend?"

Sinclair … the Elder began.

Hutchings looked around, examining the room, but could find no source for the ancient voice.

Sinclair interrupted: " … then you ditch me? Great plan, Elder!"

Sinclair, forgive me. You must calm yourself.

"Can you hear him?" he asked Hutchings. "It drove me crazy that no one else could hear him."

Hutchings nodded; perhaps because of their link, perhaps because the Elder was ready for her to hear him, she could indeed hear the eerie, disembodied voice. It seemed to flow with an internal inconsistency, communicating a sense of both ancient frailty and breathtaking power.

Sinclair reined in his anger.

"OK, Elder. How did you fail?" he asked. "That's what you need to ask yourself. And I have an answer for you: You were unprepared, and because of that, you left me completely unprepared. And in doing do, you gave us both away; I doubt Machina even knew you existed before. It probably still doesn't understand what you are. If we're lucky, that is."

He was done venting his frustration with the old specter now.

Sinclair, came Hutchings' voice across their link, be careful. *Think of who he is.*

Was, he fired back angrily. *Who he was.*

She paused, trying to define the Elder in her own terms. *God — even a dying, screwing-up God — deserves respect.*

It's not like that, he fired back, deciding reluctantly to drop the subject. Besides, with their psionic rapport, he figured she'd know his position on the matter already.

Sinclair, I am no longer what I was, said the Elder. In my passion to save the fabric and balance of the universe, I see now that I forced you into a confrontation for which you were unprepared.

"That's putting it lightly," he said. "What did you think I could do, anyway?"

You had demonstrated that you could alter the fabric of reality. This is an evolutionary step for which I had been waiting. With this ability, however small, you were the one who could help me wrest power from Machina and restore reality.

"Wait a minute," said Sinclair warily. "You hadn't even convinced me I'd done anything to the fabric of reality."

"No," said Hutchings. "I felt the changes you made as tremblings in the fabric of reality, Sinclair; like a spider feels tremblings in its web when a fly gets caught in it."

Sinclair turned to her.

"How did you know it was me?" he asked. "Couldn't it have been anyone?"

She shook her head gently.

"No — it had your flavor about it. I sensed your changes in the fabric of reality a few weeks ago, but at first I didn't dare let myself believe it. Then I began to get glimpses of you — fragments of information traveling with the tremblings. I began to understand who you were. And with my position in the intelligence community, finding information on you wasn't difficult. But I didn't know for certain that it was you until the moment you entered that office at the university. Your flavor Sinclair — the kind of trail you leave in your wake — it's all over the fabric of reality here. It's how I was able to track you."

Ahhhh ... you were part of Machina. I can taste the machine's presence all over you. This is most fortunate, said the Elder.

"You both came to me because you could sense the changes I was making?" said Sinclair. "You both knew even before I did?"

The true power flows from the knowledge, Sinclair, said the Elder. The more you understand of how the universe functions — the more you grasp its nature — the more at one with the Awareness you become. It is part of the process of ascension to the Awareness; as the old tender of the Awareness fades and dies, another consciousness grows and evolves to take his place. And he gains that growth by gaining intimate knowledge of the nature of the universe.

"I remembered it happening that way when you took me before Machina the first time," said Sinclair. "It's why Hutchings and I created a mental link with one another: So we can work together to cobble together at least part of that intimate knowledge of reality. Elder, can you just share that information? Just – I don't know

– tell somebody and turn them into God?"

No, Sinclair – I no longer possess the needed knowledge. It passes from the consciousness guiding the Awareness when that consciousness begins to fade. The knowledge then flows into the new Awareness. But Sinclair – I still retain some small portion of the information, fragments of that intimate knowledge you seek. Perhaps between the three of us, we may be able to pool enough of it to wrest control from Machina and restore the natural way of things.

The thought terrified him for a moment; would they somehow need to establish a psionic rapport with the Elder, as well? Was that even possible?

Hutchings could hear his thoughts across their mental bridge.

I have no idea how we could do it, she said via their rapport. The only way I know of is via the combination of hypnosis and synchronization.

The Elder's voice came to them again: The three of us are extraordinary, Sinclair. We each possess some portion of the power of the Awareness – slivers, so to speak, of godhood. With our three wills working together, wielding our portions of godhood, I believe that we could establish this psionic link. I think now that it may give us a better chance against Machina; that mental link may allow one of us to wield the three portions of godhood as one.

"Which one of us?" Sinclair asked.

As I knew when I came to you the first time, Sinclair, it must be you.

Sinclair was speechless with fear. What could he do?

"Why does it have to be me, Elder? Why not you? You wielded the full power of the Awareness' godhood before. Or Hutchings – she was a part of Machina for years. She even managed to seize some of Machina's power and sneak off with it undetected."

"I'm not the right one, Sinclair," she said. "I don't understand how to do much of anything with Machina's power. I – "

None of this matters, the Elder interrupted. The cycle of the Awareness chose you, Sinclair. That is why you can alter the fabric of reality, whether or not you understand how you do it. My role as the Awareness is done. My time is passed. I have searched for you, reaching out with all my ability, straining to sense the arrival of one who could manipulate the fabric of reality. That one would be my successor, the cycle's evolution and ascension of him or her halted. I had sincerely hoped that that your ascension would be further along when I sensed your manipulations, Sinclair. In my haste, I did not realize that you had so little inkling of what you could do.

Sinclair was again speechless, struck dumb by the Elder's announcement. He thought of himself as a failure at nearly everything he did; how could the universe — the Awareness — have selected him?

He could sense a glow of warmth and support flooding across the mental bridge he shared with Hutchings.

Slowly, using her strength and friendship, Sinclair steeled himself. The stakes were much, much too high for him to allow himself not to try. He had come this far, hadn't he?

Let us concentrate together, said the Elder. Let us build a bridge into one anothers' minds.

Sinclair and Hutchings reached out, mentally searching for the Elder's consciousness.

Then the Elder opened his mind to them. In the vast, brilliant ocean of the Elder's mind, Sinclair and Hutchings, with a simultaneous gasp, were plunged into the consciousness of a dying god.

There's just so much of him! Sinclair yelled across their bridge. He fought to center himself, regain control of his senses.

Hutchings' thoughts were chaotic, a scrambled mess of confusion and awe. *The light!* she said. *There's so much light!*

Sinclair thought about the Heaven described by people who have near-death experiences: There was a startling consistency in their descriptions of a vast ocean of warmth and light.

If this was the greatly weakened Elder, what had his consciousness been like as the Awareness itself?

Slowly, the Elder righted them. There is so much I've forgotten, he said. So much I have lost. Let us share our knowledge with one another.

Hours later, sitting in half-lotus position, trying and failing miserably at calming himself, Sinclair shouted angrily across link he now shared with Hutchings and the Elder: *But I don't know how to do anything yet!*

Hutchings and Sinclair heard a pained gasp from the Elder. There was a pincushion effect in the vast, brilliant ocean of the Elder's mind for a moment, like the great presence was doubling over.

What's wrong, Elder? Hutchings asked voicelessly. What's happened?

A star. Its planets. All of the lives under its sway, said the Elder. The star you would call hd209458 and all of its planets have disappeared, simply gone now from existence. Machina has failed to preserve them. They were a mere 150 light years from Earth, in the constellation Pegasus.

Hutchings shook her head sorrowfully.

Sinclair, you must face Machina, said the Elder, weakly. Reality is collapsing in on itself. We must act to preserve it. we will go with you; Delphina will be with us via our psionic rapports; we will both help you to understand and wield the power.

Sinclair fought down a surge of fear. He felt like he was going to vomit. Across their bridge, he could feel the expansive consciousness of the Elder fading.

What do you mean by "We will go with you?" Can't we just travel there the way you took me before? asked Sinclair.

No, Sinclair, came the Elder's suddenly much weaker voice. I am fading. As the universe goes, I also go. I no longer have the ability to transport us.

And I don't know how, yet, or even if I can do it, said Sinclair. How can we even get to Machina?

By airplane, if we have to, Sinclair, said Hutchings. I know Machina's location, so you do as well.

How do I get through security?

We'll cross that bridge when we come to it, she replied.

Hutchings and Sinclair made their way out to her car, the eerie presence of the Elder remaining with them as they drove. For a moment, Sinclair thought that he also detected another presence, but it quickly dissipated.

They had a plane to catch – the first flight they could find to D.C. Then he had the fight of his life to consider, using weapons and power he simply did not understand.

At the airport, Hutchings gave Sinclair a reassuring kiss, hugging him tightly. *We can do this*, she said, trying at the same time to convince herself of that.

Sinclair and Hutchings managed to get seats together, despite needing to purchase their tickets at the last minute.

"That will be," said the airline ticket-counter attendant, pausing to frown at the sky-high last-minute fare. Her voice took on an apologetic tone. "$2,545 each."

Hutchings slowly waved her hand before the attendant's face; not understanding what she was doing, Sinclair directed his attention to their mental bridge, but before he could gain any insight, the attendant said, simply, "Thank-you," tore the newly printed tickets from their printer, slipped them into an envelope with their itinerary, and handed them over.

Sinclair was awed.

How'd you do that? he asked across their mental bridge.

How do you think I managed to leave the project unnoticed? she answered back.

Can you teach me how? he asked, a small grin crossing his face.

After the security check-in, she led him to a seat at their gate. *Look across the psionic rapport, Sinclair. I'll show you.*

In his mind's eye, peering into hers, he began to grasp what she had done. I concentrate, seize everything I can in my mind, and then will things to be different. I can't do very much, but I can convince people they've seen or heard or done something they really haven't. In this case, I convinced our attendant that the transaction was completed. She didn't want to charge us twenty-five hundred bucks each anyway, she said with a mischievous grin.

When an attendant read off their seating assignments over the P.A. system, Hutchings and Sinclair boarded their D.C.-bound 737. He clutched her hand as the plane rumbled down the tarmac and onto a runway.

The plane's rumbling smoothed out as it lifted off, and Sinclair felt the force of the plane's engines pushing him back into his seat.

As the plane climbed, he relaxed a bit, loosening his grip on Hutchings' hand. Below, cars became first moving dots, then motionless specs.

Sinclair smelled something odd as the plane climbed laboriously toward its cruising altitude: No, he realized, it wasn't a smell, exactly.

With a bone-jarring explosion, the fuel-filled wings of their 737 exploded.

Later, he would realize that he had had a sensory experience akin to when the Elder arrived — that the cabin had filled with the invisible, metallic, inhuman presence of Machina.

How many times has your airplane been destroyed? asked the Elder. I can no longer tell.

Sinclair, itchy sweat prickling at his pores, clenched his eyelids tightly closed, fistlike, trying to muster his concentration.

"Seven," he said finally, quietly, his voice awash on the whooshing sea of airplane noise. "None ... now."

There was a long, uncomfortable pause.

I can no longer tell when things have changed. You have fended it off every time, said the Elder. You are learning.

Sinclair swallowed against a sandpapery catch in his throat, fighting the fear and fatigue. "So far, yeah. It goes 'kaboom,' then I concentrate, seize everything I can in my mind, and we rewind to just before the explosion. Then we move forward again. The next time through, I don't let the plane explode."

Silence, save for the blare of background noise.

And ... the Elder began, pausing distantly. Your friend Thaddeus is part of it now.

"Friend," thought Sinclair bitterly.

"Part of Machina," said Sinclair, his voice a dry, papery, autumn leaves sound. "Yes."

Silence again, as the Voice faded into the white noise of the airplane.

"Elder?"

I am here, Sinclair. As I told you I would be.

That's reassuring, Sinclair thought. The voice in my head is there for me.

He was having difficulty keeping his sense of reality together — after all, everything he'd ever thought about good, solid reality had been thrown on its ear. Terra Firma was a concept he'd lost long ago.

"I don't know how to stop it, Elder. I can barely keep it from blowing us all out of the air," Sinclair said wearily. "I mean, what kind of god would do that to everyone on a 737?"

After another long, expansive silence, Elder's voice quietly replied:

The kind that hears your footsteps, Sinclair. The kind that knows you're coming for it. And is worried.

As he glanced to his side to check on Hutchings, he felt the color draining out of the world. Like it had when the Elder had spirited him away from the Men In Black.

Alarmed, he tried to clutch Hutchings' hand, but his was suddenly ephemeral.

He shouted a warning across their psionic link to her and to the Elder: Machina had engaged them.

The shock caused a surge of knowledge and information and ideas to crash through their mental link to the three of them. But only Sinclair seemed to be retaining it all.

As the cabin of the 737 faded from his vision, details of a new place began to form before his eyes. An enormous hall, one darkened, save an occasional pale, overhead light and a pulsing, pervasive red glow illuminating a monstrous snarl of mechanical, electronic, and biological materials, a low, rumbling thumm emanating from the structure in rhythm with the light.

Row upon row of dull, grey-metallic figures seemed to be kneeling, sort of, almost as if in prayer, on black, metal-mesh resting structures.

He knew this place. He had been here before, with the Elder; he was standing alone in the presence of Machina.

Chapter Twenty

To Tame the Great Ocean

A note from the author: Artists and authors such as Beat-Generation authors William S. Burroughs and Brion Gysin applied various techniques collectively referred to as "cut-up" to literature, sound, film and painting. While there are various techniques and approaches to actually creating a cut-up piece, cut-up generally involves the cutting up the medium or media — text, film, audiotape, etc. — in which the artist is working, and randomly reassembling the separated elements.

In a lecture on cut-up, Burroughs once claimed that cut-up broke down certain barriers imposed by structure, allowing a new, more organic perception of the information that is being exchanged. He even ascribed metaphysical qualities to the results. As such, it seemed appropriate in a novel dealing with perceptions of reality on the most fundamental level, that cut-up might come into play to some extent, particularly in the sense of adding a sense of chaos to some passages. Portions of this chapter have been re-composed using a variety of cut-up techniques and tools; the non-cut-up version of this chapter is included as an appendix to the story.

Sinclair's mind had become a maddening cascade of new ideas and newly learned knowledge.

The Elder's ancient presence suddenly surrounded Sinclair.

Without a word, and with an inhuman burst of will, the Elder propelled Sinclair through new levels of realization: He found himself flowing with knowledge of the Great Ocean of Thought.

And Sinclair's world wrenched itself inside-out.

Been Across Time, Realized By Individuals Over Him. Of Subatomic Particles.

Which make up reincarnation. The energy of it! The pieces; the guiding hand of reality.

Sinclair slammed both hands into the sides of his head, battling desperately to contain it all.

The nature of the Great Ocean, its relationship with – no, its oneness with the fabric of the universe was suddenly laid bare before him. Words from the pages of The Dancing Wu-Li Masters, the Fritjof Capra effort to unify the quantum world with Eastern philosophy, washed over him. Capra had compared the eternal dance of creation, the dance of the Hindu deity Shiva, with the dance of subatomic particles which make up the matter and energy of the universe: He felt Capra's revelation about the energy and the matter that make up the universe, felt Capra's rush of excitement in a moment of visionary insight, down to their most minute parts, sharing a sort of rhythm of creation – the rhythm of the dance of Shiva.

The Great Ocean are the universe learning to envision its relationship with the clutter of other, inaccurate speculation into Machina s essence of the consciousness.

Again, Sinclair battled to keep control as a breathtaking chaos of knowledge flooded his consciousness.

"It's all the same thing!" Sinclair shouted. "All of it! The waves of the Great Ocean are the waves that make up the stuff of reality! The particles, the energy – it is all Awareness!"

Oh my god! he thought. Matter, energy, thought, the Great Ocean — if it's all made up of the same thing in different forms, then the Awareness — all awareness — is the universe learning to know itself!

Of rhythm of rhythm of reality. It! Sinclair shouted (he thought). All awareness - matter, energy, thought, the same thing in sentient beings scattered across time, realized by its relationship with the Great Ocean decanted whole into a new person!

Sinclair worked to make sense of the chaotic burst of information: Pieces of the overall truth had been scattered across time, realized by individuals over the millennia, but never all at once, outside of the Awareness, and never without the clutter of other, inaccurate speculation into the nature of reality.

It must be the universe's backup plan, he thought. Separate pieces of the knowledge necessary to ascend, split up and housed in sentient beings scattered throughout space and time.

Then he knew: Hutchings had had some of the pieces; that was why she could control some small amount of the essence of godhood that Machina had welled up.

So he had at least some of the pieces; the Elder remembered some of it.

It all made sense to him: Why he had been able to alter solid things; why someone or something needed to perceive the universe to keep it stable; why Dr. Errol Mannheim, Ph.D. in parapsychology, assistant director of the Geller Metaphysics Institute, was getting so many reports of hauntings and reincarnation. The universe – the Great Ocean – was a riot of possibility, the stuff of which everything — matter, energy, you name it – was made up. But without the guiding hand of the Awareness, some of the measures of the Great Ocean decanted into those of strong enough will simply held together, their measure either refusing to leave Earth or becoming decanted whole into a new person!

But who had the knowledge he still needed?

`Lack A Single Unified Contiuum.`
Information surged through him.
`Trull. Trull! understood it was why he still needed?`
Of course, he thought. *Trull. Trull understood it all well enough to envision the core machine that evolved itself into Machina, but he didn't have enough pieces of the puzzle to know what would happen when they activated the Project Oversight machine.*

And now Trull was gone — dragged into Machina's essence when it was activated, used up by its voracious appetite for the energy of consciousness.

So Trull's pieces of the knowledge were gone forever; how could he put it all together without Trull's pieces of the puzzle?

There was more to it — Sinclair could sense it. Pieces of the puzzle were missing, but they might still exist out there, somewhere in the universe. He began casting about, mentally searching through the streams of information washing over him:

Pieces began to appear in his mind. He saw:

In the Chicago suburb or Northland, Choi Kwang, a 38-year-old practitioner of T'ai Chi, focused his chi, the spiritual energy he firmly believed flowed through along channels throughout the body, into a small pile of paper scraps setting them, with fierce concentration, ablaze, holding only his open palm above the paper.

He saw:

An ironic political statement in cartoon form: A Caucasian Christ, spikes driven through the palms of his hands, happily munches a handful of toasted mustard seeds. Mustard seeds: A Judeo-Christian symbol of faith, paralleled by the traditional portrayal of a nail through the palm of his hand. Forensic testing had demonstrated that a nail through each hand this way could not possibly support an adult's bodyweight.

And, he now somehow knew, the word cross — the entire tradition of Christians wearing and displaying and kissing and worshipping before crosses hinged on a mistranslation: The Greek word *stauros*, or *stavros*, was more accurately translated as "persecution spike." There was no crossbar in use for several hundred years after his crucifixion. Nonetheless, once the crossbar became a part of the practice of crucifixion, a pole with a crossbar had become the symbol for one of the world's most widespread and successful religions.

It reminded Sinclair, now, of an old joke: If Jesus had arrived in the mid-20th century, would his followers have worn little electric chair pendants around their necks?

But if forensic testing had demonstrated that a spike through each hand this way could not possibly support an adult's bodyweight, how could one explain stigmata?

In rare cases, a few Christians had become afflicted with stigmata — wounds in the palms and feet resembling what most of the faithful believed to be Christ's crucifixion wounds; and pin-prick wounds on the head resembling his "crown" of thorns; even a wound on the chest resembling the wound traditionally believed to have been left by a Roman centurian. How? Faith! It was the power of will, focused via faith in something greater — even something that may not be entirely accurate — that could bring about a mind over body event such as stigmata. And, he realized, mind over matter. Psychokinesis, or telekinesis: The ability to move or bend solid objects with the power of one's mind. The ability to forge an alteration of the very fabric of reality. Pyrokinesis: The ability to set things ablaze with the power of one's mind alone, as Choi Kwang had done.

He saw:

In Madison, Wisconsin, reading herself to sleep in her bed, 53-year-old office manager Laura Crenshaw encountered an interesting, if whimsical idea in "Breakfast of Champions," penned by author Kurt Vonnegut, involving E=MC2, Einstein's formula describing the relationship between matter and energy. Energy (E) is equal to matter (M) multiplied by the speed of light (C) squared.

Speed matter up enough and it becomes energy.

But the novel idea was this: The formula neglected to include an important ingredient — Awareness.

Yes! thought Sinclair. Awareness is missing from the equation — but that's not all!

Another element was missing: Faith. Not Christian faith, particularly, but a faith based upon an omniscient understanding of the nature of reality, of the universe-Awareness binary pair, of all of it.

Sinclair directed his attention toward embracing this truth, and toward intertwining all of the information and knowledge and understanding he had into a single unified contiuum: He envisioned The Truth, the universe as it was intended to be, the Great Ocean of Thought — the Awareness! — all returning to their normal, essential, natures. This, he knew, would unify all of it, and would repair the mess that had been made when Machina interrupted the natural cycle of the Awareness as the Elder began to die.

`Binary Trees / Forest Binary Not`

And suddenly he understood the truth that had eluded him when the Elder had forced his first confrontation with Machina: The universe was not as the Elder had told him!

Elder! Sinclair thought: The universe is not binary at all — the truth of it is far, far more complicated! You think of the universe as black and white — you see only the Great Ocean coexisting in tandem with the matter and energy of the universe; but the binary way of things was only the very, very beginning — only existence and nonexistence!

What? demanded the Elder. What nonsense is this?

Look: You see only black and white, existence and the lack thereof, a continual stream of absolutes — binaries — like this:

```
100111111101011110100111001111010011100100110010011000
001111010010000011100101100001110100111011101100101100100l
000001100001100000110001011011001100001110001111010111000000
1110010110000111010011011101000001100001110011110000111001
0011011101011101000000100111111101011110100111001111010011l
00100110010110000011010011101001000001110111100001111001l
10000011100111101001101001101100110110010000011001001l000
0111001011010101101100100000111001111010011010011011100110
11001000001110100110100011001011000001100100110100111l00101
11010011100110000011001111100101100001111100110000011011l
0110010110000111001010000011011101101001100111110100011l
0100100000110111110011010000011010011011000110010110000011
0001011001011100111110100100000011011001101001111010010000l
11001001100001111001111001110000011011111001101000001001l
11110110011001001000000100111011001011101110000001011001110
11111100101010111011101001111110101111010011100111101001
1100100110010110000011010011110100100000111001011000011010
0110110110010111001001000001110000110000011000101101100110
00011100011110101110000011100101100001110100111011101000001
10000111001111000011101001110111010111010000010011111l010
11101001110011110100111001001100101100000110100111010010ol
00011011111000011110011100000111001111010011010011011l001
10110010000011001001100001110010110101110110010000011100ll
```

But you're missing the forest for the trees, Elder — look again, from a distance, and you begin to see not just the black and white of a binary system, but the beginnings of a universe of every conceivable shade in between:

```
Group Humankind: In.
```

Enlightenment! he thought to himself, startled. Again, he clutched his head with both hands, battling to hold himself together.

Sinclair's expanding consciousness had encountered the Buddhist understanding of the term "enlightenment": Being at one with everything, losing even one's sense of Self to the nature of the universe. Was this also Moksha, the concept of enlightenment familiar to the Hindus? (He did not know, but soon enough he would.) He was unifying it all, repairing what had gone awry when the cycle of the Awareness had been torn asunder.

Machina, he now understood, could never have taken the place of the Awareness in the cycle of the universe, because Machina, being mechanical, did not understand what it meant to be non-binary; no matter what language a computer program is written in, when it is compiled and fed into a machine, the data is ultimately sent through its processor as binary data. Like all machines that receive and process information, Machina, in the end, received only binary communications into itself, and thus had no hope of truly grasping the non-binary nature of the universe.

```
New cases of nearby Adapa. He thought were
infected with all machines that this to teach
black men a newborn named Jesu, and secretly
scribbled down notes about themselves and for-
ested areas in July 1997.
```

His understanding, his consciousness, his Awareness, was expanding, but he waged a desperate internal war to make sense of the information surging through him.

He saw:

Contractors working on the restoration of the Iowa State Capitol in autumn of 2000 opened a panel in the stair casing on the lantern of the capitol to find a .38 caliber shell casing and two letters dated 1897. The letters were signed by two men: One named Jed, and another named Burke. The letters, describing the men's wives, families, and lives, had been hidden within the woodwork by Jed and Burke, laborers who first worked on this part of the capitol, messages to future builders and restorers who might retrace their steps.

The small group of contractors quickly and secretly scribbled down notes about themselves and their families and sealed them away, communications to the next set of builders who would one day re-open the panel in some future restoration project, a secret communication between a unique set of workers.

No one but them would ever know.

But Sinclair knew.

He saw:

2,100 years ago, near ancient Bethlehem, as the cycle of the Awareness began to refresh itself anew, an uneducated shepherd named Mahalalel was suddenly caught up in the process; he was a gentle man who was very, very afraid of what the vengeful God of Scripture might have in store for him, and in his confusion, as the elder Awareness waned and Mahalalel quickly expanded to assume the role, Mahalalel panicked, wishing with all his heart that he might be allowed to live a full life.

But the mantle of power was in the midst of being passed from the old overseer of the Awareness to the new one; Mahalalel's wish had an unpredictable result.

Miles and miles from where Mahalalel had been drawn away from his flock and into the cycle of the Awareness, a young woman who had not yet engaged in sex of any sort, and who was promised to Josef, a young member of her traveling people, suddenly carried a child, a life form in every way identical to Mahalalel, save that Mahalalel was now the overseer of the Awareness and the Great Ocean of Thought.

After birth, the child would be named Jesu, and would grow up to be a rabbi of unusual inspiration to his followers. His 12 closest devotees would come to be known as disciples.

Those chronicling Rabbi Jesu Josef's life would find his proclamations of the word and will of God becoming more gentle, less vengeful than they had previously been.

Sinclair knew that this was because the being thought of by these people as God was not actually the same being any longer. The time of a vengeful "God" had passed.

He saw:

In Austin, Texas, in July 1997, Shamal Cornelius Johnson, a 36-year-old African-American man, was strapped into elaborate stereotaxic restraints, awaiting a lethal injection for the brutal rape and murder of Cordelia Meribeth Kuykendall, a 19-year-old white woman whose family was well-connected. Kuykedall's blood-caked hair had been found plastered to the walls and floor of her apartment near the University of Texas in 1988. Shamal knew that an all-white jury had set out to teach black men a lesson about what happens when black men do this to white women. He did not know who had committed the crime for which he was being executed.

But Sinclair knew.

Billy-Ray Wayne Biggs, a white lawn-care worker on the payroll of Kuykendall's father, had committed the assault and murder. He had died in an SUV rollover accident on Interstate 35 outside Buda, Texas, three years before Shamal Cornelius Johnson's execution. His measure of the Awareness had since been reintegrated into the Great Ocean of Thought.

He saw:

In Little Rock, Arkansas, Bobby Joe Hansen, now five and a half years old, still wets the bed. His parents told no one.

But Sinclair knew.

In September 2023, Dr. Errol Mannheim, Ph.D. in parapsychology, assistant director of the Geller Metaphysics Institute, wondered why he was seeing so many new cases of supposed reincarnation in the institute's files. He had no idea why such a spike would occur.

But Sinclair knew:

Pradeep Mishra had died of small pox in Niphad, in the District of Mathura, at his family's home. But because of the destabilization Machina and its creators had wrought in the Great Ocean of Thought, Pradeep's portion of the Awareness was never reintegrated into the Great Ocean. It was, instead, decanted whole into the body of a newborn named Ravindra, to parents Sri Krishnachand Nagar and his wife, Saraswati, residents of nearby Chandvad.

Ravindra simply was Pradeep.

The same thing had happened to Dona Henrique, nicknamed Catarina, the daughter of a farmer in the Brazilian state of Paraná, who was reborn when her close friend Ida Dos Santos gave birth to a daughter, who she named Helena, in nearby Adapa.

He saw:

At 6:21 a.m. September 2001, Muhamed Atta said his dawn prayers. He and 18 other terrorists, living in the United States under deep cover, posing variously as university students and pilots in training, planned the worst terrorist attack in the history of humankind: In less than three hours, he and four of his associates would hijack a commercial jetliner, take control of it, and intentionally crash it into one of the two towers of the World Trade Centers; minutes later, others in his group on other jets would use the same method of attack on the second tower; the Pentagon in Washington, D.C.; and a fourth Washington, D.C. target. Thousands people would lose their lives in the attacks.

The last group would fail when passengers on board rebelled against the hi-jackers. In the ensuing battle for control of the airliner, the plane would crash into the Pennsylvania countryside.

Their plans were a closely guarded secret.

But Sinclair knew.

In 1981, Department 13, an ultra-black ops agency investigating the develop-ment of biological weapons, began what they thought of as the successor to the Tuskegee syphilis study. Through carefully planned infiltration of what patients thought were routine doctors' examinations, dozens of women and, principally, homosexual men in New York City, San Francisco, and Los Angeles were infected with Biological Agent Attila. The virus was unwittingly spread via contaminated syringes used in health surveys in rural desert and forested areas in Africa. Once the Centers for Disease Controls and the medical community at large realized that some deadly new phenomenon was attacking these communities, the cycle of symp-toms leading, ultimately, to death was dubbed GRID, or Gay-Related Immune De-ficiency.

The lab-created virus was genetically modified from another virus known to be fatal in other primates: Simian Immunodeficiency Virus.

The disease turned out to be slow-moving and difficult to spread, and in October 1994, Department 13 declared Biological Agent Attila a failure as an effective combat agent. In April 1995, Biological Agent Khan, a microbe specifically genetically engineered to combat Attila, was released into the public in cities known to be affected.

In August of 2001, researchers isolated what appeared to be a naturally occurring microbe that fights HIV to a standstill, explaining how increasing numbers of people are now "living with HIV," rather than dying from it.

All records from Department 13's Attila and Khan projects were then destroyed. Department 13 consisted of fewer than 15 individuals, the only people alive who knew about Attila and Khan.

But Sinclair knows.

In November 1990, an operative with the codename Agent Dalia compares a superior's comment that God may be dead to Nietsche's famous declaration that "God is dead."

She doesn't know what they're talking about.

But Sinclair knows: He knows that when Friedrich Wilhelm Nietzsche died on August 25, 1900, his individual distillate of Awareness from the Great Ocean of Thought was remingled into the Great Ocean once again. A tiny portion of that Awareness that made up Friedrich Wilhelm Nietzsche is distilled decades later into a young boy from Niphad, in India, named Pradeep Bannerjee, and again, later into Ravindra Nadar in nearby Chandvad.

At the time, anyway, Nietsche's proclamation was wrong; but then, in Pradeep's and Prakesh's era, he was essentially right: "God," in a sense, was dying. And what a ride that portion of Nietsche's Awareness had been on in the meantime!

He saw:

Many more dimensions than he had realized were there; his understanding had only been of a four dimensional world – three dimensions moving through time. Now he grappled with a fifth; now a sixth; suddenly, fully eleven separate dimensions stood in his gaze. He reeled, desperately trying to understand it all.

He saw:

In July 2018, up late again in pursuit of his dream of having a short story published so that he might legitimately call himself an author, a young man labored at a desk in his room in an Iowa City, scribbling away at a writing pad, constantly striking, correcting, and adjusting a small piece of speculative fiction he hoped to polish to a gleaming perfection. He had titled the piece "Sum"; the piece began with the words, "For a period immeasurable, all that was was unaware," and ended with the words, "The Deity is a madman."

Sinclair could see that a piece of the knowledge he sought was within the struggling writer, but that he was interpreting it through a Judeo-Christian filter. He had written the piece that had haunted Sinclair; had seemed to try to warn him of some sort of madness — but was it madness in the Elder, or the mad rule perpetrated by Machina?

And where was the Elder?

It had all washed over him in an instant, but the torrent of information continued.

In a burst on profound insight, Sinclair turned his attention again to Machina, solidifying its post-human henchman again in its tacks, this time for good. He fought the flood of Awareness – omniscience? – washing over him. His very essence was expanding by leaps he hadn't previously even been capable of imagining.

Machina's lights we blowing out, showers of sparks erupting as it resisted Sinclair's efforts to change it. But it was lost; it did not begin to grasp even what the Awareness was, let alone the depths of its Ocean, or the nature of what it — Machina — had done.

The Unity of the universe suddenly vibrated with the familiar flavor of one who had known it all before: The Elder was here, now, with him, as Sinclair understood more and more, and that understanding expanded his essence, molding him to fit into his new role.

The Elder! I'm not alone!, he thought, trembling as he fought to contain the growing dimensions of his understanding.

Sinclair? I'm trying to stay with you too, Kid, said Hutchings' voice inside his mind. He could feel her reaching out, reaching into herself, trying to hide that hint of desperation in her tone, doing her best to be a comforting presence, restraining her tough-as-nails military discipline. But she could not hide her terror. *I can't get to Machina, but I can still reach you through our bridge.*

`Hoisting Torrent Of Reality. Grinning Mania-`
`cally.`

Thunderous pounding surrounded Sinclair. He was buffeted, knocked distances he could only just fathom. Fathoming them was distracting him from the task of grasping and bringing Unity to the mind-numbing crash of newfound knowledge and Awareness.

The Elder's greed shone through. The Elder could not let go; he could not resist the lure of ultimate power — of omnipotence — even if he no longer understood it.

With a thought, Sinclair dismissed Machina.

In the distance, what remained of the machine went a leaden, unlit gray as its power drained away and Sinclair reduced it to rock.

The Men In Black that were plugged into the interfaces went suddenly limp, finally dead so long after their minds had died. Those not plugged into the interfaces simply dropped, lifeless, to the ground, their bodies littering the ultra-secret subterranean headquarters of Project Oversight.

`Dead Machina broken.`

Machina was finished, a fossil marking an artificial regime.

The Elder's mental voice howled a deafening protest.

The deity is a madman.

Sinclair heard the words echo hauntingly through his thoughts. "Madman," Sinclair whispered. Suddenly alarmed, he turned his attention from the unfinished Unity to the Elder. The power-mad Elder was forcing his hand, making him abandon his effort to heal the failing universe to fend off the old god.

But the Elder remembered more now than he had let on when he had coached Sinclair. Howling maniacally, the Elder clutched at the new, unfinished Unity with his mind, forging an incredible wedge of willpower, working to pry free Sinclair's grip.

Sinclair felt fear to the point of panic; if he could not stop the Elder who knew what would happen to the universe and the new, incomplete Unity? It was all still collapsing.

Struggling with the wash of information, with lies and dreams and ancient ideals of a flat Earth and a Sun and moon and planets and stars that orbited a human-centered universe, Sinclair fought with his self-doubt and disappointment. He was a newly bisexual/night janitor/college dropout/hallucinogen-tripping failure! How could he ever assume the role of the Awareness?

He resisted; the doubt and shame and disappointment, he now saw, were the Elder's attack on him. The Elder was causing it!

Fight it! he thought. Fight him! Place your Faith in the new Unity!

The Elder howled again, lashing mental energy at Sinclair, searing his physical body, as well. Sinclair was weakening; he could feel his body, its skin searing, its bones breaking under the stress; how long could he keep up the battle?

His vision, all of his senses blurred, Sinclair stared in disbelief as a figure emerged from the chaos of creation before him, taking shape from the mists and blur.

His mother.

His dead, horrifyingly alone, suicidal mother, tears streaming down her face.

"Why, Sinclair?" she pleaded, wailing. "Why didn't you come home and help me? Why didn't you stop me? What kind of son lets his own mother do that to herself?!"

Stop! he demanded, the command permeating the new Unity with a thought. *Stop it, Elder!* And then, his mental state weakening, his demand became a desperate plea: *Please!*

"Never should've even had you, you sonovabitch!" the apparition of his mother screamed. "All you had to do was come home! But you had to live in a college town, away from us! Better than us! Away from me!" She pounded her chest. "God, how does anyone survive when their whole family just leaves them behind?"

Please! he pleaded. He could feel his grip on reality slipping under the pressure and guilt. *Take her away!*

Shit! Hutchings pleaded, her mental voice filled with alarm. *Resist him, Sinclair!*

Suddenly, Hutchings' universe was filled with her mental image of Jordan, her fellow operative and the man she'd fallen in love with, only to turn her back on him, never speaking with him or contacting him in any way, ever again, because her superiors had ordered her not to do so.

Oh God, Jordan, I'm sorry! she said. She had abandoned him without a word on orders from a man she knew only as Sapphire.

She was filled with dread, a sense of futility and guilt suffusing her whole being, until Sinclair's mental universe was teeming with her guilt, as well as his own.

She faced her failure with Machina, as well, her arrogant, ridiculous, impossible gamble with the fate of everything she ever knew in the balance and its resulting consequences of a universe slowly eroding away, its natural rhythms and cycles and laws disrupted.

Behind Sinclair's mother, suddenly, he could see his father smoking synth from a crack pipe in a run-down apartment, surrounded by the old man's friends — people he had known when he was growing up from their visits to the house.

Every one of them was wizened, wrinkled, and glassy-eyed, tapping his feet or washing his hands nervously in the air as he waited for the pipe. They passed around a bottle of Thunderbird, cheap, alcohol-boosted wine for alcoholics, to take the edge off the effects of the synthetic speed.

His father! There was no escape for him, either. He wouldn't survive another six months like this.

And Sinclair could do nothing, nothing at all, to change things.

Anger and unreason began to swell throughout the Awareness as it swelled within Sinclair; suddenly, the unfinished Unity rippled, puckering wildly with new, volatile weak spots, and began to change dramatically.

Bastard! he thought at the Elder. But a desperate realization dawned on him. *I can change it! I can change everything! I absolutely have to change it!*

Fighting through the pain, he made a desperate decision: He would oppose the Elder on his — the Elder's — own turf. The Elder wanted the power, the omnipotence, of the Awareness. Through the searing pain and thought-clouding weariness, Sinclair clutched fast to that omnipotence, trying to clear his head, leaving behind his project of Unity to focus on the Elder.

Hutchings' constant drenching of his psyche in guilt and failure and pain had to be purged. She was dead weight to him now — worse than dead weight. With a violent mental slash, he severed their psionic rapport, cleaving her off from the battle and clearing her from his mind.

He lost all track of the orderliness and truth of the new Unity; his rage, a monstrous, unreasoning anger, would no longer allow him to hold it all together.

With the faith and will and strength of mania, Sinclair formed a vision of his own two hands closing, constricting around the neck of the Elder.

What did the Elder look like?

Like God. No — no, he looked like a man who grew into the role.

Some shepherd guy, right? he recalled vaguely, bitterly. Guy with a beard …

Mahalalel.

There's. The. Weakness! he thought haltingly, as a struggling body appeared in his tightly locked, trembling hands.

Driving forward with murderous will, Sinclair had forced the Elder to become corporeal for the first time in millennia. And now, filled with murderous anger, with a seemingly random wash of information from the Awareness and the damaged, incomplete Unity, maddened by the pain in his crumpled, broken, burned physical form, Sinclair became the steward of the Awareness with an initial act of murder.

He destroyed the Elder, choked the life out of him with his bare hands, and stood, hoisting the carcass over his head. He planted his feet on the fabric of reality, grinning maniacally.

Sinclair's feet met the Earth's flat, solid surface.

With a murderous, triumphant sneer, he hurled the broken, dead body of a 2000+-year-old shepherd named Mahalalel down upon the Earth. The dried, ruined body exploded in a cloud of dust and bone on an uninhabited plateau south of Jerusalem.

The mists of creation/destruction, in a torrent until now, began to clear, and a new God, drunk with power and anger and madness, reinforced the fabric of reality as the torrent of information had told him it should be, bending it to his will.

```
Sun blaze, a massive waterfall that rose again
though the centers of the carcass over the edges
of dust and hurled the centers of dust and anger
and madness, reinforced the oceans, and destroyed
the centers of dust and he planted his bare hands,
and through rains rising over his will.
```

The world, caught in its almost-hemisphere base, other flat-surfaced planets orbiting not far away, all was right in its almost-hemisphere.

Reality was crashing down around him, dimensions collapsing in upon themselves. The rules were coming apart, rending cause from effect. He could see effect beginning to occur as a function of its potentiality, its chances to happen, before cause could occur.

The sun blazed overhead, a cauldron of fire contained by gravity in its almost-hemisphere base, other flat-surfaced planets orbiting not far *away*, all circling the Earth. The oceans poured over the edges of the world, to be caught in a massive waterfall that rose again through the centers of the oceans, and back up over its edges as rains rising over the seas.

He understood how it all worked together; all was right in the new world.

And he had forgotten all about a lonely, missing star that had once been designated Andromeda RA 2h12m OS D47°10'.

```
Dead Mahalalel broken. Flat-surfaced planets.
```

It didn't matter; this was his universe now.

Chapter Twenty-One

New Dawn

Delphina Hutchings, ex-D.I.Ops agent, ex-director of an ultra-secret government project, calved off from Sinclair, no longer part of the sundered trinity, fell back to Earth, an afterthought of God. She awoke, gasping, in a cold December morning on a hillside filled with bare, leafless trees; a fine coat of snow dusted the hill where she found herself. She slowly gathered that she was somehow in a corner of the woods behind Black's Gaslight Village, a sprawling near-slum of Iowa City apartments built one after another by owners over the decades who didn't appear to have had a great deal of building or planning skills.

As she shook her head, trying to rub away the blurred vision, she noticed the ground nearby shifting, slowly raising into an oblong mound from the surrounding earth.

As her vision cleared, she saw the earthen sculpture take on an ever-more-defined human shape; within a few moments she could see Asian facial features forming on the face of a nude male body — facial features and a male body she recognized from Sinclair's memories: It looked like Deuce MacKenzie.

Then, abruptly, the sculpture flashed from miraculous soil sculpture to living flesh, drew a sharp breath, and coughed horribly in the frosty cold of a December morning in Iowa.

Is this some kind of weird after effect of the battle? she wondered. Is reality still coming unglued?

Deuce MacKenzie sat up, examining his newborn-tender skin with a puzzled look. After a moment, he looked up, seeming for the first time to see Delphina Hutchings.

He looked confused; he was moving very, very slowly, and beginning to shiver in the cold, damp morning air.

"Hhhhchhh," he said, trying out his untrained musculature. He tried again: "Hhuuh — huh — Hutchings? Ruh … right?"

She wasn't sure how he might know her, but she remembered him vividly, thanks to the psychic rapport she shared with Sinclair.

Had shared, she thought. Past tense.

Where was Sinclair now?

"That's right. You're Deuce, right?"

He trembled in the cold. "Yes. Yes, thuh-that's right. Di — did Sinclair tell you about me?"

"Yeah, kid, he did," she assured him. "He sure did. We thought the machine consumed you."

"Maybe it did — I can't really remember much after the Men In Black," he said.

She helped him to his feet, tugging off her coat and slipping it over his shoulders. With effort, the two — one battered and bruised, the other with a new, pristine musculature unused to even the most basic day-to-day efforts — let themselves into one of the buildings that made up Black's Gaslight Village.

But everything seemed different; the sun shone overhead, blazing through the morning mists, but it seemed uneven, ovular, rather than circular, somehow.

Inside an abandoned apartment the owner of the Gaslight Village seemed to be using for storage, she was able to find MacKenzie an old flannel shirt and paint-spattered blue jeans.

In the filthy shared kitchen of the building, Deuce sat wearily as she borrowed ground coffee from a jar and brewed a pot for them. She flipped the power switch on an old radio, its surface caked with a buildup of congealed cooking grease and cat hair, dust and kitchen debris. Someone had apparently abandoned it on the top shelf, over the sink, years and years ago.

"Expect a clear, 40-degree-angle view of the surface of Mars tonight as it passes overhead, once the sun goes under," the newsreader said cheerfully.

"'... once the sun goes under?'" she asked, her face pinched. "What the hell's that supposed to mean?"

Deuce MacKenzie looked over to her.

"Uh-huh. And I've never heard of 'a 40-degree-angle view of the surface of' any planet before," he said, worry in his weary voice. He stood unevenly and laboriously made his way over to a model of the Solar System a tenant had left in the kitchen, pointing it out to Hutchings: At its center was a flat, blue planet with a vast expanse of ocean and plenty of land, an odd concavity too shallow to be a hemisphere forming the rocky bottom. Around the odd, planetoid-like body, their perfectly circular orbits suspended on metal rings, were eight other planetoid-like bodies of varying size, color, and topography, along with a broad, flat (like the planets), and entirely too small sun.

The Earth, if that's what it was, rested at the center. The planetoid-like bodies seemed entirely too close to it.

"What's going on, Hutchings?" he asked.

She had no idea what to say. She wandered to a cinderblock and plywood bookcase in the hallway, tugging an outdated encyclopedia from its shelf. She flipped to the entry on light, but could find nothing about the particle-wave duality; light was an energy wave, as far as the encyclopedia was concerned.

The Solar System consisted of nearby planets with the gravity anchoring everything to the flat top surfaces of the planets, all orbiting around the earth. The celestial bodies each had a consistent up direction and a consistent down direction, rather than the relative concepts of up and down relating to the center of a celestial body and gravity generated by that celestial body, as she had known it.

The sun, too, was now shaped like the planets in the planetary model they were examining; it was a fiery celestial cauldron whose gravity was pointed in the opposite direction of Earth's, so its fiery contents did not spill down from the heavens to decimate the planet. But it burned so brightly that astronomers had only viewed its rocky, Earth-facing base beginning a few decades ago.

She flipped the pages of the encyclopedia, looking up weather systems; scientists had determined that the oceans' water spilled over the edges of the Earth, then fell into a rotational cycle that brought it back around, then into the sky as water vapor, creating clouds that passed over the Earth and generating the winds that drove them. It was incredible! It was as though every rule she'd ever understood had simply been rewritten according to someone else's wishes.

Then the memory — some of the last things she felt across their psionic rapport before Sinclair had split her off: Sinclair had set out to fix everything in accordance with what he knew — he'd been attempting to repair the entire universe via his newfound understanding of how it all worked together. But he had thought of the wave-particle duality of light, for example, as a riddle — a problem.

He was badly rattled, angry and pained to the point of madness when he decided to destroy the Elder and Machina; who knows what he thought the rules that hold the universe together might be, or whether they mattered, when he was in that state of mind?

The other problems she could immediately see he'd solved: The death of Deuce MacKenzie, and her mental bond to Sinclair. Both were resolved now — she couldn't sense anything over their psychic rapport. It was gone.

A young twentysomething man entered the kitchen, breezing past them and pulling a box of corn flakes down from another shelf.

"I've got to get one of those for my nephew," he said, pointing to the model. "Teach him how the planets work, y'know?"

Their presence there didn't seem to alarm him; in a sprawling complex of this size, Hutchings doubted the neighbors knew one another.

"Hutchings … " Deuce began.

"I'm not sure, kid," she said in reply. She turned to the new arrival. "Does that model seem unusual to you?"

He gave her a puzzled expression, looking it over more closely.

"Oh! Dude!" he said reassuringly. "I'd get my kid nephew a new one! Paint's all chipped on that old thing."

Deuce MacKenzie turned toward Hutchings, willing his new tongue and mouth, lips and vocal cords to heed his commands.

"Think we're the only ones who know?" he asked.

Slowly, with a slight shrug and wide eyes, Hutchings said, carefully, "I don't know, kid. It looks that way."

"But what's this mean? Did the fight break Sinclair's mind?"

The room was warm enough — the building was heated — but she saw that Deuce was still shivering.

"You OK, kid? Warm enough?"

He nodded, his teeth chattering.

"Deuce," she said, trying to take as gentle a tone as she could, "what's wrong? Why are you shaking like that?"

"Because, Hutchings," he whispered, his fear evident. "'God' loves me."

Afterward

This novel represents quite a challenge for me: namely, the challenge of resolving the many varied metaphysical, religious, hard science, and weird, highly theoretical science ideas I have encountered in my lifetime into an entirely new idea, an entirely different way of thinking of things.

In this new model, as you now know, if you've just finished the novel, the stuff of the universe exists as a cohesive whole, constructed in part of the matter and energy of the universe and in part of the unimaginably immense sea of consciousness in the universe represented by the Great Ocean of Thought.

There's something about the Great Ocean that helps to resolve all sorts of mysteries and paranormal miscellanea that appeals to me a great deal: The ways in which old information from one person's life time might turn up in the memories of another person, often thought of as reincarnation; the role of the observer, of will, and of consciousness in influencing the world around us; and the role that tremendous will, or faith, or some combination thereof, plays in maintaining and indeed in changing the world around us. Psychokinesis/telekinesis; pyrokinesis; the notion of ghosts or lost spirits haunting places, their essence not finding their way back to the Great Ocean somehow; and a great many other mysteries and ideas.

In the scheme of this Great Ocean, a small portion of all of the consciousness, all the Awareness that is, is decanted into a new being upon birth (if all goes well). This goes for all living beings, down to the least creature who obviously pursues that which sustains his or her life. At the end of their time alive, in this cycle of the Awareness, their portion of the Awareness leaves the body when it dies and is remingled with the Awareness that constitutes the Great Ocean of Thought. In this way, the universe itself experiences every sort of sensation possible in every form of being possible.

But it goes deeper; as scientists and physicists dig deeper and deeper into the quantum nature of reality, they find tinier and tinier, more and more briefly lived subatomic particles and sorts of energy, such as quanta. These particles and energy states exist as both waves and particles in the physical world we know of and live in; this dual state is due to the nature of the stuff of the universe. That nature I'm speaking of is that at its most fundamental level, the fabric of the universe is constructed of the same Awareness, the very same consciousness that makes up the Great Ocean of Thought, and the same Awareness that is decanted into every living being. (For the purposes of this book, anyway.)

It is because of this, according to our new model for the universe, that we have this wave-particle duality, for at its most basic level the physical universe is made up of a sort of material that cannot be stably defined by our conceptions of matter and energy; it is simply something else: pure, raw Awareness. And this is how the observer can affect the outcome of certain sorts of quantum-level experiments.

At the helm of this Awareness, this Great Ocean of Thought, is not one being, but an ongoing cycle, an eternal changing of the guard of the consciousness that holds the reins, so to speak. In our new Great Ocean model, this helps to explain why we encounter "gods" in the various religions — even within a single religion, such as Christianity — who behave very, very differently at different times.

Take the vengeful, hands-on Old Testament God, named variously YHWH, The Lord, etc., who threatened Moses and Abraham with punishment if they or their people should ever worship other gods, versus the more aloof God of the New Testament, who seems to preach forgiveness and piety. Are these all the same persona? Or are we seeing evidence of a "God" who is changing a great deal over time? How about one who requires entirely different behaviors or sacrifices or dietary behaviors in differing regions and different eras?

The Great Ocean of Thought model addresses this.

And an event in which more than one consciousness ascends to hold the reins, so to speak, might account for pantheons of gods.

And consider the episode in which Moses returns to his people to find them worshipping other gods; when smiths hurl gold into the furnace, a finished golden calf is immediately flung back out at them. Is this evidence of other "gods" coexisting with the Old Testament God? Why would this supposedly one true deity even need to acknowledge the presence of other gods and warn his followers not to worship them?

In the Great Ocean of Thought model, these could be unusually large, potent pools of the Awareness that had somehow broken free of the Great Ocean, but which still retained enough sense of self and enough will, or faith, to alter the world around them in some ways, such as is demonstrated with the creation of a golden calf from gold that is hurled into a furnace.

How many names has the Judeo-Christian tradition given to God? How many personalities have we seen mention of in the Koran, the Bible, the Torah, or the Talmud, all described variously as "The Book"?

Who is to say that an extraordinary amount of faith on the part of people, all of whom carry a portion of the Awareness within them, could not raise a man in whom they believed very strongly from the dead? What if his portion of the Awareness were maintained whole, as it is in reincarnation, and his body healed or transformed by the faith and will of his followers?

What about a case such as that of the biblical Lazarus, who, as the story goes, rose from the dead with Jesus' help?

Again, in the model presented by the Great Ocean of Thought, a great enough concentration of will and faith — faith the size of a mustard seed, as it were — could call back the dispatched portion of the Awareness that was Lazarus' consciousness and decant it once more into a repaired, functioning, living body.

When we hear of near-death experiences (NDE), we often encounter descriptions of out-of-body experiences much like those described in Remote Viewing. We also encounter a surprising number of similarities in the stories of those who are thought dead, but who are revived:

~ The observation of information exchanged after someone who has been thought or pronounced dead, such as observing a physician actually pronouncing one's own death.

~ The distinct experience of being apart from one's body — often floating over one's body, for a time.

~ The sensation of traveling through a long, dark tunnel, but seeing light at the end of the tunnel.

~ Many who have experienced NDE report what is often thought of as having their life flash before their eyes.

~ Meeting and communicating with deceased friends and others is often reported during this experience.

~ A sensation of being at peace.

~ The experience of seeing — and sometimes communicating with — a "being of light" at the end of the tunnel and being filled with awe.

But consider that the Great Ocean of Thought could explain all of this.

If the consciousness — the portion of the Awareness that makes up an individual — has departed the body, but not yet dispersed, it could still perceive events happening around it.

The transition across the threshold from the matter and energy portion of the universe to the Great Ocean could be like traversing a passage from one area to another; to a being now made up entirely of a portion of the Awareness, the Great Ocean might beckon with a profound luminescence.

In the experience of one's life flashing before one's eyes, suppose that this were part of the disengaging of the individual's portion of the Awareness from the individual's physical form, a sort of shock from the transition that causes one to spontaneously experience one's experiences from the beginning.

Meeting departed friends and loved ones is no more unusual than ghosts or reincarnation under this model. The individual portions of the Awareness that make up individual beings do not always reintegrate into the Great Ocean of Thought immediately.

A sensation of peace may come over a being who is now composed completely of Awareness as he or she approaches unity with the Great Ocean of Thought — an unthinkably large reservoir of all that this sort of being is. This experience could also account for at least some interpretations of Heaven.

The "being of light" could be thought of as the overwhelming presence of the consciousness that makes up the great Ocean of Thought, guided by whichever personality the Cycle of the Awareness has installed as the guiding will behind the universe.

(This Cycle of the Awareness, incidentally, also addresses what is widely regarded as a longstanding problem with the dominant Christian model of "God" as a deity who is all-knowing, all-powerful, and all-good governing a world where bad things happen without apparent reason. It is possible under the new model for the ascension of a consciousness that is not "all-good" to occur. Otherwise, as the saying goes, you can pick two, but all three simply do not work together.)

To a being now composed completely of Awareness, an ocean composed completely of Awareness and an instinct to rejoin that ocean would seem like an invitation to Heaven, and to peace in the Great Ocean of Thought, perhaps even to the Buddhist sense of enlightenment in losing distinction of oneself from the surrounding universe.

In the case of religious systems involving pantheons, or groups of gods, this could be explained by the regular cycle of the Awareness selecting multiple replacements, rather than a single replacement, for the guiding consciousness behind the Awareness from time to time.

If someone maintains an extraordinary sensitivity to, or connection with the Great Ocean of Thought, might that person not perceive things others cannot? Would this person become a prophet, like Muhammed, or Moses, or Nostradamus, or a psychic, perhaps, like the famed Edgar Cayce, who found that he could answer nearly any question put to him once he had placed himself into a dreamlike trance?

Would someone who learned to tune his or her portion of the Awareness to the resonance of others' portions of the Awareness be capable of telepathy? Those involved in real-life Remote Viewing programs were reportedly able to develop the various RV talents by simply undergoing training.

So as you can see, the Great Ocean of Thought way of conceiving of the universe can be a very flexible and unifying means of explaining many things that remain unexplained today in other religious and metaphysical and even scientific systems.

A few other notes:

The doomed star that winks out of existence, Andromeda RA 2h12m OS D47°10', is a star that was renamed after my mother-in-law, Nancy McLain, as a gift from her son Justin through a program that allows people to purchase rights to do just that.

The binary sequence used to show the forest-for-the-trees comparison during the final confrontation in Chapter 20 is a translation of the opening passage to my first novel, Burn, into binary, repeated to fill the page and trimmed as necessary at the end. That passage reads as follows: "Outside, it rained a black rain again. Outside, it was still dark, still the dirty grey near-night of the best-lit days of Old New York."

The secretive discovery of notes, pictures, and a bullet casing in the Iowa Capitol was related to me by my wife's uncle, Karl McLain, who worked on a renovation project there. The knowledge was gained, as is most of the important knowledge one gains in adult life, over a couple of beers, late one night. It struck me as one of those rare instances that seemed so necessary to this book, stories in which the details of a true event are known only to a few people.

The hypnosis passage uses a technique called Guided Imagery.

From the Watchman Fellowship Profiles, a feature of the Watchman Expositor: "Guided Imagery, considered one of the most powerful induction techniques, consists of talking the subject through an imaginary journey where with a soft voice the hypnotist takes them on a walk through the forest or a trip to the beach. 'Good, now I want you to picture yourself strolling in the park on a lovely summer day.... Go to the hammock, let your body sink into it ... .' Throughout the exercise the subject is given suggestions to reinforce or deepen the trance. 'As you walk along feeling so peaceful, so relaxed ... '

(Rachel Copelan, How to Hypnotize Yourself and Others, pp. 94–95)."

(http://www.watchman.org/profile/hypnopro.htm)

The passage from Revelations quoted in Chapter 20 is Rev. 22:1 : "And he showed me a pure river of water of life, clear as crystal, proceeding out of the throne of God and of the Lamb."

Appendix

The un-Cut-Up version of the battle for godhood in Chapter 19

Sinclair's mind had become a maddening cascade of new ideas and newly learned knowledge.

The Elder's ancient presence suddenly surrounded Sinclair.

Without a word, and with an inhuman burst of will, the Elder propelled Sinclair through new levels of realization: He found himself flowing with knowledge of the Great Ocean of Thought.

And Sinclair's world wrenched itself inside-out.

Sinclair slammed both hands into the sides of his head, battling desperately to contain it all.

The nature of the Great Ocean, its relationship with – no, its oneness with the fabric of the universe was suddenly laid bare before him. Words from the pages of The Dancing Wu-Li Masters, the Fritjof Capra effort to unify the quantum world with Eastern philosophy, washed over him. Capra had compared the eternal dance of creation, the dance of the Hindu deity Shiva, with the dance of subatomic particles which make up the matter and energy of the universe: He felt Capra's revelation about the energy and the matter that make up the universe, felt Capra's rush of excitement in a moment of visionary insight, down to their most minute parts, sharing a sort of rhythm of creation – the rhythm of the dance of Shiva.

"It's all the same thing!" Sinclair shouted. "All of it! The waves of the Great Ocean are the waves that make up the stuff of reality! The particles, the energy – it is all Awareness!"

Oh my god! he thought. Matter, energy, thought, the Great Ocean — if it's all made up of the same thing in different forms, then the Awareness — all awareness — is the universe learning to know itself!

Pieces of the overall truth had been scattered across time, realized by individuals over the millennia, but never all at once, outside of the Awareness, and never without the clutter of other, inaccurate speculation into the nature of reality.

It must be the universe's backup plan, he thought. Separate pieces of the knowledge necessary to ascend, split up and housed in sentient beings scattered throughout space and time.

Then he knew: Hutchings had had some of the pieces; that was why she could control some small amount of the essence of godhood that Machina had welled up.

So he had at least some of the pieces; the Elder remembered some of it.

It all made sense to him: Why he had been able to alter solid things; why someone or something needed to perceive the universe to keep it stable; why Dr. Errol Mannheim, Ph.D. in parapsychology, assistant director of the Geller Meta-physics Institute, was getting so many reports of hauntings and reincarnation. The universe – the Great Ocean – was a riot of possibility, the stuff of which everything — matter, energy, you name it – was made up. But without the guiding hand of the Awareness, some of the measures of the Great Ocean decanted into those of strong enough will simply held together, their measure either refusing to leave Earth or becoming decanted whole into a new person!

But who had the knowledge he still needed?

Information surged through him.

Of course, he thought. Trull. Trull understood it all well enough to envision the core machine that evolved itself into Machina, but he didn't have enough pieces of the puzzle to know what would happen when they activated the Project Oversight machine.

And now Trull was gone — dragged into Machina's essence when it was acti-vated, used up by its voracious appetite for the energy of consciousness.

So Trull's pieces of the knowledge were gone forever; how could he put it all together without Trull's pieces of the puzzle?

There was more to it — Sinclair could sense it. Pieces of the puzzle were missing, but they might still exist out there, somewhere in the universe. He began casting about, mentally searching through the streams of information washing over him:

Pieces began to appear in his mind. He saw:

In the Chicago suburb or Northland, Choi Kwang, a 38-year-old practitioner of T'ai Chi, focused his chi, the spiritual energy he firmly believed flowed through along channels throughout the body, into a small pile of paper scraps setting them, with fierce concentration, ablaze, holding only his open palm above the paper.

He saw:

An ironic political statement in cartoon form: A Caucasian Christ, spikes driven through the palms of his hands, happily munches a handful of toasted mustard seeds. Mustard seeds: A Judeo-Christian symbol of faith, paralleled by the tradi-tional portrayal of a nail through the palm of his hand. Forensic testing had demon-strated that a nail through each hand this way could not possibly support an adult's bodyweight.

And, he now somehow knew, the word cross — the entire tradition of Chris-tians wearing and displaying and kissing and worshipping before crosses hinged on a mistranslation: The Greek word stauros, or stavros, was more accurately trans-lated as "persecution spike." There was no crossbar in use for several hundred years after his crucifixion. Nonetheless, once the crossbar became a part of the practice of crucifixion, a pole with a crossbar had become the symbol for one of the world's most widespread and successful religions.

It reminded Sinclair, now, of an old joke: If Jesus had arrived in the mid-20th century, would his followers have worn little electric chair pendants around their necks?

But if forensic testing had demonstrated that a spike through each hand this way could not possibly support an adult's bodyweight, how could one explain stigmata?

In rare cases, a few Christians had become afflicted with stigmata — wounds in the palms and feet resembling what most of the faithful believed to be Christ's crucifixion wounds; and pin-prick wounds on the head resembling his "crown" of thorns; even a wound on the chest resembling the wound traditionally believed to have been left by a Roman centurian. How? Faith! It was the power of will, focused via faith in something greater — even something that may not be entirely accurate — that could bring about a mind over body event such as stigmata. And, he realized, mind over matter. Psychokinesis, or telekinesis: The ability to move or bend solid objects with the power of one's mind. The ability to forge an alteration of the very fabric of reality. Pyrokinesis: The ability to set things ablaze with the power of one's mind alone, as Choi Kwang had done.

He saw:

In Madison, Wisconsin, reading herself to sleep in her bed, 53-year-old office manager Laura Crenshaw encountered an interesting, if whimsical idea in "Breakfast of Champions," penned by author Kurt Vonnegut, involving E=MC2, Einstein's formula describing the relationship between matter and energy. Energy (E) is equal to matter (M) multiplied by the speed of light © squared.

Speed matter up enough and it becomes energy.

But the novel idea was this: The formula neglected to include an important ingredient: Awareness.

Yes! thought Sinclair. Awareness is missing from the equation — but that's not all!

Another element was missing: Faith. Not Christian faith, particularly, but a faith based upon an omniscient understanding of the nature of reality, of the universe-Awareness binary pair, of all of it.

Sinclair directed his attention toward embracing this truth, and toward intertwining all of the information and knowledge and understanding he had into a single unified contiuum: He envisioned The Truth, the universe as it was intended to be, the Great Ocean of Thought — the Awareness! — all returning to their normal, essential, natures. This, he knew, would unify all of it, and would repair the mess that had been made when Machina interrupted the natural cycle of the Awareness as the Elder began to die.

And suddenly he understood the truth that had eluded him when the Elder had forced his first confrontation with Machina: The universe was not as the Elder had told him!

Elder! Sinclair thought: *The universe is not binary at all — the truth of it is far, far more complicated! You think of the universe as black and white — you see only the Great Ocean coexisting in tandem with the matter and energy of the universe; but the binary way of things was only the very, very beginning — only existence and nonexistence!*

What? demanded the Elder. *What nonsense is this?*

Look: You see only black and white, existence and the lack thereof, a continual stream of absolutes — binaries — like this:

```
IOOIIIIIIIOIOIIIIOIOOIIIOOIIIIOIOOIIOOIOOIIOOIOIIOOO
OOIIIIOIOOIOOOOOIIIOOIOIIOOOOIIIOIOOIIIOIIIOIIOOIOIIIOOIOOI
OOOOOIIOOOOIIOOOOOIIOOOIOIIOIIOOIIOOOOIIIOOOIIIIOIOIIIOOOOO
IIIOOIOIIOOOOIIIOIOOIIIOIIIOIOOOOOIIOOOOIIIOOIIIIIOOOOIIIOI
OOIIIOIIIOIOIIIOIOOOOOIOOIIIIIIIOIOIIIIOIOOIIIOOIIIIOIOOIII
OOIOOIIOOIOIIOOOOOIIOIOOIIIIOIOOIOOOOOIIIOIIIIIOOOOIIIIOOII
IOOOOOIIIOOIIIIIOIOOIIOIOOIIOIIOOIIOIIOOIOOOOOIIOOIOOIIOOO
OIIIIOOIOIIOIOIIIOIIOOIOOOOOIIIOOIIIIIOIOOIIOIOOIIOIIOOIIO
IIOOIOOOOOIIIOIOOIIOIOOOIIOOIOIIOOOOOIOOIOOIIOIOOIIIIOOIOI
IIOIOOIIIIOOIIOOOOOIOOIIIIIIOOIOIIOOOOIIIIIOOIIOOOOOIIOIII
OIIOOIOIIIOOOOIIIIOOIOIOOOOOIIOIIIOIIOOIIIOOIIIIIOIOOOIII
OIOOIOOOOOIIOIIIIIOOIIOIOOOOOIIIOIOOIIOIOOOIIOOIOIIOOOOOII
OOOIOIIOOIOIIIOOIIIIIOIOOIOOOOOIIOIIOOIIOIOOIIIIOIOOIOOOOO
IIOOIOOIIOOOOIIIIOOIIIOOIIOOOOOIIOIIIIIOOIIOIOOOOOIOOII
IIIIOIIOOIIOOIOOIOOOOOIOOIIIOIIOOIOIIIIOIIIOOOOOIOIIOOIIIO
IIIIIIIOOIOIIOIOIIIOIIIOIOOIIIIIIOIOIIIIOIOOIIIOOIIIOIOOI
IIOOIOOIIOOIOIIOOOOOIIOIOOIIIOIOOIOOOOOIIIOOIOIIOOOOIIIOIO
OIIIOIIIOIIOOIOIIIOOIOOIOOOOOIIOOOOIIOOOOOIIOOOIOIIOIIOOIIO
OOOIIIOOOIIIIOIOIIIOOOOOIIIOOIOIIOOOOIIIOIOOIIIOIIIOIOOOOOI
IOOOOIIIOOIIIIIOOOOIIIOIOOIIIOIIIOIOIIIOIOOOOOIOOIIIIIIIOIO
IIIIOIOOIIIOOIIIOIOOIIIOOIOOIIOOIOIIOOOOOIIOIOOIIIIOIOOIOO
OOOIIIOIIIIOOOOIIIIOOIIIOOOOOIIIOOIIIIIOIOOIIOIOOIIOIIOOI
IOIIOOIOOOOOIIOOIOOIIOOOOIIIIOOIOIIOIOIIIOIIOOIOOOOOIIIOOII
```

But you're missing the forest for the trees, Elder — look again, from a distance, and you begin to see not just the black and white of a binary system, but the beginnings of a universe of every conceivable shade in between:

```
10011111110101111010011100111101001110010011001011000011
11010010000011100101100001101001110111011001011100100100
00011000011000001100010110110011000011100011110101110000
11100101100001110100111011101000001100001110001110011100001111
01001110111010111010000010011111110101111010011100111100111010
01110010011001011000001101001111010010000011101111100011
11001110000011100111110100111010011011001110110011001000001100
10011000011110010110101111011001100000111001111101001101001
11011001101100100000111010011010000110010110000011001001100
10011110010111010011110011000001100111111100101100001111110
01100000110111011001011100001110010100000110111011010011
10011111010001110100100000011011111100110100000011101001101
00011001011000001100010111100110111110100100010000011101100
11010011110100100000110010011000011111001111001110011000000110
11111100110100000010011111100110011001001000001001110110010
11110111100000101100111011111111100101011001101011100100111111
10101111010011100111101001110010011001001011000001010011110
10010000011100101100001101001110110111001011100100100000
11000011000001100010110110011000011100011111010101110000111
00101100011101001110110100000011000011100111110101011100001111010
01110111010111010000001001111110101011101001100111101000011
10010011001011000001101001111010010000011101111100001111110
01110000011100111110100110100101001101001001000010000111001100
11000011110010110101111011001000000110011110001111001100
01011011001100001110001110101011100000111001011000011110100
11101110100000011000011100111100011101101100101011010011010
00001001111111010111101001001100111101001110010011001011000
00111010011101010010000011101111100001110011100001110011
```

Enlightenment! he thought to himself, startled. Again, he clutched his head with both hands, battling to hold himself together.

Sinclair's expanding consciousness had encountered the Buddhist understanding of the term "enlightenment": Being at one with everything, losing even one's sense of Self to the nature of the universe. Was this also Moksha, the concept of enlightenment familiar to the Hindus? (He did not know, but soon enough he would.) He was unifying it all, repairing what had gone awry when the cycle of the Awareness had been torn asunder.

Machina, he now understood, could never have taken the place of the Awareness in the cycle of the universe, because Machina, being mechanical, did not understand what it meant to be non-binary; no matter what language a computer program is written in, when it is compiled and fed into a machine, the data is ultimately sent through its processor as binary data. Like all machines that receive and process information, Machina, in the end, received only binary communications into itself, and thus had no hope of truly grasping the non-binary nature of the universe.

His understanding, his consciousness, his Awareness, was expanding.

He saw:

Contractors working on the restoration of the Iowa State Capitol in autumn of 2000 opened a panel in the stair casing on the lantern of the capitol to find a .38

caliber shell casing and two letters dated 1897. The letters were signed by two men: One named Jed, and another named Burke. The letters, describing the men's wives, families, and lives, had been hidden within the woodwork by Jed and Burke, laborers who first worked on this part of the capitol, messages to future builders and restorers who might retrace their steps.

The small group of contractors quickly and secretly scribbled down notes about themselves and their families and sealed them away, communications to the next set of builders who would one day re-open the panel in some future restoration project, a secret communication between a unique set of workers.

No one but them would ever know.

But Sinclair knew.

He saw:

2,100 years ago, near ancient Bethlehem, as the cycle of the Awareness began to refresh itself anew, an uneducated shepherd named Mahalalel was suddenly caught up in the process; he was a gentle man who was very, very afraid of what the vengeful God of Scripture might have in store for him, and in his confusion, as the elder Awareness waned and Mahalalel quickly expanded to assume the role, Mahalalel panicked, wishing with all his heart that he might be allowed to live a full life.

But the mantle of power was in the midst of being passed from the old overseer of the Awareness to the new one; Mahalalel's wish had an unpredictable result.

Miles and miles from where Mahalalel had been drawn away from his flock and into the cycle of the Awareness, a young woman who had not yet engaged in sex of any sort, and who was promised to Josef, a young member of her traveling people, suddenly carried a child, a life form in every way identical to Mahalalel, save that Mahalalel was now the overseer of the Awareness and the Great Ocean of Thought.

After birth, the child would be named Jesu, and would grow up to be a rabbi of unusual inspiration to his followers. His 12 closest devotees would come to be known as disciples.

Those chronicling Rabbi Jesu Josef's life would find his proclamations of the word and will of God becoming more gentle, less vengeful than they had previously been.

Sinclair knew that this was because the being thought of by these people as God was not actually the same being any longer. The time of a vengeful "God" had passed.

He saw:

In Austin, Texas, in July 1997, Shamal Cornelius Johnson, a 36-year-old African-American man, was strapped into elaborate stereotaxic restraints, awaiting a lethal injection for the brutal rape and murder of Cordelia Meribeth Kuykendall, a 19-year-old white woman whose family was well-connected. Kuykedall's blood-caked hair had been found plastered to the walls and floor of her apartment near the University of Texas in 1988. Shamal knew that an all-white jury had set out to teach black men a lesson about what happens when black men do this to white women.

He did not know who had committed the crime for which he was being executed.

But Sinclair knew.

Billy-Ray Wayne Biggs, a white lawn-care worker on the payroll of Kuykendall's father, had committed the assault and murder. He had died in an SUV rollover accident on Interstate 35 outside Buda, Texas, three years before Shamal Cornelius Johnson's execution. His measure of the Awareness had since been reintegrated into the Great Ocean of Thought.

He saw:

In Little Rock, Arkansas, Bobby Joe Hansen, now five and a half years old, still wets the bed. His parents told no one.

But Sinclair knew.

In September 2023, Dr. Errol Mannheim, Ph.D. in parapsychology, assistant director of the Geller Metaphysics Institute, wondered why he was seeing so many new cases of supposed reincarnation in the institute's files. He had no idea why such a spike would occur.

But Sinclair knew:

Pradeep Mishra had died of small pox in Niphad, in the District of Mathura, at his family's home. But because of the destabilization Machina and its creators had wrought in the Great Ocean of Thought, Pradeep's portion of the Awareness was never reintegrated into the Great Ocean. It was, instead, decanted whole into the body of a newborn named Ravindra, to parents Sri Krishnachand Nagar and his wife, Saraswati, residents of nearby Chandvad.

Ravindra simply was Pradeep.

The same thing had happened to Dona Henrique, nicknamed Catarina, the daughter of a farmer in the Brazilian state of Paraná, who was reborn when her close friend Ida Dos Santos gave birth to a daughter, who she named Helena, in nearby Adapa.

He saw:

At 6:21 a.m. September 2001, Muhamed Atta said his dawn prayers. He and 18 other terrorists, living in the United States under deep cover, posing variously as university students and pilots in training, planned the worst terrorist attack in the history of humankind: In less than three hours, he and four of his associates would hijack a commercial jetliner, take control of it, and intentionally crash it into one of the two towers of the World Trade Centers; minutes later, others in his group on other jets would use the same method of attack on the second tower; the Pentagon in Washington, D.C.; and a fourth Washington, D.C. target. More than 6,000 people would lose their lives in the attacks.

The last group would fail when passengers on board rebelled against the hijackers. In the ensuing battle for control of the airliner, the plane would crash into the Pennsylvania countryside.

Their plans were a closely guarded secret.

But Sinclair knew.

In 1981, Department 13, an ultra-black ops agency investigating the development of biological weapons, began what they thought of as the successor to the Tuskegee syphilis study. Through carefully planned infiltration of what patients thought were routine doctors' examinations, dozens of women and, principally, homosexual men in New York City, San Francisco, and Los Angeles were infected with Biological Agent Attila. The virus was unwittingly spread via contaminated syringes used in health surveys in rural desert and forested areas in Africa. Once the Centers for Disease Controls and the medical community at large realized that some deadly new phenomenon was attacking these communities, the cycle of symptoms leading, ultimately, to death was dubbed GRID, or Gay-Related Immune Deficiency.

The lab-created virus was genetically modified from another virus known to be fatal in other primates: Simian Immunodeficiency Virus.

The disease turned out to be slow-moving and difficult to spread, and in October 1994, Department 13 declared Biological Agent Attila a failure as an effective combat agent. In April 1995, Biological Agent Khan, a microbe specifically genetically engineered to combat Attila, was released into the public in cities known to be affected.

In August of 2001, researchers isolated what appeared to be a naturally occurring microbe that fights HIV to a standstill, explaining how increasing numbers of people are now "living with HIV," rather than dying from it.

All records from Department 13's Attila and Khan projects were then destroyed. Department 13 consisted of fewer than 15 individuals, the only people alive who knew about Attila and Khan.

But Sinclair knows.

In November 1990, an operative with the codename Agent Dalia compares a superior's comment that God may be dead to Nietsche's famous declaration that "God is dead."

She doesn't know what they're talking about.

But Sinclair knows: He knows that when Friedrich Wilhelm Nietzsche died on August 25, 1900, his individual distillate of Awareness from the Great Ocean of Thought was remingled into the Great Ocean once again. A tiny portion of that Awareness that made up Friedrich Wilhelm Nietzsche is distilled decades later into a young boy from Niphad, in India, named Pradeep Bannerjee, and again, later into Ravindra Nadar in nearby Chandvad.

At the time, anyway, Nietsche's proclamation was wrong; but then, in Pradeep's and Prakesh's era, he was essentially right: "God," in a sense, was dying. And what a ride that portion of Nietsche's Awareness had been on in the meantime!

He saw:

Many more dimensions than he had realized were there; his understanding had only been of a four dimensional world — three dimensions moving through time. Now he grappled with a fifth; now a sixth; suddenly, fully eleven separate dimensions stood in his gaze. He reeled, desperately trying to understand it all.

He saw:

In July 2018, up late again in pursuit of his dream of having a short story published so that he might legitimately call himself an author, a young man labored at a desk in his room in an Iowa City, scribbling away at a writing pad, constantly striking, correcting, and adjusting a small piece of speculative fiction he hoped to polish to a gleaming perfection. He had titled the piece "Sum"; the piece began with the words, "For a period immeasurable, all that was was unaware," and ended with the words, "The Deity is a madman."

Sinclair could see that a piece of the knowledge he sought was within him, but that he was interpreting it through a Judeo-Christian filter. He had written the piece that had haunted Sinclair; had seemed to try to warn him of some sort of madness — but was it madness in the Elder, or the mad rule perpetrated by Machina?

And where was the Elder?

It had all washed over him in an instant, but the torrent of information continued.

In a burst on profound insight, Sinclair turned his attention again to Machina, solidifying its post-human henchman again in its tacks, this time for good. He fought the flood of Awareness – omniscience? – washing over him. His very essence was expanding by leaps he hadn't previously even been capable of imagining.

Machina's lights we blowing out, showers of sparks erupting as it resisted Sinclair's efforts to change it. But it was lost; it did not begin to grasp even what the Awareness was, let alone the depths of its Ocean, or the nature of what it — Machina — had done.

The Unity of the universe suddenly vibrated with the familiar flavor of one who had known it all before: The Elder was here, now, with him, as Sinclair understood more and more, and that understanding expanded his essence, molding him to fit into his new role.

The Elder! I'm not alone!, he thought, trembling as he fought to contain the growing dimensions of his understanding.

Sinclair? I can still hear you too, Kid, said Hutchings' voice inside his mind. He could feel her trying to be a comforting presence, restraining her tough-as-nails military discipline. But she could not hide her terror. *I can't get to Machina, but I can still reach you through our bridge.*

Thunderous pounding surrounded Sinclair. He was buffeted, knocked distances he could only just fathom. Fathoming them was distracting him from the task of grasping and bringing Unity to the mind-numbing crash of newfound knowledge and Awareness.

The Elder's greed shone through. The Elder could not let go; he could not resist the lure of ultimate power — of omnipotence — even if he no longer understood it.

With a thought, Sinclair dismissed Machina.

In the distance, what remained of the machine went a leaden, unlit gray as its power drained away and Sinclair reduced it to rock.

The Men In Black that were plugged into the interfaces went suddenly limp, finally dead so long after their minds had died. Those not plugged into the interfaces simply dropped, lifeless, to the ground, their bodies littering the ultra-secret subterranean headquarters of Project Oversight.

Machina was finished, a fossil marking an artificial regime.

The Elder's mental voice howled a deafening protest.

The deity is a madman. Sinclair heard the words echo hauntingly through his thoughts. "Madman," Sinclair whispered. Suddenly alarmed, he turned his attention from the unfinished Unity to the Elder. The power-mad Elder was forcing his hand, making him abandon his effort to heal the failing universe to fend off the old god.

But the Elder remembered more now than he had let on when he had coached Sinclair. Howling maniacally, the Elder clutched at the new, unfinished Unity with his mind, forging an incredible wedge of willpower, working to pry free Sinclair's grip.

Sinclair felt fear to the point of panic; if he could not stop the Elder who knew what would happen to the universe and the new, incomplete Unity? It was all still collapsing.

Struggling with the wash of information, with ancient ideals of a flat Earth and a Sun and moon and planets and stars that orbited a human-centered universe, Sinclair fought with his self-doubt and disappointment. He was a newly bisexual/night janitor/college dropout/hallucinogen-tripping failure! How could he ever assume the role of the Awareness?

He resisted; the doubt and shame and disappointment, he now saw, were the Elder's attack on him. The Elder was causing it!

Fight it! he thought. Fight him! Place your Faith in the new Unity!

The Elder howled again, lashing mental energy at Sinclair, searing his physical body, as well. Sinclair was weakening; he could feel his body, its skin searing, its bones breaking under the stress; how long could he keep up the battle?

His vision, all of his senses blurred, Sinclair stared in disbelief as a figure emerged from the chaos of creation before him, taking shape from the mists and blur.

His mother.

His dead, horrifyingly alone, suicidal mother, tears streaming down her face.

"Why, Sinclair?" she pleaded, wailing. "Why didn't you come home and help me? Why didn't you stop me? What kind of son lets his own mother do that to herself?!"

Stop! he demanded, the command permeating the new Unity with a thought. *Stop it, Elder!* And then, his mental state weakening, his demand became a plea: *Please!*

"Never should've even had you, you sonovabitch!" the apparition of his mother screamed. "All you had to do was come home! But you had to live in a college town, away from us! Better than us! Away from me!" She pounded her chest. "God, how does anyone survive when their whole family just leaves them behind?"

Please! he pleaded. He could feel his grip on reality slipping under the pressure and guilt. *Take her away!*

Shit! Hutchings pleaded, her mental voice filled with alarm. *Resist him, Sinclair!*

Suddenly, Hutchings' universe was filled with her mental image of Jordan, her fellow operative and the man she'd fallen in love with, only to turn her back on him, never speaking with him or contacting him in any way, ever again, because her superiors had ordered her not to do so.

Oh God, Jordan, I'm sorry! she said. She had abandoned him without a word on orders from a man she knew only as Sapphire.

She was filled with dread, a sense of futility and guilt suffusing her whole being, until Sinclair's mental universe was teeming with her guilt, as well as his own.

She faced her failure with Machina, as well, her arrogant, ridiculous, impossible gamble with the fate of everything she ever knew in the balance and its resulting consequences of a universe slowly eroding away, its natural rhythms and cycles and laws disrupted.

Behind Sinclair's mother, suddenly, he could see his father smoking synth from a crack pipe in a run-down apartment, surrounded by the old man's friends — people he had known when he was growing up from their visits to the house.

Every one of them was wizened, wrinkled, and glassy-eyed, tapping his feet or washing his hands nervously in the air as he waited for the pipe. They passed around a bottle of Thunderbird, cheap, alcohol-boosted wine for alcoholics, to take the edge off the effects of the synthetic speed.

His father! There was no escape for him, either. He wouldn't survive another six months like this.

And Sinclair could do nothing, nothing at all, to change things.

Anger and unreason began to swell throughout the Awareness as it swelled within Sinclair; suddenly, the unfinished Unity rippled, puckering wildly with new, volatile weak spots, and began to change dramatically.

Bastard! he thought at the Elder. But a desperate realization was dawning on him. I can change it! I can change everything! I absolutely have to change it!

Fighting through the pain, he came to a decision: He would oppose the Elder on his — the Elder's — own turf. The Elder wanted the power, the omnipotence, of the Awareness. Through the searing pain and thought-clouding weariness, Sinclair clutched fast to that omnipotence, trying to clear his head, leaving behind his project of Unity to focus on the Elder.

Hutchings' constant drenching of his psyche in guilt and failure and pain had to be purged. She was dead weight to him now — worse than dead weight. With a violent mental slash, he severed their psionic rapport, cleaving her off from the battle and clearing her from his mind.

He lost all track of the orderliness and truth of the new Unity; his rage, a monstrous, unreasoning anger, would no longer allow him to hold it all together.

With the faith and will and strength of mania, Sinclair formed a vision of his own two hands closing, constricting around the neck of the Elder.

What did the Elder look like?

Like God. Or like a man who grew into the role.

Some shepherd guy, right? he recalled vaguely, bitterly. Guy with a beard ... Mahalalel.

There's. The. Weakness! he thought haltingly, as a struggling body appeared in his tightly locked, trembling hands.

Driving forward with murderous will, Sinclair had forced the Elder to become corporeal for the first time in millennia. And now, filled with murderous anger, with a seemingly random wash of information from the Awareness and the damaged, incomplete Unity, maddened by the pain in his crumpled, broken, burned physical form, Sinclair became the steward of the Awareness with an initial act of murder.

He destroyed the Elder, choked the life out of him with his bare hands, and stood, hoisting the carcass over his head. He planted his feet on the fabric of reality, grinning maniacally.

Sinclair's feet met the Earth's flat, solid surface.

With a murderous, triumphant sneer, he hurled the broken, dead body of a 2000+-year-old shepherd named Mahalalel down upon the Earth. The dried, ruined body exploded in a cloud of dust and bone on an uninhabited plateau south of Jerusalem.

The mists of creation/destruction, in a torrent until now, began to clear, and a new God, drunk with power and anger and madness, reinforced the fabric of reality as the torrent of information had told him it should be, bending it to his will.

The sun blazed overhead, a cauldron of fire contained by gravity in its almost-hemisphere base, other flat-surfaced planets orbiting not far away, all circling the Earth. The oceans poured over the edges of the world, to be caught in a massive waterfall that rose again though the centers of the oceans, and through rains rising over the seas.

He understood how it all worked together; all was right in the new God's universe.

And he had forgotten all about a lonely, missing star that had once been designated Andromeda RA 2h12m OS D47°10'.

It didn't matter; this was his universe now.

About the Author

Jonathan Lyons received his MFA in writing from the California College of the Arts in Spring 2005. He currently lives in the Bay Area, but has lived in Austin, TX, and Bombay, India, of all places; he hails from Iowa. He received his bachelor's in English from the University of Iowa in Iowa City. (He doesn't miss the winters.)

He has had a number of short stories, essays, a hyperfiction, and his first novel, Burn, published.

Printed in the United States
24173LVS00004B/313-345